D1136437

A Cake for the
Gestapo

Jacqueline King

First published in the UK in 2020 by ZunTold
www.zuntold.com

Text copyright © Jacqueline King 2020
Cover design by Isla Bousfield-Donohoe

A catalogue record for this book is available
from the British Library

ISBN 978-1-9162042-0-1
1 2 3 4 5 6 7 8 9 10

Printed and bound in the UK by
Short Run Press Limited
25 Bittern Road
Sowton Industrial Estate
EXETER
Devon
EX2 7LW

For the brave children of Jersey,
past, present and future.
Salut!

Extract from Interview
with Bernie Robert, Jerseyman

We kids thought the German Occupation was an adventure, a bit of fun. I was seven when the soldiers arrived, so I got up to all sorts of dangerous things, using caps from my toy guns and making them jump. I stole from them too.

I didn't understand the danger, because our parents hid the dark side from us. They were so brave.

But in the end, we were starving. When the islands were liberated, I was given a piece of white bread. It was the most delicious thing I'd ever eaten and I thought it was cake. My mother cried then.

Jersey, Channel Islands
June 1940

June 17th 4am

Joe Le Carin wriggled out of bed, dragged on a ragged shirt and shorts, then checked the baby in his cot next to the window. 'All right, kid?' he whispered.

Moonlight shone through a hole in the blackout curtain on Arthur's sleeping face and the bubbles he was blowing from his little nose. Joe wiped them away with the tail of his shirt then tiptoed along the corridor past his sister's makeshift bed.

Diddie was deep in dreams as well, thumb in mouth. If she woke, she'd scream. That would set off Arthur. If Dad heard about it, Joe would get the hiding of his life, no kidding. So he hurried past on silent feet. But when he pushed opened the kitchen door, he gasped. 'Flipping heck, Mum. You forgot the blackouts.'

The moon lit every corner – cooking pots and tin plates, the clock on the shelf, the flowers on the table and the shiny buckle on his father's spare belt behind the door. Joe hurried from window to window, yanking down blinds and muttering, 'Anyone could've seen what we got and nicked it. Auntie Vi down the road, Percy Du Brin, German spies. Bombers. *Anyone.*'

He added, 'Not that we got much to nick, except Dad's fags.'

Beside baby Arthur's rattle, an opened pack of cigarettes lay ready for his father to enjoy after his night's fishing. Joe hesitated for a second, then took one. He slipped outside and made his way to the sea wall between the lobster pots that littered the garden.

For a moment, he listened in case the enemy had arrived. Slowing his breathing, he strained his ears for the scrape and splash of boots in rock pools, or foreign voices. But all he could hear was crackling seaweed and herring gulls trumpeting the end of night.

Anyhow, the enemy wouldn't know about the full moon and the tides it brought, pulling the sea off the rocks for miles, then racing back six hours later until it lapped sea walls and flooded roads. They wouldn't understand how the big tides turned the gullies and rocks into death traps. Joe pictured them shouting as tentacles grabbed them in deep pools. Serve them right,' he murmured. 'If they try and steal our island.'

Picking up his bucket and rake, he felt his way down the steps to the beach in the half-light. Then he set off, running over sand. When he reached wetter ground, his bare feet stamped splat, splat, splat in the puddles, however hard he tried to muffle them. Soon he was knee deep in gurgling waters, wading through ribbons of seaweed in gullies edged by towering rocks.

A mile out, he left the rocks behind and raked for sand-eels under the fading stars. He whistled softly as he worked over a sandbank, but there was nothing and the tide was on the turn already, foaming at its edge. He tried again and again, dashing from one sandbank to another as the sun tipped them all with colour.

Soon, the German planes would arrive, buzzing over the island, spying.

'Asking for it,' muttered Joe, resting his arms for a moment. He scanned the sky and fingered his catapult, hoping for a pilot in an open cockpit. Then he raked again, putting his back into it. But still there was nothing. His family would go without breakfast again.

Just as he was about to give up, there was a thunderous explosion on the French coast. 'ASKING FOR IT,' Joe bellowed, adding a string of words his father would belt him for. Then he jumped, yelping with amazement. Sand-eels were leaping over his feet like tiny silver arrows, throwing themselves out of the water and twisting and turning, their tails shimmering as they landed on the sand around him.

'Blimey,' he said, grabbing his rake. 'That was a big bomb. No wonder you lot jumped.' He set to work, scooping up sand-eels until the bucket was full, chucking in a few cockles as well. Then he turned for home, the heavy bucket banging against his legs.

The tide streamed back through the gullies, flecked white, twisting round the rocks ahead. But Joe knew his route, every rock and every puddle and every hole. 'Risk it or drown,' he shouted. Then he plunged through the icy tug of the tide, jumping and slipping. Seaweed grabbed his feet. 'Out of my way,' he yelled. 'Out of my way, damn you.'

At last he left the main body of the tide, whistling as he splashed over wet ground dimpled with worm casts until he was on dry sand below his home on the sea wall. He dumped the bucket, felt in his pocket and smiled.

The cigarette he'd nicked from his father was dry. That was the important thing.

As he lit up, coughing and spluttering, there was another explosion across the water.

Joe spat out a plume of smoke and yelled, 'Oi, Mr. Hitler. Shut your noise.' He spat out tobacco shreds. 'Flipping fags, you're just not the same since the war started.' He took a deep pull, coughed and yelled at the French coast again. Then he stubbed out the cigarette on a rock, cooled the hot end in a puddle and stuck it behind his ear. He carried his bucket up the steps, through the gap in the sea wall and into his house.

In the kitchen, he cut a slice of the week's butter ration into the frying pan and turned on the gas. As the butter sizzled, he rolled sand-eels in flour, then fried them. While they cooked, he nipped into the corridor and flapped a wet sand-eel at his sleeping sister. 'Get up Diddie, breakfast in five minutes.'

Diddie shot upright, opening her mouth to yell. But Joe stuck a fishy finger over her mouth. 'Don't wake the baby, 'cos I'll tell Dad. He won't like that.'

She glared at him for a minute, then pushed back the bed covers, yawning. 'Course I won't wake Arthur.' She grinned. 'You got some sand-eels, haven't you? Good old Joe.'

Next, he stood at his mother's door and said softly, 'Rise and shine. I've caught you a treat.' After he was sure his mother was awake, he went to the stove. 'Mmm,' he said, eating a crisp sand-eel. He rolled it round his mouth until the last buttery scrap had gone then covered the pan to keep the rest warm.

Then he set off along the coast road with his bucket. He'd give the cockles to his Auntie Vi. That'd cheer her up after her bad dreams about Mr. Hitler. Checking his back pocket for his catapult, he grinned at a sudden thought. Percy, the local bully, might be somewhere close.

If Percy tried to frighten Spinner any more, he'd have to sort him out. Grabbing Spinner by her plaits was bad enough, but Percy kept telling her terrible things about the enemy and how they were getting closer and closer to the island. Spinner was terrified enough already.

June 17th 8am

Up the lane, Spinner Braye sat at her desk in her attic room, still in pyjamas. She was writing in a blue book, twitching her nose at the smell drifting upstairs. *Parsnip coffee stinks*, she wrote. *It's a bit like sick. Acorn coffee's just as bad. But nothing's as bad as Percy. Not even the enemy.* Then she froze. Someone was in the garden. From the lane came the rattle of foreign words. *'ACHTUNG! HANDE HOCH!'*

Spinner gulped. So, the enemy was here after all. She listened again, then frowned. The voice was familiar.

'ACHTUNG,' came a yell. 'I will catch Spinner by her plaits. *JA? HA HA!*'

Flinging open the window, Spinner leaned out. The boy she hated most at school was goose-stepping through a gap in their hedge far below. His arm was raised in a Nazi salute as he headed for her vegetable patch. She leaned out further and bellowed, 'Don't you dare tread on my radishes, Percy Du Brin.'

The boy looked up at her and laughed. But just as he was about to stamp on her radishes, he stopped abruptly. His eyes widened and his mouth opened in a big O and he stepped backwards, staring wildly into the farmyard on the other side of Spinner's garden. He reversed further and further until he bumped into the raspberry canes and shot between them, pulling them in front of him like camouflage.

Spinner looked down at him, all covered with leaves. Then she gasped. Percy was sticking his hands into the air. She dived behind the curtains, whispering, 'I was right after all. The Germans are here.'

But just as she was about to rush downstairs to find her father, someone outside gave a booming laugh. Spinner hesitated. She knew that sound.

Only her friend Clem had a laugh like that, slow and friendly. If Clem was laughing, she needn't worry. She crawled back to the window and stood behind the blackout curtain, peering down. Percy lowered his hands and screeched, 'What the heck are you doing with a gun, Cowpat Clem?'

Spinner leaned out again. Clem with a gun? He didn't have one, unless it was his brother Bill's and he'd borrowed it for shooting rabbits.

Then she saw him clattering over the cobbles next door in his farm boots, heading for her garden gate. He dumped a pair of dead rabbits on the gate-post, pushed open the gate and ran towards Percy. Prodding him in the chest with the gun, he hissed, 'Clear off. Quit teasing Spinner.'

Percy shrieked, 'That thing better not be loaded.' He grabbed the barrel with both hands and yanked it to one side.

Clem shoved it back, pushing the other boy down. He growled, 'Go away, Percy.'

'Keep your hair on.' Percy pulled himself out of the raspberries, tearing his shorts. Then he sniggered, before scuttling off. 'When the Germans come, I'll tell them about you and your rabbiting gun.'

'Air rifle, you twit,' shouted Clem as Percy ran off, clutching a rip in his shorts so he didn't show his pants. He picked up his rabbits and looked up at her. 'All right, Spinner?' As Spinner nodded, he shouldered the rifle. 'I'd best get on. Got to do the milking for Dad.'

'Thanks Clem. I'd come and help, but I want to finish my letter to Mum so it'll catch today's post.'

Clem nodded and she watched him walk back through her garden into his farmyard, his curly black hair and the gun barrel both catching the sunlight. Then she stared out to sea from her attic window. Her mother was so far away. It was time to write her a letter.

Dearest Mummy,

We are all missing you like mad but we are coping well. I hope Granny is feeling better, then you will be able to come home.

Here, it's a lovely sunny day. Clem is milking his father's cows as usual. Daddy and I are all full of plans and we're thinking of keeping animals too.

Thousands of people are leaving the island. They think the enemy is coming, but I'm not at all worried, because Daddy doesn't think it's true. He says Mr. Hitler will need his soldiers for other things.

Yesterday, Daddy gave me a lovely new book to make notes in about the war so I can tell you when you are home. It's blue and I've drawn a kittiwake on the cover. Joe says it looks like a pelican.

In Guides, I've passed my poultry keeper's badge. Clem's mother is teaching me to make potato flour, which is a horrible boring job. Lots of grating and peeling because there are heaps of potatoes on the island, but not much flour. If the enemy comes we will be making potato flour every day. Let's hope it doesn't come to that!

Lots of love, Spinner.

She decorated the letter with cows, chickens, potatoes and a grater. Then suddenly she jumped. There was a terrible noise going on downstairs.

KERBANG! KERBANG! KERBANG!

Spinner threw down her pencil. Her father had begun his morning routine already. She sprinted to the banisters and belted downstairs, whizzing to the ground floor. Then she leapt rodeo style to the hall floor. The daily racket was worse than usual.

Her father was making as much noise as possible, like an animal blundering around with its head stuck in a tin. The gramophone was turned up loud. Spinner skidded to a halt in the sitting room doorway, giggling. 'Dad, Dad, you'll wake the whole island.' She stuck her fingers in her ears to show him how noisy he was. 'It's EARLY.'

But her father took no notice. He was singing a song he loved, recklessly smashing together a saucepan and lid. His checked shirt hung over ancient corduroy trousers, his hair stuck up wildly and there was oil on his cheek. The gramophone was turned up full volume and so was his voice. 'I hate you baby, 'cos your feet's too big,' he boomed, dancing in slow circles and clapping a raucous rhythm. Large dusters were tied round his feet and there was a strong smell of polish. The duster drawer was open, spilling yellow. 'Oh baby, I like your smile, but your feet's too big.'

So, Spinner equipped herself with dusters too, tying

them to her bare feet with itchy string. Then she danced, her long plaits whipping into her father's face. 'My feet's too big,' she sang, whirling through the sunlight.

After a while, Mr. Braye stopped the music and wiped the oil slick off his face with his cuff. Spinner said, 'Why's there oil on your face?'

'I've been mending the boat engine. Stupid old thing. It's always breaking. Needs replacing really.' He dabbed his face again and looked at the floor. 'Dancing's the best way to polish, don't you think? It'll be such a lovely welcome when Mum comes home.'

They stared triumphantly at the gleaming floor, then Spinner's eyes lit. 'Do you think she'll be here soon? She's been in England forever. That's what it seems like, with poor old Granny being so ill.'

Her father took off his dusters. 'Mum's finding it so very difficult to buy a ticket back to Jersey. The boats are full to bursting.'

'You know what she's like,' said Spinner. 'She'll find a way to get back to us.'

'Of course she will.' Mr. Braye pinched his daughter's cheek, gently. 'Come on, a quick breakfast. I'm going to France for the day, now the engine's all right.'

'*To France?* But the enemy's there,' protested Spinner. She waved her hand at the window, towards the French coast a few miles away. 'All those explosions.'

'The thing is, our own British soldiers are stuck in St. Malo. We've been asked to fetch them, all the boats possible from Jersey.'

'Oh.' Spinner felt her stomach heave. She stared at the black clouds over France and imagined burning villages, so very near to their own little island of Jersey.

Mr. Braye said, 'It does seem a bit crazy, but the

enemy are still a long way from the coast and the Prime Minister says we must fetch them. So we will.'

'Mr. Churchill?' Spinner pictured the man with the cigar.

Her father nodded and sipped his cup of parsnip coffee. 'Eeeugh. This coffee's disgusting.' He tipped it down the sink. 'Look Spinner, I know it sounds a little dangerous, but I'm sure it won't be. If we don't help these stranded soldiers, we'll let them down. They could die. It's our duty, you know.'

Spinner nodded slowly. 'Supposing the engine breaks down again?'

'Mr. Jument's coming with me and we can always sail back. There's a steam ship going too. We'll stick close.'

Spinner managed to swallow her breakfast without crying. When they'd finished, she found a tin of toffees in the kitchen dresser. She went out with him to his bike and put it in the basket. 'For the soldiers,' she said. 'Mum was saving them for a special occasion.'

Mr. Braye kissed her on her forehead. He swung his leg over the saddle. 'We'll be back tomorrow unless we have to pick up stragglers. Will you ring your cousin Ginger and cancel his trumpet lesson today? The operator will put you through.'

'Yes, I'll do that. And I'll stay at Clem's house. The Percherons are very kind. They always give me Bill's old room.'

Before he was round the corner, Spinner shot next door and found Clem leading his father's cows back to the field. He nodded as she rattled off the news. 'Give me a few minutes, then I'll take you to the harbour on my bike, so we can see them off.'

Spinner's cousin, Ginger Martin, lived in the west of the island. His house was miles from Spinner's house, but he never minded cycling there for trumpet lessons with his uncle. Anyhow, he loved riding mile after mile towards Town, then on to the parish where the others lived on the coast.

He had a racing bike with drop handle bars and enjoyed showing off its red metal frame and derailer gears. When Spinner rang, he said, 'I'll come and wave goodbye too. Won't be long.'

Soon he was cycling between the high flat fields of the west. In no time he was speeding down St. Peter's Valley, weaving round cows going for milking and being splattered with cow muck. His precious trumpet was strapped to his back and a tin of biscuits rattled in his saddlebag. Across the water, guns still grumbled over France.

Ginger pounded the pedals with his spindly legs, his glasses misted with sweat. At last he was on to the sea-front. He gave a last burst of speed and nipped between potato lorries as they waited for their loads to be shipped to England.

Then he braked and stared about him in amazement. The quays were jammed with soldiers and people. Hundreds of islanders queued for tickets, each carrying one suitcase. There were men in uniform. 'Off to fight for King and Country,' murmured Ginger. 'Like Father.'

A girl had her arms clamped round a black dog. She sobbed into its shiny coat as her mother tried to prise her fingers away. He heard her say, 'Sorry, darling. But there's no room on the boats for pets.'

Ginger cycled slowly past, concentrating so hard that

he didn't notice when a stick was hurled at his front wheel, wedging itself into the spokes and stopping the bike dead. He cart-wheeled over the handlebars and thumped to the ground, trumpet thrown out of its straps and the biscuit tin flung out of reach.

The bike wheels whirred behind him and there was a sudden burst of laughter. 'Look where you're going, Four Eyes.'

Don't cry, Ginger thought. *Don't show you care.* He took a deep breath and pushed his glasses back in place. Someone loomed over him, sniggering, pressing his foot between Ginger's shoulders, keeping him down. There was a strange sweet smell, the scent of Percy's Brylcreme.

Ginger shouted, 'You flipping coward, Percy Du Brin.' He heaved his shoulders, then staggered to his feet as Percy lifted the pressure for a moment.

'Posh boy.' The snigger came again as Percy pushed him against the harbour wall, kicking him with his size ten shoes, grabbing his shoulders.

Ginger shoved with his elbow. 'Cut it out.'

Percy laughed his peculiar, high-pitched laugh. Then he stopped abruptly and glanced anxiously into the crowd. Somewhere in the crowd a boy was shouting, 'Oi, Percy. Percy Du Brin. What are you doing to my mate?'

Joe, thought Ginger.

Percy let go of Ginger's shoulders and raced away to a sour-looking woman. She took him by the arm and shouted in his face.

'OK, Ginger?' Joe stood close, looking his friend up and down.

'Thanks,' said Ginger. 'Thanks, Joe. I'm not too bad.' He nodded in Percy's direction. 'His mother doesn't look very nice.'

'That's the problem,' said Joe. He crouched down and peered at Ginger's knees. 'Get that stuff out of your cut.' He spat on his finger and wiped off a dob of cow muck, then rubbed it off on his shirt. 'Muck's not good in a cut.' He wiped his fingers again.

Ginger said, 'I don't know why Percy picks on me and Spinner.'

'He's jealous,' Joe said quietly. 'He's thinks you've got everything.' Then he added, 'You have to fight back with people like Percy.'

'I hate fighting. It's a waste of time.'

'But you can't just let people bully you, mate.'

'I don't care, though sometimes I think of using Father's shotgun.'

'What?' Joe's eyes widened. 'I can't believe you said that. I can't even see you aiming, let alone pull the trigger. Anyhow,' he looked behind him at the crowd. 'Keep your voice down. It's best no-one knows about your dad's gun. Stick to catapults.'

'It's a brilliant gun,' Ginger whispered. 'A Holland and Holland. I keep it oiled for Father. Single barrel. He's got a couple of...'

'Shhhh. Don't tell me,' said Joe. 'Now, are you OK if I leave? Got things to do.'

Ginger nodded, so Joe vanished into the crowds. He leaned his battered bike against the wall and limped to the pier head with his trumpet and biscuits, just in time to wave at his uncle. Two boats were heading towards the pier head, their engines on full. The tide was so high they were level with the quay, a steamship first, followed by Mr. Braye's yacht, its engine throbbing and red sails flapping.

On the foredeck, Mr. Jument coiled an anchor rope, his navy jumper tight under oilskins. He helped everyone on their boats. He knew all the tides and winds and rocks. Everyone trusted Mr. Jument when there was a job to be done at sea.

His uncle was in safe hands.

Mr. Jument tipped his flat fisherman's hat at Ginger as they sailed close. Ginger roared, 'Catch, Sir.' He chucked the tin into the boat. 'Mother sent them for the soldiers. Lovely biscuits, a bit broken.'

Mr. Jument caught the biscuit tin with one hand and tipped his hat again with the other. Then Ginger's uncle pulled the tiller and the boat went about, whipping away from the pier head. It raced away from the outer harbour, foaming at the bow as its sails filled. Mr. Braye shouted, 'Thanks Ginger, thanks for coming all this way.'

Ginger shouted, 'Good luck, Uncle Hedley.' He put the trumpet to his mouth and soon he was playing *Roll out the Barrel*, then *A Life on the Ocean Wave*, with the crowd joining in the singing. Finally, he played *God Save the King*, and they all stood in silence as the boats vanished round the point towards France.

'Hey,' said a tall boy when Ginger blew the last note. 'Nice playing.'

'Clem!' Ginger slapped him on the shoulder. 'You're a bit late. Did you see them go?'

'We were up there.' Clem pointed at the steps leading to the high harbour wall. Spinner and her friend Lizzie were dancing on the top step, whirling gas masks in a goodbye salute as the boats headed south.

The boys ran up the steps to join them and Spinner nudged Lizzie, pointing at Ginger's shoes, splattered with cow muck. Then they saw his scraped knees and Spinner said, 'What's happened to your poor legs?'

Ginger shrugged. He said quietly, 'Nothing much'

'Cow muck?' said Clem. 'It's me that does cow muck. Ruddy hell, things are changing.'

'Ruddy hell,' said Ginger, reddening. 'They are.'

'You boys.' A woman in a hat shook her finger. 'Language. Whatever's happened to you? And you, Clem Percheron, from a good church family.'

Clem pushed back his dark, curly hair and smiled. 'War. That's what's happened.' He pointed at Ginger's bleeding knees. 'Bloody war.'

The woman gasped and scuttled away. When she was out of hearing, Clem added, 'I tell you something. If the enemy lands, we'll fight back, won't we?'

'Ruddy right,' said Ginger. 'Let's work out a plan. Today. This afternoon.'

2pm

The old potato store was up the hill from Clem's farm, a perfect meeting place where Clem kept his punch bag with its drawing of Hitler's face on it. Although the roof needed mending and the room was dusty, it was away from prying eyes.

Ginger held up a notepad. 'First we make a list of those present.'

Joe frowned. 'We're all here.'

'Not Lizzie,' said Spinner. 'She's packing. They're leaving Jersey.'

'Why don't they stay and fight?' Clem rolled his eyes. 'Too many people are running away. Rats leaving a sinking ship.'

Spinner frowned. 'You *know* they have to leave. It's their religion.' She paused to draw breath. '*They aren't cowards.* They have to go.'

'Right,' said Ginger. 'I'm sorry about Lizzie. So, I'll write "everyone is present except Lizzie".' Spinner nodded so Ginger went on. 'I reckon that if the enemy invades, we need a proper plan, even if they aren't as bad as we think.'

'*What?*' Clem glared at him. 'They're blowing up half Europe.'

'Well,' said Ginger. 'Spinner's father knows plenty of nice Germans.'

'Yes, he does,' said Spinner. 'Loads. He used to play the trumpet in an orchestra in Berlin. So did Mum.'

'Flipping heck,' said Joe. 'They wouldn't want to do that now.'

'Let's get on with the plan.' Ginger cleared his throat. 'Actually, what we'll have to do is dent enemy morale. We're not murderers like Hitler.'

'What the heck does *dent enemy morale mean?*' said Joe.

'Make them fed up,' explained Clem.

'Let's work out what we could do.' Ginger licked his pencil and began to write.

Joe said, 'We'll invite them to swim in the pool and fill it with conger eels.'

'We could force them to eat conger soup…'

'Octopus.' Clem grinned. 'Chuck octopuses at them when they're sunbathing.'

'We could use catapults,' suggested Joe. 'Though we'll need to practise.'

Ginger wrote carefully, then went on, 'We need pigs. Train them to knock down soldiers. Pigs are cunning. They can be vicious.'

'Pig muck stinks,' Clem said. 'If we get some pigs, I could spread it on the roads where they march. And cow muck. They'll get filthy and they'd hate that.' Then he shrugged. 'Look everyone. We're being stupid, aren't we?'

'Why?' Joe frowned. 'It'd be a laugh.'

'We can't fight proper soldiers with pigs and catapults and cow muck. They'll have bayonets.'

'Don't,' said Spinner, shutting her eyes. 'Don't mention bayonets.'

'That's what we're here for,' said Joe. 'To talk about the enemy. None of the adults are making any plans, apart from running away, like…'

Spinner pinched his arm. 'Don't be horrible about Lizzie.'

'Maybe Joe's right.' Clem leaned forward, lowering his voice. 'We don't need to fight, just put them off a bit so they don't think it's such a smart idea to be here.'

'We know the back roads, the tides, the rocks.' Joe's eyes glinted.

'Not half,' said Clem, 'and Joe and I speak Jersey French. They won't have a clue what we're on about.'

Spinner said, 'I'll ask Dad if we can have some pigs.'

'Good thinking, Spinner.' Ginger scribbled furiously on his notepad. He read out: 'OK. We're getting there. So, our aim will be to defy the enemy and destroy their morale by being a general nuisance with tricks, pigs and catapults.' He looked over his glasses. 'That is, if they come here at all.'

The others nodded.

Ginger continued, 'If the situation declines, other weapons may be employed.'

'You're doing it again, Professor,' said Joe. 'What do you mean *other weapons may be employed*?'

Ginger indicated Clem. 'Clem has his Bill's rabbiting gun and I think Father hid his guns at home, too. I can learn to use them.'

'Ha ha,' said Joe. 'Ginger Martin with guns, I do *not* think.'

Spinner stood up impatiently. 'Let's stop arguing and sign in blood. We must swear.'

'This isn't bleedin' Girl Guides, Spinner.'

But she held her hand up. 'Like this. I Spinner Braye promise to be a loyal member of our Resistance Club, even under interrogation.'

Joe said, 'I've got a really good scab.' He picked at a scab on his knee and stirred a matchstick to find some blood.

'That's disgusting,' said Spinner. 'One of your worst scabs ever.'

Joe looked hurt. 'Well, I'm disappointed in you, when it's lovely stuff like this.' He waved his knee about so blood spattered on the floor.

'Nice one,' said Clem.

Ginger stuck out his knees. 'I've got some good cuts from Percy this morning.'

'Not deep enough,' said Spinner, peering at Ginger's knobbly knees. She grabbed the matchstick from Joe, stuck it in his scab and signed Ginger's piece of paper. When everyone else had done the same and the blood had clotted on the paper, they each held a corner of the Jersey flag and swore loyalty.

7pm

Spinner liked staying at Clem Percheron's house. She often stayed there on Saturday nights while her father played jazz for dances at the Pavilion.

'It's nice at your house, Mrs. Percheron,' she said, helping her to lay the table.

'You're always welcome, my love,' said Mrs. Percheron.'

After they'd said grace, Mr. Percheron tucked his table napkin into his collar, sniffed his stew and said, 'Well caught, son.'

Mrs. Percheron gave him a look.

Instantly, Spinner knew that the stew was made from the rabbits Clem had shot before milking the cows. Perhaps, she decided, rabbit was all they had. So she managed to eat up, slipping tiny bones up her cuff when no-one was looking.

There was only one thing she didn't like about staying at the farm next door. Under every bed was a potty for night-time use. They were beautiful potties, with roses round the rim. But Spinner knew she couldn't use one, not ever. Even thinking of it made her blush. The Percherons didn't have a bathroom, so if she needed to, she would have to go into the yard to the outhouse in the middle of the night.

In daylight, the outhouse was sunny. The seat was polished and neat squares of newspaper were threaded on string and hung on a nail.

But night time was different. She'd gone there once and spiders had dropped on her head. She'd dashed out, slamming the door on them. In the yard, her torch made shadows that moved and she'd been sure the place was full of German spies. Clem's father, Mr. Percheron was an important church man. He always said, 'The Lord will keep you safe, wherever you are, *Ma Chiethe*.'

She liked it when Mr. Percheron spoke Jersey French. '*Ma Chiethe*. My dear.' But she didn't think the Lord had much time to worry about a spidery outhouse in a little island like Jersey. He had a lot on His hands.

Before bedtime, Mr. Percheron read from the

illustrated family bible about Jonah and the whale. Spinner clamped her eyes shut. The whale was huge, with teeth, thrashing about in stormy waters with Jonah's legs sticking out of its mouth. She had a sudden vision of her father's boat sinking, the engine on fire. Her stomach churned and she said, 'I'd better pop next door to pick up my pyjamas.'

Crossing the yard, she listened for footsteps. But there was only the sound of the cows tugging at the grass in the last of the evening light. Soon, she was inside her own house and it was still warm from the heat of the day. It smelled of her father's cigar smoke and her mother's soap, even though they weren't there.

Spinner wandered around picking things up and putting them down. She visited the bathroom with its gleaming taps, wishing she could give such a room to the Percherons. Before she left, she stood at her bedroom window, watching the fires rimming the French coast all round the horizon.

'Good luck, Daddy,' she whispered. 'Come back soon.' She took her parents' wedding photo from her bedside table, ferreted for one of her mother's letters under the pillow, together with her pyjamas, toothbrush and her blue book. Then she pulled down all the blackout blinds and hurried back to the farmhouse.

Upstairs, in Bill's old room, the bed was high and Spinner almost had to take a running jump to get in. But the sheets were soft and smelled of lavender and there was comfort in the familiar tick of the grandfather clock in the hall. On the opposite wall hung a painting of Clem's brothers Bill and George when they were young, both in sailor suits, smiling. Big, jolly boys with sunburned skin and dark curly hair like Clem's.

She said a prayer for them.

Bill was dead, his ship hit by a torpedo in the Atlantic Ocean. There was no news of brother George, who'd been missing for months. 'Keep him safe,' she whispered in the dark. She thought for a moment. 'Don't forget to send me a pig. If You possibly could. Thank You. Thank You ever so much.'

9pm

As Spinner fell asleep in the feather bed at the Percheron's farmhouse, Joe was crouching under an upturned boat on the beach below his house. He'd been there for hours, hiding from his father. He didn't want any more shouting, just because he'd been out before sunrise fishing for his mother and sister's breakfast and pinching his father's fags.

Mr. Le Carin had yelled, his bony face close to Joe's. 'You'll find yourself on the wrong side of the big gully, then you'll never get home.' He'd yanked Joe by his collar and hauled him towards the belt that hung behind the kitchen door. But Joe had wriggled free and bolted to his hiding place under the disused boat. His father never belted him on the beach, in case people saw.

Joe waited until dusk, when he heard his father's boat chugging out to sea for the night's fishing. Then he crawled from his hiding place and nipped up the road, pausing outside Percy's house.

He heard Percy's mother yelling indoors. 'Get up to bed. Now.' Something hit the front door on the inside, hard, and there was a sound of shattering glass. Percy whined, 'I only wanted a second helping before bed.'

The shouting went on. For a moment, Joe felt sorry for him. He muttered, 'Poor old Perce.'

Then Percy yelled, 'I hate you. You never cook enough pudding.'

At that, Joe laughed and hurried towards his Auntie Vi's house. Percy's mother knew every way of getting round the ration book. He'd caught a glimpse of her once on the bus, her string shopping bag bursting with treats that Joe's mother could never dream of.

The evening was still warm. There were plenty of people about, chatting in the lane and smoking. Joe heard one say, 'Jerry won't come here tonight. There's a sea getting up.'

At Auntie Vi's house, the full moon shone on the marigolds that lined the square of gravel in her front garden. He took out his penknife and cut flower after flower, keeping the stems long and making a bunch. Then he ran to Spinner's house.

Her bedroom was in darkness, with the blackouts shut. He tried the door, but she'd locked it. Then he remembered that she was next door at the Percheron's. So he rooted around in Mr. Braye's shed in the moonlight and found a tin of nails. Tipping out the nails into a neat pile, he filled the tin from the water butt and stuffed the flowers into it. Then he left them on the back-door step for her.

Wednesday June 19th 8am

Mr. Braye didn't come back the next day. On the Wednesday morning, Spinner nipped home before breakfast. The wind was shaking the trees and the telegraph wires whined above. Her heart sank as she hurried through the gate into her garden. Beyond the garden walls and down the lane, the sea roared as it galloped back to the island and over the rocks where Joe fished.

Why was her father away so long? All the other boats had come home, every one of them, straight away. What on earth could he be doing? Surely one of the other boats would have seen him if something had happened? Didn't they travel together?

Then she saw Joe's marigolds in their tin on the door step and smiled. 'Good old Joe,' she murmured. Picking them up, she sniffed the flowers' clean scent, took a deep breath and unlocked the back door.

Upstairs, the wind rattled her bedroom window and a seagull tapped at the glass. A seagull carries the soul of a drowned sailor, everyone knew that. She banged the glass and yelled, 'Go back to sea, you horrible thing,' and pulled up the blackout blinds and hurried back to the Percherons, pulling her mother's cardigan around her shoulders.

As Mrs. Percheron handed out boiled eggs, Mr.

Percheron straightened his tie and cleared his throat. 'Your father's a brave man, sailing to France in this weather. Force Six, they say.'

Mrs. Percheron kicked her husband under the table before passing toast and butter. 'He's a hero, going to the rescue. They all are. '

'Battleships,' said Mr. Percheron. 'That's what we need against Hitler, not boats the size of matchboxes sailing into the jaws of death.'

Spinner dropped her spoon and a piece of egg-white wobbled to the floor.

Clem glared at his father.

Mrs. Percheron said, 'Take no notice, my love.'

'All the other boats are back. Joe said yesterday he'd seen them in the harbour, every single one except Dad's.'

Mrs. Percheron gave her husband a stern look. She smiled at Spinner. 'Daddy would like you to eat that egg, my love. Waste not, want not, as they say.'

'He's probably picking up stragglers,' Clem said.

Mr. Percheron muttered, 'More cannon-fodder for Hitler.' But when they'd finished breakfast, he put on his jacket and took Spinner to choose a rose for her hair and one for his button-hole.

They walked together round his fields as he did every day, first up the hill behind the farm towards the steep fields which Mr. Percheron called the *cotils*. That was where he and Clem planted potatoes in every nook and cranny of soil, where they caught the sun and grew quickly.

From the top of the hill, they could see the flat fields nearer the coast where his tomatoes grew in tidy rows. Spinner said, 'Daddy thinks the tomatoes are ripening early this year.'

'We'll soon be picking,' said Mr. Percheron. 'Nearly all

the potatoes are dug, except over there.' He pointed at a small field of potato plants, then leaned down and grubbed a few tubers that had been left in the ground. He handed them to her and said, 'Your father loves new potatoes.'

'I love them too, thank you.' Spinner looked out to sea. 'It's not so rough now and look at all those ships.'

'Carrying troops,' said Mr. Percheron. Then he added, 'I bet your father's home right now. Go and see.'

11am

Her father was asleep at the kitchen table, covered in ash like a grey stone statue. Even his trouser turn-ups were full of it and his wild hair powdered. She inched forward, whispering, 'Daddy.'

Mr. Braye lifted his head from folded arms, opened his eyes and turned to the other side. He'd slept so heavily that his cheek was dented from his fingers. She trod silently backwards, her hands behind her so she didn't bump into the dresser. 'Dad... Dad...' She bit her lip. He looked so tired.

Perhaps, she decided, she should fetch a blanket to wrap round him. It wasn't really cold, but that's what you did with people who'd come back from war. Blankets and cups of tea. She edged backwards a little more, planning to creep out of the room and find the rug that was kept in the sitting room for cold evenings.

Then her fingers touched something horrible behind her, a wet, cold piece of something that felt like flesh.

'AAAARGH,' she screamed, so loudly her father woke with a start, jumping from his chair so it fell to the floor with a clatter. 'What is it? What's happened? Who's hurt...?' Then he burst out laughing and Spinner did too.

She picked up a heavy plate from behind her and staggered to the table, trying not to look too closely at what was on it. 'Sorry I screamed, but I touched this and it was...' she made a face. 'Ugh, it was horrible. But it's only a conger eel.'

'A conger eel? How extraordinary. What on earth is it doing on the dresser?'

Spinner giggled. 'Auntie Vi must have left it, or Joe. But I thought it was... oh, I don't know. Something else.'

'Goodness. What a fierce looking fellow.'

They both stared at it, curled round itself, its eyes gazing back at them like grey glass. Mr. Braye picked up the plate, shedding ash from his clothes. 'I'll put him in the meat safe until we decide what to do with him. I suppose we'll make soup.'

Spinner put the chair back in place. 'Conger eels look like Hitler, don't they?'

'No moustaches though.' Mr. Braye put the plate in the meat safe outside the back door, then slumped into the chair again.

'What happened?'

'So much,' said her father. He wiped ash off his mouth, then went on. 'Our boats lifted the men off the French docks. We ferried them to troop-ships in the bay, over and over again, thousands of soldiers and some civilians as well.'

'Did they eat my toffees?' Spinner said.

'I gave them to the soldiers who'd waited longest. Poor chaps. They were so tired.' He felt in his pocket. 'One of them gave me this for you.' He handed her a French lollipop on a wooden stick. 'He'd bought some on his way up France, God knows how, for his daughter. She's twelve like you, waiting for him in England.'

'Do you think I could find him and say thank you?'

'I'm afraid you can't. The troop ships took all the soldiers to England. Actually,' Mr. Braye took a deep breath, 'they're taking them out of Jersey as well. And Guernsey.'

'What?' Spinner stared at him, open mouthed. 'But if the British army isn't here, what will we do if the Jerries invade? What will we *do*? We're a TINY island.' Her voice rose. 'The grown- ups say it's nonsense, as if we kids don't understand. They should tell the truth.'

'You know what I think?'

Spinner shook her head.

'Mr. Churchill knows we islanders are tough, whatever happens.'

'Not *that* tough,' said Spinner. 'Not *fighting* tough.'

'Of course we are.' Mr. Braye gave a wry smile. 'There's no need to be frightened of the enemy. You see, German helmets look like tin potties. We mustn't be scared of potty-heads, Spinner. That would be cowardly.'

12 noon

In her kitchen, Mrs. Percheron was packing a bag. 'Cake, jam, bread,' she murmured. When she saw Spinner, she smiled. 'I hear Daddy's home.'

'He's sleeping,' said Spinner. 'Where's Clem?'

'Off to see Ginger for the day.'

'What are you doing?' Spinner asked as Mrs. Percheron tucked another pot of jam into the bag.

'Just packing some provisions for a neighbour. We have to help each other out in these tough times.'

Spinner nodded. She chose apples for the bag and went on, 'Some of my school friends are going to England today. Lizzie's leaving.'

Mrs. Percheron's hands shook, but her voice was firm. 'Lizzie has to go to safety, my dear. Hitler doesn't like her religion. It's a wicked shame, but at least she won't be hurt.'

'Daddy says the Germans are nice really. They drink coffee and eat cake like us and they have Beethoven and all those composers, so why would they hurt Lizzie?' But then she stopped, suddenly thinking of Bill Percheron tumbling out of his ship in the Atlantic and wishing she hadn't opened her stupid mouth.

'There's good in every nation.' Mrs. Percheron gave a ghost of a smile. 'I think I'll send the family a pot of cream too.'

Spinner said that would be wonderful. Then she returned thoughtfully home.

Her father was washed and dressed, talking on the phone. His face was white and he was shaking his head. 'Dear God. I can't believe it.'

When he saw Spinner standing there, he put down the phone and said nothing.

'I heard you, Dad. Sorry. I didn't mean to. What's happened?' She held her breath. 'Is it Mum? Has something happened to her?'

Her father shook his head.

'Then what's happened?' Spinner felt her stomach churn.

Very quietly, her father said, 'France has fallen to the enemy.'

Spinner caught her breath. 'Oh, the poor things.' She looked out of the window at the French coast. 'So near us.'

Mr. Braye frowned. *'There are rules of war.* The enemy can't just… lay into them… they will be all right.'

'Are you sure Daddy?'

'I'd like to think so.' Mr. Braye put back his shoulders.

'Come on, let's cheer up and cook conger soup? The enemy will smell it from France. That'll put them off.'

'It does stink, doesn't it?' Spinner said.

When it was safely in boiling water, she slapped on the lid because the head was staring at her. She thought of what her father had said. 'There are rules of war.'

Then she noticed the time. 'Dad, the mail boat's coming in soon! Mum might be on it.'

Mr. Braye looked at his watch. 'Oh my word. Time has vanished today.' He turned off the gas. 'Let's go! Straight away!'

Soon they were on the edge of town on his bike, weaving round lorries stacked with barrels stamped *Jersey Royals*. 'It's worse than Monday,' said Spinner, jumping off the luggage rack. She gazed at the thousands of people waiting patiently to leave the island. 'Oh. There's Lizzie. Lizzie! LIZZIE!'

But her friend couldn't hear her. The mail-boat was chugging into harbour and everyone was cheering and waving. 'Oh Daddy, I don't know what to do. I want to look for Mum. But I must say goodbye to Lizzie. *I must.*'

Her father nodded. 'I'll watch the mail boat. If Mum's on deck I'll wave my hat.' He patted her shoulder. 'Don't worry. It'll be ten minutes before the gangplank's down. I'll stay here, beside the lamp post.'

Spinner raced into the crowd, forging on towards Lizzie, pushing past old ladies as politely as she could. 'Lizzie! Lizzie!' she shouted. At last she found her friend sitting neatly on a carpet bag, her violin case beside her. 'Oh Lizzie, I so wanted to say goodbye to you.'

Lizzie looked up and smiled. 'I knew you'd come.' She felt in her pocket and said, 'I kept something for you.' She pulled out two small, warm stones, rounded and smoothed by the waves on the beach they both liked best. 'In my religion, we give stones to our friends when we part. I'll keep one, and you keep the other.'

Spinner felt a lump in her throat. 'Of course I will. I'll keep it safely until you come back home.' She held out the lollipop her father brought from France. 'This is for you, for emergencies. It's got a long story...'

She was about to tell Lizzie about the soldier in St. Malo and his daughter, when Lizzie's mother bustled through the crowd, pulling her daughter away with an apologetic nod at Spinner. 'We must go. There's just room for us. Please, Spinner, look after yourself. And if your parents want you to leave Jersey, you can stay with us in Devon.' She gave Spinner a piece of paper with an address on it and rushed away with her daughter and their pitiful pieces of luggage.

Lizzie shouted, 'I left my cat with Clem.' Then she was gone, dwarfed by the crowd, all bulky in layers of clothes even though the weather was hot, because there wasn't enough room in the suitcases.

'Goodbye, goodbye,' shouted Spinner. She hurried over to her father, but he wasn't twirling his hat. He was watching the last passenger coming down the gangplank. 'I don't think she made it,' he said.

Spinner put her arm through his. 'Maybe she'll get here tomorrow. She'll do her best, won't she?'

'You bet,' said Mr. Braye. He scratched his head and thought for a moment. Then he said, 'If Mummy can't find a place on a boat, would you like to go to England, too, like Lizzie?'

'No thank you, Dad. She'll definitely come back. She hates being away from home. So there wouldn't be any point, would there?

Monday June 24th 9.30am

Joe plaited his sister's hair, tied her ribbons and checked that her shoes were clean. He settled the baby in the pram and waited for Mrs. Le Carin as she changed into her best green dress. She said, 'It'll be lovely to go shopping, after my silly illness.'

'Everyone's stocking up,' said Joe. 'We'd better be ready.' He watched her walking away, her face held to the sun. Diddie held the pram-handle, chattering to Arthur and dancing excitedly along. As Joe watched, for no reason whatsoever, he had a terrible feeling. 'Everything's going to go wrong,' he whispered. 'It isn't Hitler and his plans. It isn't Percy or even Dad, 'cause everything's gone wrong with him already.'

When he went indoors, he noticed there was no jam-jar of flowers on the table. Mrs. Le Carin always found flowers, scavenging from the hedgerows and telling the children their names. 'Buttercups and daisies,' she always sang. She'd done it all Joe's life, even when there was only dry bread to eat. 'Flowers on the table,' she'd say, 'make us civilised.'

Then he looked round. His heart began to thump.

The kitchen cupboards were dusty. A coat of grease clung to surfaces. A broken cup waited to be mended.

The ironing sat in a crumpled heap. His mother loved to keep her house clean, even though it wasn't much of a place, just a narrow cottage on the sea wall. But she always made it feel like home.

Why hadn't he noticed these things before? He should have helped more. Perhaps he'd clean the house while she was out, he thought.

On the other hand, he really wanted to improve his catapult, because Auntie Vi said Hitler's men were coming for sure, any day now. He'd definitely need something to defend his family with.

He hurried out to the garden, dodging the washing line of nappies which flapped at his face like grey bats. Standing on the sea wall, he checked to see if his father was still fishing. Yes, his boat was still out at sea, just a dot on the horizon, chugging along between the flags that marked his lobster pots on the sea bed. He wouldn't be back for hours.

Back in the kitchen, he dragged a chair under the shelf to reach for his dad's shed key. As he pulled aside the shelf curtain, his eyes widened. 'Jam,' he gasped. 'Blimmin' piles of it.'

Mrs. Percheron had done the Le Carins proud. There must have been twenty shiny glass jars full of jam, scarlet and sweet. He stroked their lovely clean sides and felt the gleaming lids. Then he forced his hands away, wavering until he finally shook his head. He unhooked the key and climbed regretfully off the chair to head outside.

The shed reminded him of his father – the neatness, the cruel pincers and instruments for dealing with lobster claws, the cans of diesel lined up in size order, each a finger-width apart. All the same, the place was stuffed with useful things. Soon Joe had found the reel of elastic he wanted, strong and thick.

He usually pinched Auntie Vi's knicker elastic from her sewing basket when she wasn't looking. It was good for ordinary catapults, but not man enough for wartime. Anyhow, she'd blown up when he'd taken it last time, and hadn't given him cake for days.

He drilled larger holes in his catapult and sanded them, shouting at seagulls as they strutted on the shed roof overhead. When the holes were perfect, he wet the ends of the elastic and began to poke them through.

As he knotted the ends, he stopped mid-knot, catching a reflection on a tin. Something was moving in the garden behind him. For a horrible moment he thought his father was home early. 'Dad?' he whispered, glancing at the mess he'd made in the shed, curls of elastic and piles of sawdust.

He peered outside and his eyes widened. The kitchen door was open, flapping in the breeze. 'What the heck? What's going on?'

He stepped outside and glanced out to sea, giving a sigh of relief. Mr. Le Carin's boat was only just chugging into the harbour. When he was alongside, he'd still take ages to sort out his catch and hose down the boat.

'Must be flipping seagulls,' Joe said, nipping across the garden to shut the kitchen door. He went back to the shed and picked up his catapult. Using empty crab shells as ammunition, he hit the chimney pot bang in the middle over and over again.

After a couple more satisfying hits, he heard a sound on the beach, a rustling of paper, followed by loud crunches. He leaned silently over the wall. Percy sat on the sand below him, ripping off sweet papers, hurling them into the breeze and cramming sweets into his mouth.

'Litter lout,' yelled Joe. 'Don't make such a blimming mess.'

Percy looked up and sneered, spitting shards of humbug. 'I popped into your house for a look while you were in your dad's shed. Your house is disgusting. Don't your mum do any cleaning? Lazy, isn't she?'

'You nosy pig.' Joe glared at him and whipped another crab shell from his pocket. He pulled the new elastic as far as it could stretch, then let go. 'Bull's eye,' he yelled as the shell flew at double the speed it would have from Auntie Vi's knicker elastic.

Percy bellowed and clutched his shoulder.

Joe aimed again and got him on the bottom.

'Ow,' yelled Percy. 'Ow.'

As the boy raced away, scattering humbugs, Joe yelled, 'I'll kill you if you ever come near my house again. Nosy pig.' Then he made sure the latches on both gates were tightly shut so Percy would have to make a lot of noise to open them again.

First, he checked the metal one that led on to the road, then the old wooden gate on the other side of the house, in the sea wall where the steps were to the beach. After a sudden thought, he went indoors and peered under all the beds in case Percy had left something disgusting, maybe some dog's mess he'd found, or a dead seagull.

When he was sure the house wasn't tainted by Percy's visit, he hurried to tidy the shed. He dusted the work bench, coiled the elastic and straightened the fuel cans. As he finished, there was a familiar bang, bang, bang from a lorry stopping outside the house.

In the road, someone swore and a lorry door slammed shut. The metal road gate swung open and crashed against the garden wall. A heavy load was hurled to the gravel and there was an exchange of shouted goodbyes.

Joe locked the shed with shaking hands and raced into the kitchen to hang up the key. Then he jumped over the gate in the sea wall and down the steps, slipping underneath them to hide on shadowed sand.

'I know you're down there, son,' shouted his father from the garden. 'Come here, right now.' Joe tucked himself into a ball, wishing that his father was like Spinner's or Clem's, or even Ginger's.

Mr. Le Carin yelled again.

Tuesday June 25th 3pm

Mr. Braye stood with Spinner in the garden admiring the chicken coops he'd made, as well as a large rabbit hutch and pen. Lizzie's cat wound itself round Spinner's legs, purring.

'Off we go then,' said Mr. Braye.

Spinner followed her father to his car, an Austin Ruby. Mr. Braye poured some of his precious petrol ration into the tank then turned the key in the ignition and cranked the car until the motor turned and the engine began to purr.

The Austin Ruby took them up the hill behind their house and past Mr. Percheron's steep potato fields. From the top, Spinner had a clear view of the sea and the French coast. On every side, wild flowers bowed in the gust caused by the speeding motor and she felt like a queen. She beamed at her father. 'Mum will enjoy meeting the chickens.'

Her father pressed the accelerator hard, although the car was going perfectly well. 'She'll love them to bits. Make them little coats and hats, I bet.'

'She must be having a horrible time trying to get a ticket home.' They'd been to the harbour every day, she thought, and they still didn't know if her mother would find her way back to the island.

Spinner sat quietly all the way to the chicken farm, staring out to sea until her father distracted her by bursting into song. 'My feet's too big...' He took his eyes off the road for a moment and looked at her. 'We must keep singing, you know.'

At the chicken farm, hens, a cockerel and rabbits were waiting for them in cardboard boxes. Soon they were home and the new animals were settled contentedly into their home-made coops, staring hopefully at Spinner's radish patch. Mr. Braye said, 'The pigeons arrive tomorrow. What a menagerie we'll have.'

'And maybe a pig?' asked Spinner, hardly daring to ask.

'Come with me.' Her father led her through the gate to the Percherons' farmyard. 'Notice anything?'

Spinner looked round, puzzled. Clem had begun the evening milking. They could see his back, his blue shirt like a dash of sea. Everything looked the same. Mr. Braye called out, 'Are they here yet?'

'They arrived while you were out,' Clem called out. 'Lovely animals, quite big and already weaned.' He came out of the milking parlour to say hello, winked at Spinner, then turned back to the cows.

'Excellent,' said Mr. Braye. He led Spinner to the old pig sty in the corner of the yard and pushed her gently forward to look into it.

Her eyes widened in disbelief. 'PIGLETS! THREE!' She threw her arms round her father. 'Look at their curly tails. Oooh, thank you Dad.'

'You can choose one as your own,' said Mr. Braye.

Spinner leaned into the sty. The largest piglet, hairy, white and already knee-high, hustled over to be scratched.

Spinner tickled it under the chin. 'I like this one. She's smiling.'

'Animals don't smile.' Clem roared with laughter in the milking parlour.

Spinner shook her head. She was sure she could see a smile. Anyhow, she knew immediately this pig would be special. 'I'll call her Peggy,' she said, stroking the animal's coarse, wiry coat. 'Peggy the Piggy. That fierce one could be....'

'Hotspur,' shouted Clem. 'He's mine.'

Spinner looked at the black piglet with its red eyes and mean look. 'Good name,' she said, adding, 'The spotty one could be Patch. She's got a splodge over her eye.'

'Peggy, Hotspur and Patch,' said Mr. Braye,

Clem appeared with full milk buckets. 'I hear you've got rabbits and chickens as well as pigs.'

'Yes,' said Spinner, jumping up and down. 'It's so *exciting*.'

Clem looked at her kindly. 'Don't give them names. War makes people hungry. They're eating their pets in Holland. If the war goes on, we'll all have to think like farmers and remember that animals are food.'

'I'll never eat Peggy,' said Spinner, her voice fierce. She tickled the piglet's back again, then jumped as Lizzie's cat leapt from the farmyard wall to her shoulders, purring like an engine.

Clem gave his big grin. 'How do you fancy roast cat, with a nice little garnish of parsley?'

Friday June 28th 5.30pm

On the last Friday in June, Mr. Percheron said he had a few potatoes to dig in the top *cotil* and he'd be glad of help with them. He said, 'I want them on the boat for England tomorrow. I'll give you all half a crown if you can finish the job.'

In the afternoon, Spinner, Clem and Ginger waited ages for Joe to come and join them, but he didn't turn up. 'Joe loves digging for spuds,' said Spinner. 'He *always* helps and takes some home.'

'His dad's probably making him clean the boat again,' said Clem. 'Joe's had to do it every day this week, because he used his tools.'

'Poor Joe,' replied Spinner as they climbed the hill to the potato field. 'His father's horrible to him.'

'Dad says Mr. Le Carin was all right when he was a kid. Something happened to him in the trenches. Blew his mind to bits. ' Clem handed out baskets and forks. 'Let's start.'

After she'd dug her tenth basketful, Spinner said, 'Mum still hasn't come back. She rang again, then the phone got cut off. I didn't even get to say goodbye.'

'We haven't heard from Father for ages. I don't even know what ship he's on.' Ginger pushed his glasses back into place. 'Oh heck, my blooming glasses keep slipping off.'

'Mummy said she'd catch a boat if it killed her.'

Clem looked at her. 'Best if she gets here alive.'

Spinner glared at him. 'You know what I mean.' Wiping sweat off her face, she said, 'I think Peggy would like a swim. I could take her into the water on a string.'

'Pigs love swimming,' said Clem. 'They're very clean. They even do their business in the same place and don't roll in it. Like people.'

Spinner roared at this and when Ginger joined in, his glasses fell into a potato basket. As he flung out potatoes in his search for them, one hit Clem, who hurled it back. Then another hit Spinner, splattering dust onto her dress. She grubbed up more in the ground and chucked them at her cousin, but Clem moved in front of Ginger and bellowed, 'Stop wasting them.'

So Ginger lobbed a couple more, catching him on the neck.

Clem lunged at him, his fingers stained green from potato leaves. 'Surrender,' he shouted, grabbing Ginger by his collar.

Soon they were getting down to a good fight, with Clem trying to catch potatoes and save them. But all of a sudden, Clem froze, pointing at a dot on the horizon. '*Shut up*. There's a plane coming in from France.'

'Probably German,' said Ginger. He whipped a pocket telescope from his shirt. 'They were snooping at Town harbour yesterday.'

Spinner felt her insides turn over. Why didn't the enemy leave them alone? She shook the dust from her hair. The plane was flying nearer, very close, just off the Jersey coast.

As it flew close, Clem clamped his huge hand round her

wrist and shoved her to the ground, shouting, 'Jesus. Put that ruddy telescope away, Ginger. The sun's reflecting on it. They'll see us.'

'Crikey,' said Ginger. 'That one's a Heinkel. The pilot's aiming at us.'

Clem yanked the telescope out of his hands. 'Don't be daft. He's going *over* us, not *at* us.'

'Stop arguing,' shrieked Spinner. The German plane swept over the flat tomato fields towards the coast, then swooped upwards over them so she could see the pilot's smirking face. She crouched lower behind Clem and the stink of fuel caught the back of her throat.

Then he was gone.

'Advance party,' said Ginger faintly. 'They always do that. I read about it.'

Spinner dropped her basket. '*Look.*' She pointed towards France. 'Hundreds more.'

'Six actually,' admonished Ginger. 'Can't you count?'

The six planes roared towards them, until three wheeled away, heading north. 'Going for Guernsey,' said Clem. He swallowed, adding, 'Swine.'

Spinner gasped, 'The other three… look!' She pointed again. Those ones are going to *bomb* us.'

'Course they aren't.' Clem watched the planes, his eyes narrowing. Then suddenly he jumped up so he was in full view, cursing just like Joe and his father. 'You're right, Spinner. They're going to bomb, they really are. Look,' he pointed 'They're going for La Rocque harbour. You'd have thought they'd go for something more important …'

Spinner pulled him down again so he was hidden among the potato plants. Her voice was shaky. 'Joe's down there, cleaning his dad's boat.' She covered her face in horror.

The Heinkels angled towards the little harbour beyond

the tomato fields, machine guns rattling. Flames flared as the bombs dropped, then explosion after explosion ripped through the air. Even from far away on the sloping potato field, the children could hear screams.

Spinner joined in, her mouth square with terror.

Clem put his arm round her. All round La Rocque, they could see people scattering like ants, finding shelter inland. 'Jesus,' he said. 'The bloody, bloody...' But before he finished his sentence, the planes turned and headed straight for the three of them, machine guns strafing. 'Get down, further,' he yelled. 'They're coming for us.'

Spinner screamed as Clem threw himself on top of her and Ginger, so they were all in a heap. There was an ear-splitting growl above their heads, then a sudden spiftt spiftt, spiftt as bullets ripped through the soil all round them and the planes flew so low they scraped the tree tops.

'They're shooting us,' screeched Spinner. She pulled herself out from under Clem and peered between potato leaves. Then she gasped, 'I can see the pilots, laughing.'

'Get down, idiot,' shouted Ginger, yanking her flat.

The planes swooped away, stinking of fuel, then round in a circle and suddenly back over them. 'They're ruddy having a joke,' growled Clem. He pulled leaves over Spinner, trying to shield her with his own body as well. But the planes begin to lift again until suddenly, they were gone, racing away towards Town over the hill, flak cracking and popping like whips, circling upwards and roaring back over the sea to their base in France.

'Hilarious game,' stammered Ginger. He stuck his head above the potato plants. 'Bit close though.'

Spinner stuck her fingers in her ears. 'I saw their faces when they were over us,' she whispered.

'Course you didn't,' said Clem. 'They were too quick.'

'I did. They were laughing.' Staring at the others, she noticed that Clem, always sun burned like a true Jersey boy, had turned white. 'The planes had crosses on them,' she said, sobbing. 'Like ambulance planes. That's cheating, pretending to be doctors. There are rules of war, and they've broken them. *Bombing children.*'

'Different crosses, Spinner.' Ginger pulled an I Spy Book of planes out of his pocket and flipped it open at a well-thumbed page. 'Look.'

Spinner pushed the book away. 'I bet Mr. Churchill didn't think they'd break the rules when he left us all alone without any soldiers to protect us.'

They sat in silence, too shocked to talk any more. Then Spinner said, 'What about Joe? He was in his father's boat.'

Clem said, 'Joe'll be all right. He always is.'

Spinner clasped her hands round her knees, curling up into a ball. 'Daddy promised the Germans wouldn't hurt us.' She went on, 'I bet something's happened to Joe. *Something awful.*' She scanned the land below them. 'I want to go home,' she whimpered. 'I want to see if Dad's all right.'

'He'll be fine. He fought in the trenches like the rest of them. He knows how to hide,' said Clem, adding, 'Let's wait until we're sure the coast's clear.' So they sat in the evening sunshine, looking out for Mr. Braye on his bicycle on the road back from Town and taking it in turns to use Ginger's telescope and check for more bombers.

7.20pm

At last they decided the planes had gone for good, although there was no sign of Mr. Braye. 'He knows you're safe with us,' said Clem as they ran down the hill.

Ginger shot off on his bike. 'Got to check up on Mother and Rosie. They'll be worried,' he said, 'without me to look after them.'

Clem went to bring the cows to safety while Spinner rushed home past the pig sty. She skidded to a halt, wondering if they were frightened. But the pigs were calmly chewing turnips as if nothing had happened. She picked up Peggy, staggering a little at her weight, and cuddled her tightly, feeling her warm, wriggling body. 'Don't be frightened. Spinner's here,' she said, stroking the piglet's head.

But just as Peggy made a bad smell, Mr. Braye ran round the corner shouting, 'Spinner, Spinner, where are you?'

As she ran towards him, she dropped the piglet back into the sty and her father rushed towards her. 'Thank God,' he said. 'I didn't know where you were. I raced back from Town straight away and I've been searching ever since – under the stairs, under the table, even under your bed.'

'And we've been looking out for *you*!' Spinner's voice wavered. 'We watched the road for ages.'

'I came home the other way,' Mr. Braye said. 'Kept to the hedge, cycled like the devil. Where were you? What were you doing?'

'We were in the top field, the *cotil*, digging potatoes and…' she took a deep breath… 'we saw everything and after the planes bombed the harbour, they came for us. We could see the pilots, laughing.'

'Could you?' Mr. Braye looked horrified. 'My poor girl. How terrifying.' He stroked her head, his hands shaking.

'Now I've probably hurt Peggy, dropping her like that. I'm as bad as the bombers.' Spinner wiped her eyes. She lifted up the piglet and checked all her legs were working before putting her gently back. 'But I didn't. She's quite all right. So that's one good thing.'

Her father put his arm round her and led her indoors. 'Sit down, darling. Let's put the kettle on.' He looked out of the window. 'The bombers have gone.'

'How do you know they won't come back?'

Mr. Braye checked his watch. 'It's too late in the day.'

'Are you sure?' Spinner said.

Mr. Braye nodded. 'I hope so, darling.' The kettle began to hiss and as he took it off the gas, he said, 'It's very important to eat after a shock. What would be an extra lovely treat? Bread and treacle?'

'I'm not hungry, thank you. You choose.'

While her father searched in the cupboards, she nipped upstairs to wash her face and brush the ends of her plaits. Then she put on her mother's old blue cardigan and picked up Lizzie's stone, coming down to the kitchen slowly and checking out of every window that the bombers had really vanished.

Mr. Braye handed her a cup. 'Weak tea, with a little sugar,' he said. 'That'll help.'

Spinner edged round the kitchen table, putting down her cup and picking it up again over and over while Mr. Braye fried bread. 'You said there were *rules* of war.'

'They've been broken.' Her father spread treacle fiercely on the fried bread and handed it to her, but she pushed it away.

'What's happened to Joe? Why doesn't anyone tell me? I think,' she paused, staring wildly at her father, 'I think I should go and look for him.'

Mr. Braye took her shoulders and gently sat her down. 'Everyone will help each other down at La Rocque. I'll see what's happened when you feel better.'

'I don't want to be left on my own,' Spinner said quickly. She gulped some tea, then said, 'Sorry. That was selfish. If you go, I'll check the chickens and the rabbits, then I'll stay next door until you're back.'

Her father nodded. 'Whatever happens, you have to eat.'

Spinner wiped more tears from her face. 'I can't eat a thing.' Her face suddenly crumpled. 'Mum won't come back now, will she? Now they're bombing, the boats won't come from England.' Her father was washing the pans and didn't answer, so she picked up Lizzie's cat under one arm for comfort. Then she carried her bread into the garden in her spare hand. Outside, a strange smell of burning lingered in the air.

A few minutes later, Mr. Braye checked to see if she was all right, then made his way down the lane. Spinner listened to his footsteps fading away and chucked the remains of the bread at the cockerel because he kept trying to peck her. She dropped the wriggling cat and held a spade in front of her like a shield, dodging his beak and hoping he'd get stuck in the treacle.

'Watch yourself, Spinner,' said a familiar voice. 'Don't get a peck on the cheek.'

Spinner said, automatically, 'Shut up, Joe,' then whipped round, yelling, '*Joe!* We were worried sick.'

'Like my new look?'

Spinner gasped. Then she whispered, 'Well, at least you're alive.'

'Depends on how you see things,' replied Joe. He was covered in soot; his hair was wet and thick with pieces of gravel and he dripped blood from his nose and chin. Holding up a piece of shrapnel triumphantly, he said, 'They missed our place, but you should have seen the roofs catching. BOOM! It was like fireworks night.'

'Was anyone else…?' Spinner clutched Lizzie's stone in her pocket. 'Was anyone hurt?'

'Didn't stay to watch,' said Joe. 'There was explosions all over the place. People running in all directions, hiding under hedges and screaming and God knows what.' He paused then said, 'There was even a man burning.' His voice shook. 'Even Percy was running.'

'Poor Percy,' said Spinner, blinking. 'I don't like him. But that's horrible.' She blinked again. 'That poor man. Burning. That's just…'

'Them bombers are cowards, Spin. They gunned everyone as we ran, even a little girl on the beach. Flippin' b…' He staggered and held on to the fence. 'Dad's boat's been wrecked. Got an 'ole right through it.'

Spinner gasped. 'That's terrible Joe. You'd better come inside and sit down. How's he going to fish? What'll he do?' She held his arm as they walked to her house.

Joe felt in the pocket of his tatty old shorts. 'Got a spare hanky?' He staggered. 'A sticking plaster for my chin, too? The blood keeps messin' up my lovely clothes.'

Spinner gave him her hanky. 'I'd better wash your cut. I've got my First Aider badge in Guides.' She took a deep breath 'There are bits and bobs in it.' She dabbed at his chin, trying not to hurt. Then she gave Joe a clean hanky to cover it.

Joe stuck it on to his wound, cracking jokes about his pure blood not spoiling her hanky. Then blood suddenly gushed from his nose like water from a tap. It seeped through the hanky, scarlet and purple and he collapsed and fell with a thump to the kitchen floor.

A moment later, Spinner fainted too.

8pm

That evening, Joe's mother washed his cut properly and

gave him a cup of cocoa. Mr. Le Carin made up a camp bed for him in the kitchen, covering his son with his old army blanket. He put a pot of strawberry jam nearby, ordering Diddie not to touch it or there'd be trouble.

All night, Joe swam in and out of consciousness. His father sat with him for once in his life, but by morning he'd gone and Joe woke to hear his mother singing to the baby. She smiled gently at him. 'How's my Joe? *Man p'tit crabin? My little crab?'*

Then she washed the cuts again and squeezed his hand. 'Most of them have dried, but there's a small, deep cut. We'd better watch out or it'll get infected.'

Diddie offered him a wobbling spoon of jam. But Joe didn't feel like eating and his mouth hurt. He murmured, 'You have it, Diddie.' She shook her head and said she'd better not, because their father might be back soon from fetching Auntie Vi who was going to help them. She tidied his blanket and went out as Joe drifted off to sleep again.

Some hours later, he woke to a loud voice. 'Crumbs, Kenny Le Carin, your wife's ill, and you're a lazy beggar. *This place is a pig sty.* What a mess. Why don't you help her?'

There was fierce, low discussion about the bombing.

Mr. Le Carin said, 'Look Vi, I got other things to worry about than women's work. My boat for a start. And them stupid bombers thought the potato lorries in town was tanks.' He lowered his voice, but Joe heard. 'There's plenty dead. Just farmers, going about their business.'

'What's happened has happened,' said Auntie Vi loudly, 'Now we got to deal with it. Kenny Le Carin, we'll keep up our standards. We don't want them Germans thinking we're peasants, which is what this place looks like. A houseful of dirty peasants.'

Then Auntie Vi swept off with Mrs. L Carin, Diddie and the baby, saying over her shoulder, 'Pull yourself together, Kenny Le Carin. Soak those nappies in bleach. They're disgusting.'

With that, the door slammed and Auntie Vi could be heard commanding Diddie and the baby to behave and encouraging Mrs. Le Carin to hold her arm. Joe closed his eyes, listening to his father grumbling and picking up the scrubbing brush.

Auntie Vi was the only person who could deal with his father. Her own son had rescued Joe's dad in the last war, then died himself in the trenches. No-one talked about it, but everyone knew that if it hadn't been for Kenny Le Carin's cousin, he'd be dead himself.

Sunday June 30th

Joe drifted in and out of sleep for a day and a half. When he woke properly at Sunday lunchtime, the house smelled of polish. Auntie Vi stirred soup at the stove, a bleached apron round her waist. Diddie sat at the table, her hair and face shiny clean.

'Joe first,' ordered Auntie Vi. She spooned soup gently into his mouth, tutting at the deep, oozing cut. Then she gave soup to Diddie. 'Custard for afters, if you finish every scrap.'

Mr. Le Carin walked in and said, 'Where's Mavis?'

'At my place.' Auntie Vi gave him a fierce look. 'If she isn't better soon, I'm getting the doctor. Conger soup?'

'She didn't tell me she was feeling bad.' Mr. Le Carin sat, obedient as his children, holding out a bowl like Oliver Twist.

'You got eyes, haven't you?' Auntie Vi ladled soup.

Joe pulled up the blanket to hide his smile. No-one ever talked to his father like that.

Auntie Vi said, 'Your boat's got a hole in it. So you won't mend it. You're too damn sorry for yourself. You'll be back at that pub as soon as that.' She clicked her fingers.

His father murmured something, but Auntie Vi flapped a dishcloth at him and continued. 'Well, you'll have to do something else for a living, won't you? You've got three children and a wife, more's the pity.'

Joe fell back asleep and heard no more. When he woke, it was hours later and he was alone. He got up and ate the remains of the custard. Eating hurt, so he went outside, clutching his sore chin and nose. On the line, a row of dry, bleached nappies flapped in the breeze.

As he stood there, Spinner called out over the wall. 'Hello, Joe. How are you doing?'

Joe turned round gingerly. 'I'm all right. How about you Spin? I heard your mother hasn't made it back to Jersey?'

Spinner was silent, then she said, 'She got a call through last night. We all talked and said goodbye. She's tried to get on a boat for days, but it's too late now. There won't be another one.'

'That's really bad luck,' said Joe. 'Chin up, though.' He gave Spinner a wink. 'The Germans won't be here long. We kids will get rid of them. Then your mother'll be home in two shakes of a lamb's tail.'

'Course we will.' Spinner looked away and blinked. She put a basket on the wall beside him. 'There's some raspberry pies in there and a pot of cream. Mrs. Percheron said…' She stopped and turned round. 'Who's that?'

Joe looked behind her, hearing racing footsteps as well. 'Someone's in a hurry,' he said, as Diddie charged into the garden, her face red with excitement.

She snatched a breath and said, 'I just been to Sunday school and had a free bun and squash and the Germans are gonna send letters to say they're coming tomorrow and we got to give in our guns and we got to be good and if we don't hang up white flags, they'll bomb us to Mr. Keen's, Percy says.'

'Mr. Keen's? You mean *Smithereens*, Diddie. *Smithereens*.'

'I don't care where.' Diddie's voice was rising with excitement. 'We've got to paint white crosses on our houses and everywhere.'

'White crosses?' Spinner frowned. 'They're dead keen on crosses, those Germans.'

'Well,' replied Joe, 'That's very exciting, Diddie. Matter of fact, I don't mind the Germans coming. The bombs have done Dad no end of good. He's been quite nice ever since they dropped a load on his boat. If Hitler's lads come, he'll turn into a flipping angel.'

Diddie giggled at this. 'Clem hasn't got a flag, so he's flying a dirty hanky. '

'Right.' Joe grinned. 'Well I don't do white flags either. White flags are for cowards. But we'll leave these nappies on the line.'

'Auntie Vi's hung up her flags, already.'

'Them aren't white flags, Diddie. Them's Vi's bloomers.'

July 1940

Tuesday July 2nd 7am

For the first time in his life, Ginger wished he lived nearer his friends. He'd hardly slept because his mother's best sheet had hung under his window all night. He'd had to stop himself from ripping it down, because it looked like a coward's sign. But Monday, the enemy sent orders. 'If you don't hang up white flags, we'll bomb you again.'

Now it was nearly dawn, though the sky was still dark and the moon hung over the island. After groping for his glasses, he got out of bed. Soon there'd be soldiers marching through Town.

He tip-toed downstairs into his father's study and felt his way round until he'd put his hands on his father's shotgun. Lifting it carefully with both hands, he slipped outside and headed in the moonlight for his father's workshop.

He pushed open the door and laid the shotgun carefully on the work bench, stroking the long metal barrel and wooden stock and butt. Even in the dark, he could feel how carefully it was made.

For a moment, he imagined using it. Steadying his hand. Aiming. The explosion, then the terrible thud of a soldier's body to the ground. *I couldn't*, he thought. Then he thought of his little sister Rosie and his mother. He muttered, 'Don't be such a coward.'

As his eyes got used to the moonlight coming through the window, he unrolled an oil cloth he'd left ready the night before. He wrapped the shotgun in it, taking the weight again in both hands as he folded it round and round the weapon. Then he trussed it with string.

'Cartridges,' he murmured, feeling on the shelf where his father kept them, then shrugging and leaving them where they were. He murmured again, 'No point. They'll just get damp, even in a tin. I'll leave them.'

As he picked up the shotgun in its wrapping, his eye was caught by a small, hand written poster, stuck to the wall. '*Without Courage*,' he read, '*there is no virtue*.' The handwriting was his father's. Ginger smiled.

Repeating the words in time with his heartbeat, he carried the shotgun through the potato field and into a shed, where he lifted up the floor, piled the bricks and dug a long narrow hole. Soon the weapon was buried and the bricks replaced. Ginger brushed dirt over the floor until it looked like as if it had never been touched.

As the sun rose, he heard the German planes fly into Jersey from France, casting shadows on the beach and the island's dewy fields. It seemed as though this time there really were hundreds, not six like the Friday before. Looking up, he guessed they carried more troops than any of the islanders had imagined.

He fetched his trumpet and stood in his garden staring out to sea.

Lifting his trumpet to his lips he played the island's

song as carefully as he could, so that everyone who lived nearby could hear it. *'Beautiful Jersey.'*

As he walked back to the house, an ancient voice croaked, 'You're up early. Couldn't wait to see the soldiers, eh?'

Ginger gritted his teeth. Their neighbour, Old Gaston, stood staring at their house with shifty eyes. He did that all the time, ever since his father had returned to sea.

'Nobody wants the enemy here, sir,' Ginger replied politely, even though he couldn't stand Gaston.

Unshaven and stinking of cider before breakfast, the old man cackled. 'Yes, Master Martin. We islanders want to get on with our lives. We don't like foreigners.' He spat something slimy out of his mouth. 'Not that I hold anything against you, just because your pretty mother married an Englishman, wherever he might be now.'

'My father's in his battleship,' said Ginger, his voice tight with rage. 'At Action Stations, probably in the middle of the Atlantic.'

Gaston coughed again. 'That's what you say.'

Ginger clenched his fists and hurried indoors. There was lot to be said for owning a gun, he decided, even if it was hidden.

8am

On the other side of the island, Joe leaned against the upturned boat on the beach, picking scabs and counting German planes as they flew into the island. His catapults lay in a row beside him, little ones for close range, medium for bird scaring and big ones for bullies, so strong they could do triple bounces from wall to wall then on to the victim.

He'd tried the triple bounce on Percy a couple of days

ago and the result had been perfect. Percy had stared wildly around with no idea where the pebble had come from, because Joe had shot it hard against one wall and it had carried on to another, then another, then it had headed for Percy's backside.

Joe wondered whether or not he dared steal more knicker elastic from Auntie Vi's sewing basket or risk it from his father's shed. Double bounce elastic would be perfect for getting back at enemy soldiers. He laughed again at the thought, then frowned. His scabs were annoying, crusting over his chin. So he peeled another one off, wincing slightly. The cut was almost dry, but not quite. Blood welled up again.

As he flicked it into the sand, he heard a familiar voice.

He peered behind the boat at the road. Percy and his mother stood at the bus stop.

The boy wore his Sunday suit. 'Mum,' he whined, 'Why are we going to Town to meet the German soldiers? It's safer at home and why are you wearing lipstick and your best shoes as if you're going to a party?'

Mrs. Du Brin grabbed her son by the arm and Joe knew it would hurt because of her long fingernails. He could see them, scarlet and sharp. 'Shut up Percy. We've must look our best for the Germans. If we look good, they'll treat us good. All right?' She checked that her stocking seams were straight.

'But Mum,' he began, as the bus drew up. 'If we're dressed up, people will think...'

His mother kicked him sharply on the shin and Percy followed her on to the bus. Joe watched as the other passengers moved away and the Du Brins sat alone. He took a quick aim with one of the big catapults, then decided not to waste a pebble.

Up the lane from Joe, at Clem's place, Mr. Percheron opened the family bible and read, 'You shall not be afraid of the terror by night, nor of the arrow that flies by day. *For He Shall Give His Angels Charge over You.*'

Clem said quietly, 'His Angels didn't look after Bill, did they?'

'Stop that nonsense, Son,' Mr. Percheron snapped.

Clem flushed. His mother looked wretched.

George was still missing and his photograph had been moved next to Bill's on the dresser. There was a black ribbon round them both. Clem stood up, violently dragging his chair on the stone floor and shoving it back into place. 'Sorry. I didn't mean that.' He went out to finish his jobs on the farm, leaving an awful silence.

Before he fetched the cows, he kicked the wall of the milking parlour until his feet hurt. Then he hurled a pile of hay into the air, deliberately wasting it and treading it into the floor until his temper faded and he felt calm enough to fetch the cows.

After milking, he checked the pigs, tickling each one in turn under the chin and noticing how quickly they were growing. Peggy stood on her hind legs, peering over the sty wall. 'Oh no,' said Clem, pushing her gently back. 'No escaping, Peggy. Too dangerous with the enemy about.'

As he walked off, he added, 'They'll turn you into bacon.'

At that, Hotspur gave him a mean look and even Patch squealed. But Peggy charged round the sty and scrabbled energetically at the new board Clem and Ginger had added to the sty to make it pig proof.

Clem checked that it was secure. Murmuring to the cows, he walked them back to the orchard. Overhead, troop planes roared towards the island, black crosses gleaming. He tethered the cows on thick green grass, drawing comfort by leaning against their warm, thick flanks. Then he looked up at the planes. 'Damn funny angels,' he said, laughing dryly.

He could see Spinner in her garden with her father. Mr. Braye had his arm round her, and they looked too deep in talk for him to go and say hello. Spinner was clutching her recorder tightly in one hand.

When all his jobs were finished, he walked up the lane to the old potato store where he kept his punch-bag. As he boxed, he grunted with effort, shouting, '*You. God. How about sending Your Angels down to bring back Bill and George?*'

Then he punched four more times. As he punched, he thought about the stupidity of their plan to fight back. 'Hopeless,' he said, with every punch. 'Hopeless. Hopeless. HOPELESS.'

From Spinner's garden, the sounds of a defiant recorder tune floated up to him. So he changed the words. 'THIS. IS. HITLER'S. FACE. THIS. IS. HITLER'S. FACE.'

8.45am

Spinner was talking to her mother's photograph. In one hand, she held a large pair of dressmaking scissors. 'I'm sorry,' she said to the photograph. 'I know you like my plaits, but Percy says the Germans tie people by their hair.'

She waved the scissors about so they flashed in the sunshine. Then she snapped them together and metal blades sliced the air and glittered. 'Here goes,' she murmured. Taking a deep breath she snipped off her plaits with a rasping cut and each one slid to the ground with a thump. Then she shook her shorn head and glanced at herself in the mirror. What was left of her hair stuck out like a clown's.

'More,' she muttered, snipping until the floor was carpeted gold and her hair was a thumb length all over. She looked at her reflection again and laughed, before hanging the plaits from a hook beside her cupboard.

Then she peered out of the window, keeping low and listening for the tramp of jackboots. However, everything sounded the same – seagulls and waves breaking on the beach. Her father wasn't playing his usual morning music, but she'd heard him earlier, chatting on the phone.

She hurried downstairs, but he was nowhere to be seen. The kitchen door was open, so she went outside to give the animals their breakfast.

Peggy looked at her curiously, as if she was a stranger. Spinner ran her fingers through what was left of her hair. 'I'm still me,' she said, holding out her hand. 'Smell.' The pig turned her back and Spinner wandered indoors wondering if she'd been too drastic with her mother's scissors, then wondering again why her father wasn't crashing around singing.

However, there was a message from him on the table that she hadn't noticed before.

'There's nothing to worry about, hardly any Germans on the island, not Nazi types or anything, just the Wehrmacht, ordinary soldier lads. They're all behaving well. Porridge on cooker. Back soon. I've had to nip into Town.'

She ladled porridge into a bowl. As she licked the last

spoonful clean, the back door was flung open.

'ACHTUNG,' yelled a boy's voice. Spinner leapt out of her chair and shot under the table, the bowl flying out of her hands and crashing to the floor.

There was a loud chuckle, then, 'What're you doing, Spin?'

Spinner peered out from her hiding place, recognising Joe's scabby legs. 'Picking up my broken bowl because you made me jump, *idiot*. I thought you were Percy.'

'Oo-er, keep your hair on.' Joe picked shards from the floor and stared at her. 'Blimey, Spinner. What's happened to your crowning glory?' He spluttered with laughter, tried to grab at her stumps of hair, then ducked as Spinner picked up a spoon to hurl. 'Watch it Baldilocks,' he shouted. 'Don't open my scabs.'

Spinner flung the spoon at him. 'I don't care if I do. Don't call me that.'

'*Baldilocks, Baldilocks, Baldilocks*,' yelled Joe, holding his chin as she grabbed another spoon and chased him round the table. Then he held up his free hand to stop her. 'Listen. The soldiers are coming this way.'

'Oooh,' said Spinner, clutching her stomach. 'Daddy says they're just ordinary German soldiers.' She showed Joe his note. 'Perfectly nice.'

'They've got bayonets and big boots. Proper soldiers.'

Spinner's eyes opened wide. '*Bayonets?*'

'Bayonets aren't anything to worry about. They just wear them to look good. Let's throw rabbit droppings on them. I got loads in my pockets.'

'Rabbit droppings? On enemy soldiers? *Rabbit droppings?*'

'You're repeating yourself, Spin. C'mon, trust old Joe. I got my biggest catapult so we'll be quite all right.' He took her hand and pulled. After yanking herself free, she followed him outside, her stomach churning with terror.

At the end of the garden, they shinned up the conker tree that hung over the high wall next to the road. In the distance, men were singing. The tramp of heavy boots drew nearer and Spinner gulped as a platoon of soldiers rounded the corner, bayonets glinting, jackboots gleaming, their faces at the same angle facing left. '*Links, recht*,' shouted their sergeant.

'Oooh. Hilarious,' hissed Joe, loading his catapult. 'They're doing the goose-step like we saw at the flicks. Funny way to get about, isn't it?' He leaned through the branches, shouting, '*Heil Hitler*.'

'Shut up,' Spinner hissed back, pinching his arm. 'They'll hear us.'

'No they won't. They're making too much noise with their flippin' jackboots.'

The soldiers came to a crashing, disciplined halt under the tree. An order was given and the soldiers stood at ease and removed their helmets. When they'd placed them on the wall beneath the tree, she and Joe saw that they had pale, combed hair like coffee creams. She kept her voice quiet. 'Goodness. Their helmets really do look like potties.'

Joe whispered, 'Shall I nick one? We could do with an extra potty at our place.' He gave her a handful of rabbit droppings. 'Aim for the helmets, so when they put them on, they get an eyeful.'

Spinner swallowed, but Joe mouthed, '*Get on with it or I'll use my catapult.*' So she let them go one by one, dropping them carefully into the upturned helmets. Joe did the same until their supply was almost finished. Then they waited, trying not to snigger as Joe flicked the last few on the sergeant, who brushed them off his neck and looked round for flies.

He gave a sudden shout of annoyance, German style. *'Was is Das?'*

'That means What is That?' explained Spinner. 'Dad taught me. He used to live in Germany.'

The other soldiers finished their cigarettes, admiring the houses and fields. Then the sergeant barked another command and his men reached for their helmets.

'Leg it,' hissed Joe, slithering down the trunk. As they slid out of sight, the jackboots shuffled into place. There was another order, then cries of rage as helmets were hurled to the ground, bouncing and rolling along the road like skittles.

Spinner and Joe jumped off the lowest branch and raced to the farmyard, where they leapt into the pig sty, snorting with laughter. 'I can hear them coming. They'll be here in a tick.' Joe shoved Spinner into the dark hole at the back of the pen where the piglets slept. 'Ruddy heck. It flipping pongs in here.' He pulled her out of sight and Peggy nosed their faces, licking.

'Shove off,' hissed Joe, pushing her away.

'I'm going to be sick,' whispered Spinner. 'It's the smell. I'm going to be really, really…'

'Shut up,' hissed Joe. 'Hold it in.'

A soldier shouted something in German, horribly close. There was a silence and Spinner held her breath. Then his footsteps tramped away and Spinner was sick all over the pig sty. The piglets scrambled to gobble it up.

'Nice one,' said Joe as they climbed out of the sty. He looked at her with admiration. 'We could drop sick on the soldiers next time. Nice thought, eh, Spinner? Sick and muck on those uniforms.'

'I don't want to play any more tricks on them. Not one, ever. I don't think the soldiers look at all nice, whatever Daddy says. They've got mean faces, like Hotspur's.'

Joe looked serious. 'We signed in blood, Spinner. So we have to.'

Wednesday July 3rd 9.45am

Ginger raced into the farmyard and skidded to a halt in front of the others, a rucksack wobbling on his shoulders. 'Blimey everyone,' he panted. 'I just got stopped by a patrol.' His face was white. 'I forgot we have to use the other side of the road now, like in Germany. So this ruddy great soldier stepped out in front of me and...'

'I hope you smashed into him,' said Joe.

'Nearly, yes, I nearly did. I missed him by that much.' He held up his thumb and finger.

Spinner made a face. 'How horrible. What did he say?'

'Put it like this. He didn't smile.' Ginger leaned his bike against the barn and wiped his glasses with a hanky.

'Rude,' said Clem.

'Very. He shouted in my face. '*RECHTS FAHREN RECHTS FAHREN.*'

'What does that mean?' asked Spinner.

'Drive on the right like in Germany,' Ginger explained. 'But I pretended I didn't understand, like everyone else. It's a new rule. No-one's taking any notice. It's chaos out there. Horses and bikes and tractors all crashing into each other.'

'Are you sure he said that?' Joe said. '*Rechts FARTEN?*'

'*FAHREN*, you twit,' said Ginger, picking up his

rucksack. 'Look everyone, I've got loads of sticks. They're ash, very strong and bendy, better than you've got round here, nice little forks on them. Perfect for catapults.'

'I'll get some tools,' said Clem. 'We can make them in the potato store.'

Spinner hung back as Clem and Ginger sorted out tools and set off up the hill. She said to Joe. 'I don't like the sound of that soldier. I don't want to do anything that...'

'We're only making catties, Spinner. You can use yours for bird scaring if you don't want to have a go at the soldiers.' He grabbed her sleeve and pulled her along.

'Or Percy, I suppose.' Spinner pushed off his hand and quickened her pace. 'All right. I'll join in.'

Inside the potato store, Ginger tipped an untidy pile of sticks out of his rucksack. 'The soldier searched me as if I had a gun or something. I told him the sticks were fire lighters and he looked suspicious.'

'It's a hot day,' said Joe. 'Be reasonable, Ginge.'

'Yeah,' said Clem. 'But anyone could be carrying sticks for all sorts of reasons, throwing to dogs, planting seeds, anything.' He handed out tools. 'I can't understand why they look for trouble when we're such nice Jersey kids.'

'Girl Guides and Boy Scouts.'

'Church boys and girls.'

'Trumpet players.'

'Flippin' perfect, if you think about it.'

After sorting out the sticks, they stripped off bark, using Ginger's Swiss Army Knife. Ginger drilled holes while Joe sliced a broken old football into rectangles for slings. Clem punched holes in the leather with his awl and Spinner cut elastic and threaded it through, knotting each end.

When they'd finished, Clem said, 'I want to have a go at them right now. They're making so many rules already. It's not just Drive on the Right, it's...'

'Give in your Guns,' said Ginger, thinking of the gun he had carefully buried.

'Only listen to German wireless,' added Clem. 'No BBC.'

'Don't send letters to England,' Spinner added. 'And they've cut off the phone too.'

'Give us your Milk,' Clem growled, 'and your Pedigree Cows.'

'I heard,' added Joe, 'that all cars have to be given in and boats are being sent to France.'

'What?' Spinner shouted. She picked up a catapult too. 'We're not giving them our Austin Ruby, or our boat. Not for anything in the world. Why should we? Right,' she whirled it above her head. 'I'm having a go.' Rushing outside, she picked up a pebble and pulled back the elastic, yelling, 'Bull's Eye,' as she hit a gatepost.

'Blimey,' said Joe. 'You're flipping brilliant.'

Spinner pinged another.

'Bull's Eye,' shouted everyone and Clem said, 'Dark horse.' Then he let go a few pebbles, flinging them high. 'Best cattie I ever used. Brilliant.'

'Great elastic,' said Ginger, hitting the gatepost over and over again.

'Better than Auntie Vi's knicker elastic,' said Joe. 'Watch this.' His pebble whizzed at the gatepost, bounced off it at angle, then on to the farmyard wall and back to the barn again. 'Triple bounce,' he said. 'You have to get the angles right and you need a bit of power. Knicker elastic's not strong enough for a triple bounce, though it can do a double.'

'Blimey,' said Ginger. 'Impressive.'

'We need to work on it,' said Joe, 'so we're a crack team. Then the soldiers won't have a clue what's happening. A single shot's not much good. You can tell where the cattie man's hiding. But a bouncer... well, that's confusing.'

The others agreed and soon they were getting a few bounces. When they'd used up all the nearby pebbles, Spinner put down her catapult. 'An idea just whizzed into my head.'

'Pebble on the brain?' said Clem.

Spinner looked at him crossly. 'I think we should start a band. A really brilliant band.'

The boys stared at her, open mouthed. 'Right,' said Joe. 'A band. The soldiers will be so scared they'll toss their bayonets in the sea, drive the tanks over the cliffs and swim back to Germany. Ha ha.'

Spinner persisted. 'We'll make such a noise they won't even notice we're practising our catapults. We'll be the kids with a band, not the kids with the catties.'

Clem and Joe were still staring her, but Ginger said, 'Spinner's got a point. We could play jazz,' he went on enthusiastically. 'Hitler hates jazz. So they'll hate it, too.'

'Then let's go for it.' Joe pulled a couple of spoons from his pocket. He held them back to back and beat a rhythm on his knees, getting faster and faster until they blurred. When he'd done, he said, 'It's good but it flipping hurts.'

Clem was beginning to look enthusiastic. 'I'd like to play something big. Maybe a tuba, or a double bass.'

'Uncle Hedley's got a sousa,' said Ginger. He stretched his arms wide. 'Huge.'

'It's a big brass thing you move about on wheels,' explained Spinner. 'Takes a lot of breath though.'

'I'll go for that. How about you Spinner?'

She looked up at the ceiling. 'Recorder.'

'Ha ha ha, recorder.' Joe fell to the floor clutching his stomach. 'A recorder and a giant brass thing on wheels and me on the spoons and Ginger on the trumpet. It'll be horrible, blimmin' horrible.'

Spinner tapped her foot. 'We can take our band to the beach and play, especially if it's horrible. While we play, we can watch them and listen and learn.'

Joe clapped her on the back so hard she keeled over on to the dusty floor. 'Sorry, Spin.' He pulled her up. 'But you're a flipping genius.'

Spinner arranged herself neatly on a potato barrel. 'We'll go and ask Dad right now.'

'After we've hidden the catties,' said Ginger. 'We don't want Percy nicking them.'

'We'll hide Dad's car as well, under the woodpile,' said Spinner. 'We don't want that nicked, either.'

12.30pm

'A band?' asked Mr. Braye. 'What a great idea.'

'Show Clem the sousa,' suggested Ginger.

'The poor thing hasn't been used for years.' Mr. Braye brought an enormous horn-shaped piece of brass from the music room. He blew off dust and said, 'Have a go.'

Clem's eyes widened. 'Thank you, sir.' He dragged it nearer and blasted down the mouthpiece. His strong fingers pressed the keys and he produced a sound immediately, his face scarlet with effort.

'Sounds just like a cow farting,' said Joe, admiringly.

Clem blew over and over again, pressing the keys as Mr. Braye showed him what to do. Ginger took his trumpet from its case and put it together. Spinner fetched her recorder and warmed it as Joe pulled out his spoons again.

Mr. Braye said, 'We'll start with The Blues.' He played a tune on the piano that got them tapping their feet. 'Simple Blues are easy. You think of something that makes you sad, repeat it and explain it. Show them, Ginger.'

Ginger sang, 'I woke up this morning feeling sad, bumped into Percy, man it made me feel bad. That's boy's a mean boy, so I got the blues, man, I got the blues.' Then he played the same tune on his trumpet.

'Blimey,' exclaimed Joe, rattling a couple of spoons together in a rhythm. 'You're a marvel, Ginger Martin.'

Next was Spinner's turn. She played a few notes on her recorder then sang, 'I woke up this morning, sad and cross, woke up this morning, sad and cross, can't do anything 'cos Hitler's the boss. I got the blues, man, the blues, man.'

Clem blasted the sousa in salute.

'Haven't you got a quiet button?' Joe covered his ears. 'All this cow noise is getting me down.'

Clem bellowed, 'Sun isn't shining, don't know why, rain's coming on and the cows'll be a-farting till the day that I die. I got the blues, man, I got the blues.' Everyone laughed at this. Clem nudged Joe. 'Your turn.'

'I'll just play spoons.'

They played over and over again. After an hour, Mr. Braye said, 'I'd like to think you'll be famous, but really,' he laughed. 'It's a shocking noise.'

'Perfect,' muttered Joe.

Mr. Braye gave him a look. 'We'll have another go tomorrow. Seven sharp.'

They finished the evening with a watery cup of cocoa, trying to think of a good name for the band. 'The Rechts Fartens,' suggested Joe, before Clem sat on him.

Ginger leaned forward. 'How about The War Machines?'

'Are you mad?' Spinner stared at him, open mouthed.

'The Hot Trotters?' suggested Joe. 'That's more high class.'

Saturday July 6th 10am

Mr. Braye helped them for the next two evenings and on the Saturday, they all met at the old potato store.

Clem nailed up a sign on the door, THE HOT TROTTER CLUB. 'We've got to have a proper meeting room for our resistance club, so I made this.'

When they'd admired his notice, Spinner said, 'I made a club certificate using the one we signed in blood before the enemy came.' She held up a piece of paper. 'I typed the title nicely and the aims of our resistance club and stuck them over Ginger's handwriting so it looked smarter, but the blood still shows.'

Ginger looked over his glasses. 'You saying my handwriting isn't smart?'

'Typing looks more business-like,' said Spinner firmly. She went on, 'The c's don't work on dad's typewriter, so it says The Trotter lub. But who cares?'

They decided the certificate should be hidden somewhere safe, not on the wall. 'Walls have ears,' said Joe, 'and eyes too, if that twerp Percy's snooping. I'm making a den so I'll hide it there.'

Everyone agreed to this. Then Ginger said, 'So. When are we going to begin?'

'Next week?' said Clem. 'I won't be so busy digging

potatoes with Dad.'

'Tomorrow?' Joe flipped a pebble out of the door. 'I'm ready.'

Spinner bit her lip. 'When we're ready?'

Ginger shrugged impatiently. 'You're just putting it off. Let's take the band to the beach right NOW.'

'What?' Clem stared at him. 'We've only had three practices.'

Joe tapped his head. 'Crazy. Course we can't play NOW. We haven't a clue.'

Ginger took no notice. 'Look, the soldiers are off duty and they're playing football on the sand. It'll be fun, making lots of noise. Anyhow, I can play most of the time and you lot can join in randomly.'

Clem muttered, 'I can only play three notes.'

'It'll be funny whatever happens,' said Ginger. 'Hilarious.'

'Ruddy terrific,' said Joe. 'Utterly, totally, frightfully hilarious.'

Ginger frowned. 'Anyhow, the main problem isn't the enemy, it's carrying the sousa to the beach. It'll be like lugging a whale. We'll have to make a trolley for it one day.'

'Another time, we could take our old farm horse and the cart,' said Clem. 'Except he'd bolt for it if we played. We'd never see him again.'

'What about using your baby's pram, Joe?' asked Spinner. 'Arthur'll be in his cot for his afternoon nap soon, won't he?'

Joe thought for a moment. 'Dad's out, so... oh, all right, I'll fetch it. No time like the present.' He grabbed the club certificate from Spinner and shot out of the potato store. The others could hear him skidding down the hill, whistling.

'OK,' said Clem. 'Let's go too.' They shut the door and hurried back to the farm. Clem gave his sousa a polish and Ginger tuned his trumpet. Spinner went into her father's shed and returned with a painted board. 'Everyone's been painting boards,' she said. 'Dad and I made this.'

THE HOT TROTTERS
BEST BAND IN JERSEY

'The flippin' worst, really,' said Joe, rattling up with the pram.

After a quick practice, they set off to a beach with an outdoor swimming pool, a mile away. Ginger cycled with his trumpet in the basket and Clem pushed the pram, the sousa lying on its back like a big brass baby. Joe rattled his spoons all the way.

Spinner found them a warm spot on the sand and they parked the pram, looking around in amazement. Everywhere, soldiers were sunbathing and playing beach games, their laughter loud, bodies tanned and muscular. Some were diving into the seawater pool. Others were kicking footballs near a group of Jersey girls, who sat in deck-chairs trying not to watch them. Nearby, Percy was sitting with his mother, smugly eating ice cream.

'Blimey,' Joe hissed, 'You wouldn't think they was fightin' a war, would you?'

Some soldiers were taking photographs. Percy posed for them, while his mother applied lipstick. Nearby, an ice cream cart did a roaring trade. Joe propped the board against a stone and whispered, 'Their sun-cream stinks. Like flowers.'

'They're showing off to our girls,' Clem growled, glaring at soldiers demonstrating cameras. 'So many soldiers. Like 'ruddy greenfly, everywhere you don't want them.'

'Yeah, and we're not 'avin it. Play nice an' loud,' advised Joe. 'Then they'll clear off.'

Ginger picked up his trumpet. 'One, two, three.'

Clem blasted his sousa and Joe rattled his spoons then smashed them on his upturned bucket in a drum-roll. The girls shrieked and the soldiers stopped playing football. They sauntered across the beach to listen, as Spinner, with shaking hands, piped her recorder.

'Mouse farts,' mouthed Joe at her.

Some of the girls put their hands over their ears. But when Ginger joined in, his music was so beautiful that the others found themselves playing along with him, Clem giving a blast every bar and Spinner playing a sprinkling of notes.

'Sounds too good,' hissed Joe as the soldiers gathered round, clapping. 'Muck it up.'

Gradually, they all dropped out except for Ginger, who played on, hardly noticing his surroundings. The soldiers tapped their sunburned feet in the sand. One took photographs.

'Excuse me, mate.' Joe stared into the camera. 'What are you doing? Takin' our photos without permission? We charge for that.'

The photographer laughed heartily. He snapped his fingers at the ice cream man. 'We will send photographs home to show Jersey children entertaining the German troops, *ja*? Very kind kids.'

'Damn and blast,' hissed Joe, accepting an ice cream. 'Our plan's failed. They're using us as propaganda. *Typical*.'

Clem waved the ice cream man away. 'I'm not taking ice cream from them.'

Spinner and Ginger wavered, looking at each other

anxiously. After a long pause, they each accepted. Joe jabbed Clem in the back. 'Flipping take one, Clem, so I can have another.'

Clem shook his head, muttering grimly and ducking his head as Auntie Vi passed on her way home from work. 'You children,' she yelled. 'You should be ashamed. Taking ice creams from those men. BAH.' She stalked off, rimmed with rage.

Ginger sang, 'Auntie Vi is angry, man I got the blues.' The others joined him. 'Got the blues man, got the blues. Greenflies a crawling all over our ground, you see them every time you look around, I got the blues man...' As they finished, a soldier walked over to them. 'Your music, it is fun. But that man with the bristly hair and glasses, the sergeant,' he looked over his shoulder, 'he is very annoyed by you.'

Joe glanced behind the soldier. 'Blimey,' he whispered. 'He's flipping right. That sergeant's looking like thunder.'

'Shall I have a go at him?' said Clem, making fists.

Spinner clutched her stomach. 'I saw him earlier. He was writing notes in a little book.' She put her recorder into the pram. 'Let's not waste any more music on him.'

As they packed up, Percy strolled towards them. 'My mum's new boyfriend don't like your music, Cowpat.'

'Good,' growled Clem. 'He wasn't meant to like it. Stop calling me Cowpat and stop asking for it, Percy. If you don't shut up, you'll get it. Shove off.'

'Get what?' giggled Percy, licking his third ice cream. 'I don't know what you're on about. What you doing with a pram, Clem? You got a baby in there?'

Spinner took a deep breath. 'Of course we don't have a baby. But we've got something much more dangerous for big bullies like you.' Percy stuck out his tongue, thick with ice cream. She added, sternly, 'We've got *war machines* at home. Yes, *war machines*. You'd better watch out, Percy Du Brin.'

'Shut up, you twit,' hissed Clem, gripping Spinner's arm. 'Of course we haven't got war machines. She's only kidding.'

Percy sniggered. '*You* watch out, Clem Percheron. Your mate Ginger's half English. My mum's boyfriend says people like Ginger and his kid sister will be sent to a prison camp, because they aren't real Jersey people. They're not a pure race.'

Joe raised his eyebrows, but Spinner faced up to him. 'Not pure? Percy Du Brin, if anyone isn't pure it's you with your stinky Brylcreme like Adolf Hitler.'

Percy flicked the last of his ice cream cone into the sousa. Clem shoved the instrument to one side and leapt at Percy, grabbing him by the collar.

But Percy shrugged him off. 'They'll be very interested to know about your war machines.' Then he pointed at Spinner's head and said, 'Did the nit nurse shave your head?' He clutched his stomach, laughing at his own joke, then raced off.

'*P'lo*,' Joe yelled after him. He grabbed the handle of the pram. 'C'mon, you lot, I got to take Arthur's pram back or my dad'll belt me.'

As they trundled the sousa up the slipway, Spinner heard the soldiers saying, 'Stop lying, Percy. That is a children's band not a war machine. It is a terrible band so they need to spend all their time practising, *ja*? Ha ha, they are very bad musicians and will never play beautiful German music like Johann Sebastian Bach.'

'You see?' she said. 'Our cover works already. It's going to be brilliant.'

Ginger jumped on his bike and set off on the long ride home. As he left, a soldier shouted, 'Goodnight, Little Trumpeter. We liked your music on the beach. Very good of you to entertain the troops. *Guten Abend, ja?* Good Evening.'

'Little Trumpeter, eh?' Joe grinned. 'It's a better name than Ginger.'

They pushed the pram nearly as far as Joe's place. In his cottage, there was shouting. He turned swiftly into his untidy garden and didn't say goodbye.

Spinner looked anxiously at Clem as they walked home. But he shook his head as he staggered under the weight of the sousa. 'Joe'll cope. He always does.' Then he added, 'I wish you hadn't told Percy about our war machines. He's such a squealer.'

Spinner shrugged. 'They won't believe him. Even the enemy isn't that stupid.'

After that, they walked home in silence because Clem could hardly breathe under the weight of the enormous brass instrument. Spinner thought of Joe and what he had to put up with. She hoped he'd sleep at his den tonight, a place he'd told her about, the remains of a fishing shack by the sea.

'It's got a hole in the roof from the bombs,' she told Clem. 'He doesn't care about the hole in the roof. He goes there when things are bad at home.'

Wednesday July 10th midnight

The night before the schools re-opened, Joe slipped quietly out of bed at midnight. He crept along the corridor, then nipped out of doors.

His bucket was ready by the road gate, its handle oiled. He crouched low, listening. 'No-one about,' he muttered. Very slowly, he stood up, keeping in moon shadow. He scuttled across the road into a gap in the hedge on the other side and charged east along a flat farm track, holding the bucket to his chest, his bare feet feeling their way.

In the warm night, he could smell the ripeness of tomatoes. But he didn't stop. If he was caught, he'd have two hidings, one from his dad and one from the enemy, he knew that. Now and then, he checked his back pocket. His pen knife was still there, tucked well down.

At the end of the field, there was another and half way along that one, an open gate.

Joe kept low, listening again. The road bordering the tomato fields was in shadow from houses on the other side. Between the houses was a narrow lane with steps to the beach. He took a deep breath and scuttled across the road, then slunk down the sea lane, keeping to the darkest wall.

By the beach steps, he paused again, looking for refuges, noting a broken-down beach hut and an open gate into someone's back garden. 'Good,' he whispered, crouching low and moving down the steps.

He filled his bucket from a pool left by the high tide, then quickly climbed back, along the lane and into the road. Silhouettes were the danger. Everyone knew that. He shrank into the shadows, the heavy bucket of sea water weighing him down.

Then he grinned. The two army trucks were parked in the same place as he knew they would be. He listened again, but all was quiet. Quick as a flash, he'd filled the petrol tanks with sea water.

Just as he'd put on the second fuel cap, there was a shout, then another. Joe shot under the first truck, then crawled under the second and away across the fields like a deer, the bucket held tight against his chest again, laughing as he heard running soldiers and more shouts, *'HANDE HOCH! HANDE HOCH!'*

'Flipping hands up,' he muttered, sitting behind a tomato plant. 'They're scared of shadows, that lot.' He munched tomatoes until the shouting had died down, putting a couple in his bucket to give to Diddie. Then he went home by another route, stopping near a flagpole not far from his cottage.

He felt for his pen knife. The flag was at the base, rolled up and ready for Reveille at dawn. 'I'll have that,' he murmured, laying it on top of the tomatoes. Then he looked up at the halliard. 'And that.' The halliard slipped down like a snake. When it was coiled, he slung it over his shoulder and slipped home through the shadows, humming to himself.

Soon he was back in bed, the flag neatly folded under his pillow, and the tomatoes for Diddie out of sight behind the curtains.

Thursday July 11th 7.30am

Mr. Braye turned the volume extra high when the schools reopened. 'Just to cheer you up,' he said over breakfast. 'Nice piece of jazz.'

'We had so many plans,' said Spinner, tapping her feet to the music. 'Picnics and swimming, all sorts. I can't think why we have to go to school for a few weeks.'

Clem walked with her to school. 'We'll have to put everything on hold until the holidays,' he said.

'We've got time after school. We can all do double bounces so…'

'Shhh,' said Clem, pointing to a soldier standing outside the playground wall. He headed for the boys' entrance and she went to the girls' door. As she explained about her hair to her friends, she said, 'The soldiers are everywhere!'

Her friend, Lily Le Brocq whispered, 'They even listen under windows and snoop in gardens. We're keeping our pig in the attic.'

'*In the attic?* We keep ours in a pigsty.'

'He's quite happy. But he pongs. Loads of people are hiding pigs.' Lily glanced at the soldier. 'The Germans like sausages with cabbage. They call it *sauerkraut.*'

'Well,' said Spinner, folding her arms, 'they aren't

turning my pig into sausages.'

The bell began to ring and two German trucks drove past, then stopped, their engines making strange noises. Their drivers jumped out, shouting, to peer under their vehicles.

Lily whispered, 'I bet someone's put sea water into the fuel tanks. People do that.'

In assembly, Mr. Hinguette, the headmaster, cleared his throat as the children stood in rows, fidgeting in the heat, boys and girls on separate sides of the hall with a space between them. Clem stood beside him.

When the school was quiet, Mr. Hinguette announced that if anyone had problems at home they must tell him. Then he beckoned Percy. 'Percival,' he said, handing him an envelope, 'Take this to the office please and wait for an answer.'

Spinner looked at Joe. 'Percival?' she whispered.

Once Percy left the hall, the headmaster lowered his voice. 'Children, I am afraid we're no longer allowed to sing the National Anthem. I suggest therefore, that we say it instead.' He straightened his tie and everyone noticed that it was red, white and blue like the Union Jack. 'God Save our Gracious King,' he began, his voice almost a whisper.

Afterwards, he said, 'Remember our school motto. *"All that is necessary for the triumph of evil is that good men do nothing."* However,' he looked over his glasses, 'you must not hate anyone, even the enemy. That way, we become just as bad.'

His voice was kind, but he looked fierce. 'What I mean children, is the new authorities won't take kindly to jokes, so please don't start playing unpleasant tricks on them especially you, Josue Le Carin. I know what you're like.' He turned to Clem. 'Clement Percheron, as head boy, you will lead by example.'

Clem looked at his hands.

Mr. Hinguette went on. 'Do I make myself clear?

'Yes, Mr. Hinguette,' everyone chorused. But Spinner saw that Joe had his fingers crossed behind his back and he was winking at Clem, who tried to ignore him.

10am

It was hot indoors, even with the windows open. In the classroom, Spinner stared at one of Joe's paintings, which was pinned to the wall, a tea clipper bowling across an ocean. She looked out of the window at her pigeons on the school roof sunbathing and cooing. She wished she was outside like them.

Spinner straightened, suddenly noticing Clem at the classroom door. He was handing the teacher a note. The teacher cleared her throat. 'This is from Mr. Hinguette. He wants you all to know that there is a soldier listening outside and you must be careful. You know what they say, "*Walls Have Ears*".'

Joe stuck up his hand. 'Percy's mum's got a German boyfriend. He's got ears like a flippin' elephant.'

The teacher replied, 'Josue Le Carin, watch your language.'

'Sorry, Miss,' said Joe. But Spinner saw again that his fingers were crossed.

10.30am

Their class was out first, then the top one, Percy's and Clem's. Percy led the way, shoving aside his classmates and hurrying to the soldier, who still stood on the other side of the playground wall. He handed Percy a paper bag. Smirking at the others, the boy chatted to him, stuffing sweets and chucking wrappers about.

The rest of the boys kicked a football, glancing at the trucks. Their drivers were still underneath, draining the fuel tanks and shouting at each other in German.

Spinner skipped with her friends, dodging the football. She saw Clem walk up to Percy and say something, pointing at the sweet papers. Percy laughed, then whispered to the soldier, who stared at Clem.

'Percy's very friendly with the soldiers,' whispered Lily Le Brocq. 'His mother's got a boyfriend called Viktor. She kicks Percy out of the house when Viktor turns up.'

Suddenly, Clem was grabbing Percy's collar and shouting at him. 'Pick up those sweet papers!'

Sensing danger, Spinner rushed up, her heart beating. 'You know we collect sweet papers for the infants so they can make pictures. Don't waste them.' She glanced at the wall, relieved to see that the soldier had wandered off to talk to the truck drivers.

Percy sniggered. 'Cut it out, Baldie.'

'Bloody traitor,' Clem hissed. 'Eating German sweets.'

Percy stared at Clem as though he was a bad smell, all the way down from the top of his curly hair to his polished farmer's boots. 'Cowpat,' he bellowed. '*Church boy*.' Then he spat in Clem's face. 'That's for having a gun,' he shouted, turning to see if the soldier was listening. Then he spat again.

There was a long silence.

Clem wiped his face.

Joe shot across the playground like a bullet. He roared, 'Clem's right. You're a squealin' traitor.'

The pigeons rose in a grey and white wave from the school roof. Percy whipped round and pushed Joe backwards 'Learned your alphabet yet, Joe Le Carin?'

'What d'you mean?' yelled Joe.

There was another horrible silence and Spinner saw a film of red rise over Clem's eyes. He grabbed Percy's collar. '*P'lo*,' he hissed. '*Paisson d'cliave*. Stinking lobster bait.'

The other boys stopped their game. Their football bounced over the wall unnoticed and Spinner's friends moved closer. Lily shrieked as Clem jabbed Percy in the chest and sneered. 'I don't want to fight you, Percy. But I reckon I don't have a choice.'

'Cowpats can't fight,' said Percy. 'They haven't got fists.'

'Haven't they?' shouted Clem. He yanked Percy towards the sheds, pulling him out of sight of Mr. Hinguette's office. Everyone hurtled after the two big boys, yelling, 'Fight, fight, fight.'

Spinner stayed at the back, feeling sick. Clem never fought. She moved forward. 'Clem, don't.' She put her hand on his arm, but he pushed it away.

'MY FIGHT,' he growled.

Suddenly, Percy swore at Clem, a horrible word.

At this, Clem whirled back to face him. 'You blasphemous, greedy...' He stopped, as if he couldn't find words bad enough. He made a huge fist, waving it close to Percy's face.

Percy went white and backed off.

Clem danced from foot to foot, jabbing the air like a professional boxer. Then he drew back his fist hard and thumped Percy with all his strength, smack in the middle of his chest. 'You disgusting creep, frightening girls. You...'

Percy clutched his chest and moaned, but Clem punched Percy over and over again, on the shoulder and on his chest, the muscles on his arms flexing and rippling and his fists like pistons, every punch precise.

All round him, the kids stood in a circle and the boys shouted, 'FIGHT, FIGHT.'

Then Clem went for his chin and Percy groaned until at last he began to whimper, but Clem couldn't stop himself.

Spinner grabbed his shirt, but Clem wrenched away as she shrieked, 'STOP IT, stop Clem. You'll kill him. You'll kill him.' She pulled again at his shirt-tail and it ripped away, leaving long torn threads like tail feathers. She panted, 'You'll go to prison and… oh think of your parents. Your mother…'

At that, Clem froze, his huge fists in mid air. He stood still, drenched in sweat, his curly black hair plastered to his head. He gave Spinner a strange, unknowing glance and brushed sweat out of his eyes.

In the sudden silence, Percy began to cry, big blubbering sobs, like an actor.

Clem heaved Percy to his feet and said to the watching children, 'Go off and play, OK?'

Spinner turned back to Percy, wondering if she ought to help. But he sneered at her and she drew back. As he stumbled past, she saw one eye was swelling.

He suddenly lunged at her. 'You and your stupid friends had better watch out, with your war machines and catapults and kids' games. I know grown-ups who know about real war machines.' He pushed her away so hard she fell, taking Lily with her.

Then he went indoors to tell his tale.

Tuesday July 16th 4pm

Dearest Mummy,

We don't know how things are in England because we aren't allowed to listen to the BBC. I'm going to put my letters in bottles and send them on the tides. Joe said, 'They'll never reach England. Hitler's even controlling the tides these days.'

Our band's all right as long as Ginger's the only one playing! Clem's learned ten notes already. It helps that he's a choir boy and can read music, but he's not allowed to join band sessions at the moment. He's been expelled for fighting at school. Mr. P is FURIOUS and has locked him indoors. He's only allowed outdoors to go to the lav. So he hides notes for us in the outhouse.

He's had to copy the Book of Proverbs from the Bible in French and in English. 'Fools Give in to Their Anger,' and that sort of thing.

Anyhow, his fight worked because Percy's moved away and is living in the West quite near Ginger. Poor Ginger. Lucky it's holidays soon so he can come here.

The chickens are laying plenty of eggs and the rabbits have babies. Lizzie's cat is very interested in this and...

Spinner wrote two more sentences and was just signing off as her father came into the kitchen. He looked at his watch. 'I'm off to a Parish Meeting with Clem's parents. Promise you won't speak to him? It'll just make things worse.'

Spinner nodded. 'I'll do my homework. Fractions.'

Just as she'd solved a complicated problem, a pebble bounced off the kitchen window frame. Spinner pushed away her exercise book and went to the door.

Clem stood in the farmyard, finger on lips. He held up a note and gestured towards the outhouse, before going into it. A couple of seconds later he came out. He did a thumbs up to Spinner, then hurried indoors, catapult sticking out of his back pocket.

Checking that the coast was clear, Spinner went to find his note. Clem had written:

Dad let me out today to pick tomatoes. I left a bottle of sugar beet syrup in the hedge behind the flagpole. (Lower tomato field, by the road) Dad's bees are swarming and they love syrup. Maybe you can put two and two together?

She catapulted a pebble at Clem's window frame to show she'd read it, then went indoors to read about bees in her junior encyclopedia. By the time she'd made enough notes in her blue book, her father was back.

He said he'd talked to Clem's parents so they understood more about Percy. 'They still want Clem to write a letter of apology to him. Then he'll be allowed a sousa lesson. After that, he'll be able to see you all again.' He went off to his study, humming cheerfully.

Spinner called after him. 'I'll finish my homework

and then go and see if Joe's all right. His mother's not well again.'

Half an hour later, she was down the lane near Joe's cottage, recorder in hand. He was in the garden sorting lobster pots. 'How's your mother?'

'So so,' said Joe, stopping work. 'She's resting, so I'm looking after the kids. Dad's off somewhere.' He shrugged. 'No idea where the old blighter's gone.'

Spinner felt in her pocket for a toffee. 'Thanks Spin,' he said, turning it over as if it was treasure. 'I'll keep the paper and let Percy sniff it some time.'

'Want to come and tease the enemy?' she asked. 'I've got a plan.'

For a moment, Joe's eyes gleamed, but he said, 'I'd better not. The kids...'

'That's a shame,' said Spinner. 'Never mind, I can do it on my own.'

'Really?' Joe raised an eyebrow.

'Of course.' Spinner stuck her chin in the air. 'Of course I can. It's nothing bad. Just going to play them some tunes.'

'They aren't a joke, these soldiers. I know I muck about with them, but...'

Spinner frowned, 'I've got to do something myself,' she said.

4.25pm

Minutes later, she nipped through the gap in the hedge opposite his house. Crouching among tomato plants she watched through the leaves as soldiers goose-stepped past. 'Greenflies,' she muttered, taking deep breaths to steady her nerves. 'That's what Mr. Percheron calls them.'

She hurried on, keeping low until she reached the flagpole, pushing aside the long grass behind it. She gave a muffled yelp of triumph. Buried in the grass was a small glass bottle full of a thick liquid. She scuttled back into cover, eased off the stopper and sniffed. 'Sugar beet syrup,' she murmured. 'Perfect.'

Still keeping low, she slunk along until she'd reached the end of the field where Mr. Percheron kept his bees. The two hives stood in a sunny corner beside the coast road and the bees were in an angry mood. They whirled and buzzed above it as though there was no longer any room inside.

Spinner smiled. She'd read about bees doing this sort of thing in the encyclopedia.

Your bees will sound disturbed when their hive is overcrowded. This is a sign that they will soon swarm.

She hurried past the hives, keeping a wide berth. There was a country lane leading behind the hives, where she knew the patrols marched home, a shortcut to the barracks. Checking around her, she poured half the syrup into a hollow tree, sloshing it around the sides. She dabbed the rest on other trees before hiding the empty bottle.

She sat down away from the hives, but close enough to watch and began playing her recorder, shakily at first, then calmly, as if she had nothing else to do. As she played *Go Tell Aunt Nancy*, there was sudden roar from one of the hives. Spinner gasped, then flung herself to the ground, flat.

They were funnelling out of the hive like a water spout, a great black cloud spiralling upwards. 'A swarm,' she whispered. 'A wonderful, huge swarm.'

Then in perfect timing, she heard the crash crash crash of jackboots marching along the coast road. She wriggled into the hedge, peering between the leaves.

The swarm spiralled into the trees; the leaves shivered as a thousand wings thrummed.

The patrol marched closer, jackboots ringing on the road, wheeling off the main road into the country lane like puppets in perfect formation. '*LINKS, RECHTS, LINKS, RECHTS,*' ordered the sergeant.

'Left, Right,' thought Spinner, her heart thumping in time with the stamping boots. She edged out of her cover a little way, hoping for a better view. Then she gasped. The bees were whirling out of the trees, roaring round the soldiers' heads as they headed for the hollow tree and the beet syrup.

'*PAS AUF!*' yelled one, as the men raced in all directions.

'Watch out!' thought Spinner. She bit her lip as the soldiers flapped their forage caps at bees and slapped their cheeks, their arms and their legs. Suddenly, a young corporal broke away, thundering along the edge of the field, towards her.

Spinner shot back under cover, holding her breath and watching through narrowed eyes. The man's face was scarlet and sweaty, and there was a cluster of bees trying to squeeze down his shirt. He picked frantically at his collar, ripping out the bees with his fingers. Then he turned round and raced back to his men, blowing a whistle.

As if the bees had heard, the swarm picked itself up in a ball and roared into the hollow tree. There was a sudden silence, followed by a sharp order, then the sound of boots as the men marched off, their puppet feet keeping perfect time, even though they were in such a hurry.

Spinner watched a small cloud of bees flying after

them. When they were out of sight, she sighed with happiness.

'I did it. I did something of my own without the boys.' Then her legs turned to jelly, and she sat in the field as the church clock chimed six, then half past, trying to calm herself down.

Wednesday July 17th 7am

During the night, Joe got up to listen at his mother's bedroom door. She'd been very tired the night before and he was worried. The next morning, he checked again. She was still asleep. Usually she'd have been up, scraping together breakfast. He made her a cup of beetroot tea and she sat up, still very pale. 'You sit there, Mum. I'll look after the kids.'

He took Arthur from his cot and carried him to the kitchen as Diddie trailed after him, half asleep. There was nothing in the bread bin or on the shelves except the almost empty tin of cocoa and Mrs. Percheron's jam. He gave a spoonful of jam to each child, then took one to his mother. She opened her eyes, waved the jam away. 'Shall we ask Auntie Vi to help?'

'No,' said Joe. 'We'll manage.' He certainly wouldn't fetch Auntie Vi. The whole island would know their business if he did that. So he heated Diddie some cocoa-flavoured water and changed Arthur's nappy himself, jabbing him on the leg by mistake with a nappy pin.

That did it. Arthur screamed until his face was purple. Joe swathed him in the family towel and put him beside his mother in her bed. He told Diddie to wait for Spinner and walk to school with her, because he was going to follow the ebb tide to catch supper.

It had been like it since Monday – every night and every day the same – no father, no money, no food except winkles and limpets and his mother still sick. Joe got Spinner to write a letter for him to Mr. Hinguette, saying he'd caught his mother's illness and wouldn't be at school.

Mrs. Le Carin found some pence for bacon, telling Joe she didn't need the doctor because it was too expensive and she'd recover soon. But by late afternoon everyone was hungry and Joe didn't dare leave the children and go fishing for sand-eels. It would take too long and his mother still wasn't right.

Anyhow, there were soldiers putting barbed wire among the rocks. Joe longed to put sand into their boots, but he didn't have time.

Instead, he ran into town. With a racing heart, he slipped into the back of the grocer's shop, sliced off a hunk of cheese when no-one was looking and stuffed it up his shirt. Then he charged home before anyone could catch him. Not far from his house, his knees buckled and he sat against a wall, catching his breath, so hungry that he didn't think he could ever stand up again.

'I don't want to be a thief like flipping Percy.'After a while, he stood up, thrust back his shoulders and walked the last few yards home.

Later, there was a knock at the door. For a terrified moment, Joe wondered if it was the police or a soldier who'd seen him filling the tanks with sea water. He opened it a crack and saw Mrs. Percheron, smiling kindly. 'Just passing, my love,' she said, handing him a loaf. 'It's half potato flour, my dear. I made too much and it mustn't go to waste.' She didn't stare past Joe into the house, but simply patted him on the shoulder, saying, 'Come to us if you need more.'

That evening there was cheese and bread as well as the daily spoon of jam. Even Mrs. Le Carin managed a small slice of bread.

After Diddie and Arthur were asleep, Joe washed the nappies and hung them on the line.

Thursday July 18th 7.30am

The next morning, Joe stole buns. 'Family first,' he muttered, running home, his shirt stuffed with wobbling buns like a vast stomach.

'Nice,' said Diddie, tucking in. 'You 'avin one Joe?'

Joe shook his head. 'Look, I'm off for half an hour. Keep an eye on Arthur and Mum.' He knew there was only one person who'd stand up for him if he was caught thieving so he hurried up the lane to Spinner's place.

The kitchen door was open and Mr. Braye was sitting at the table with a large piece of paper in front of him. He was drawing black dots over the paper, using an ink-pen. Joe crept up behind him. 'Can I have a word?'

Mr. Braye jumped, scattering ink. 'Joe Le Carin! You gave me a right shock. Come in and sit down. Tea? Potato cake?' He glanced at Joe's face, then hurriedly put on the kettle and dabbed fat into a pan. As it spluttered, he kept his back to the boy so he could talk.

Joe began, 'I'm sorry Mr. Braye. I don't know what to do.' As he explained, he kept stopping, trying to swallow back the tears. 'I don't want to split on my dad, but we got to eat. I don't want the whole island knowing or some busybody will interfere and chuck us into the children's home.'

'I'm so sorry about your mother.'

'She's been really bad. She keeps going all weak and floppy.' He swallowed again. 'I don't know what it is, and she won't tell me and she won't waste money on the doctor,' His voice rose. 'We've got a special money tin for the doctor, and there's enough in it.' He wiped his nose on his cuff and blinked. 'Anyhow, Dr. Lewis wouldn't charge, he's that kind.'

'Do you have any idea where your father is?' Mr. Braye filled the teapot and turned potato cakes, still not looking at Joe.

'He's at the pub. Says he's looking for work. He does that every night.'

'Can I help?'

Joe shook his head. 'Like I said, she don't want any help just now, thank you. But if she changes her mind, or it gets worse, maybe...'

'I mean it,' said Mr. Braye. He went on, 'Spinner says you look after the kids a lot.'

'Someone has to. My dad don't.'

Mr. Braye handed him tea. 'I was luckier than your father, you know. I only had a month of the last war, then it was over.'

'My dad was in it two years.'

'He was a hero, your father, fighting his way through enemy lines and only fifteen years old. He saved his mates too, crawling through mud and bringing them back, some of them in a bad way.'

Joe sipped his tea. 'Dad don't say nothing about it. He just shouts about it at night and sometimes he stares at us like we're ghosts or something. Those days he walks about like he was fighting a flippin' hurricane, bent forward.'

The potato cakes sizzled and Joe's mouth watered. He cradled his mug in his hands. 'Proper tea, isn't it?' Mr. Braye nodded, saying he reckoned this was an emergency because they were all sick of beetroot tea.

'It's a pity my dad don't want to save his kids, isn't it? Like, stick together with us instead of stickin' to the pub.' The potato cakes were put in front of him and Joe ate the first proper food he'd had for days, trying not to gobble. 'I reckon my dad don't even like us.'

Mr. Braye packed a bag with porridge oats, biscuits, bacon and potatoes, tucking in a bottle of milk and the last of their chocolate bars. 'He does like you, Joe. Most people are like Russian dolls, layers and layers. Underneath, they're like everyone else. They love their kids so much it hurts.'

'D'you think Hitler's got layers? Or Percy? Or his mum's boyfriend?'

'Well, maybe not Hitler. He's a bit different. But Percy's probably all right underneath.'

'Percy's mum's nasty to him. That's why he horrible,' Joe replied, licking his fingers. 'Spinner's got layers, too. She pretends she's brave but she isn't.'

Mr. Braye said they all had to pretend these days. Then he asked, 'What do you want to do when you've left school, Joe? You could be a drummer, you're that good in the band already and we've only had a few sessions. Spinner tells me you're an artist, too.'

Joe shook his head. 'Painting's just for fun. No, I'm going to be a sea captain. Not in the Royal Navy like Ginger's dad, because I'm not posh. I'll be master of a cargo boat, carrying stuff all over the world. I'll have a sea dog called Beaufort, like the wind scale, and he's going to protect me from Dad for ever.' Then he looked at the piece of paper in front of Mr. Braye. 'What are you doing? Making up a code?'

Mr. Braye suddenly looked a little flustered. 'In a way it is. It's music which is a kind of code because each dot stands for a different sound. I'm composing a tune for my wife and Spinner's going to write the words. When the war's over and we're together again, we'll sing it to her.'

Joe's eyes filled with tears at last. He fought back a sob, hugging the bag of food to his chest. Then he said, 'Could you make one up for my mum as well?'

August 1940

Friday August 16th 8.30am

As soon as school broke up, everyone except Mr. Braye started work in the tomato fields. Her father was busy in town, Spinner explained, as they waited in the field for Mr. Percheron in the morning sunlight. 'He's gone to see the Bailiff.'

'Important man,' Clem said.

'Dad might have to translate for the Germans. I heard Dad talking to him on the phone.'

'The Bailiff's all right,' said Joe. 'He's a real Jersey man. He'll get round the Germans all right and he'll look after your dad.'

They picked on for a fortnight in the sunshine. Each lunchtime the children nipped into the sea to cool off, then ate honey sandwiches made with Mrs. Percheron's fresh potato bread. Ginger stayed for days to help, his pale skin catching the sun so he had to be covered with calamine lotion each evening. 'I hate wearing a sun hat,' he complained.

When the field was nearly picked, Joe chucked a

squashy tomato over the hedge, missing a pair of soldiers. 'Honey sandwiches are brilliant, but it's a nuisance having the grown-ups with us.' He chucked another tomato and sighed. 'I'm itching to do something to the enemy. We were going to do so much, then it was school, now it's picking. Blimey.'

Ginger pushed his sun hat to the back of his head. 'Tell you what. Let's take the band to the beach later. I'm staying the night again.'

'Hey. Nice one. I'm on. What about you two?' Clem looked at Spinner and Joe. 'Half an hour?' He picked up the full tomato baskets and carried them to the tractor trailer. When he'd emptied them, the others were waiting at the gate.

Joe said, 'I'll see you there. Need to fetch a couple of things.'

Soon they were on the beach setting up the band. Clem lifted the sousa out of the cart he'd made for it. When it was empty, Joe put two buckets in it, lids on, and pushed it in the shade. Then he pulled his spoons from his back pocket.

'Take it away The Trotters,' Ginger sang out and the others began to play.

Immediately a group of soldiers surrounded them, their lenses snapping as the band produced tune after tune.

During the break, Joe said to them, 'You must think Jersey's a lovely place, taking all them photos. But all that glitters isn't gold.'

'Jersey is *sehr schon*,' disagreed one man. 'Very beautiful.'

'It looks beautiful, but there is ugliness,' explained Joe sorrowfully. 'It's very sad, but you see, we have so much sunshine in this island that our brains have fried. It's a very unbeautiful situation.' He tapped his head.

'Ha ha, funny Jersey boy.' They laughed, offering lemonade. The others shook their heads, but Joe swigged from the bottle.

'I'm telling you, this island's full of people with fried brains.' He paused, 'You should cover your heads or you'll be just the same as us. Cooked.'

The soldiers chuckled, digging into kitbags for sweets.

Joe accepted a handful and nodded his thanks. Then he pointed at a seagull which was breaking a shell on a nearby rock. Before he stuffed a mint in his mouth, he nudged the nearest soldier. 'You want to watch out for them seagulls too. We've got a special breed of gulls here, flipping stone throwers and I tell you what...' he lowered his voice, 'they never miss.'

Ginger and Clem tapped their feet impatiently, wanting to play. But Joe said, 'Even listening to our music is dangerous. The madness is catching, you see. Of course,' he looked at them steadily, 'the other reason we aren't right in the head is that we've all been bitten by conger eels. Deadly poisonous.'

He nipped to the sousa cart and whipped off a bucket lid. 'Take a look.' Then he tipped the bucket upside down. A gigantic conger eel slithered out, snapping and lashing its tail as it headed for the soldiers' ankles. 'They can bite your leg off.'

One of the soldiers backed away but a sergeant lifted the conger eel with his bayonet, dropping it back in the bucket. 'It's wonderful that you islanders survive, *hein?* You must be strong. We Germans like strong people so we will stay here a long time.'

Soon the band was playing again. The soldiers drifted

off as the music went on, bringing sweets and drinks to them all evening until the sun was beginning to set.

As they packed up their instruments, Joe tried again. 'We have seagulls that throw stones, flying octopus...'

The soldiers roared with laughter again, slapping their knees. One said, 'Come to the beach again. You are so like German children with your blonde hair and blue eyes and love of music.'

'What?' Joe glared at them.

Clem bunched his fists. 'Let's go.' He began to drag the sousa cart up the slipway and Spinner and Ginger followed. But Joe reached into his other bucket and pulled out an octopus, sloppy and purple with big suckers on its tentacles.

'Don't,' hissed Spinner, glancing back at him.

Joe gave her a scornful look. Then he whirled the octopus round his head like a lasso and let go. It shot through the air and landed on the bare leg of an officer, who was paddling with his trousers rolled up.

The man jumped up sharply, whirling round. He limped across the sand towards the steps with the octopus wrapped round his leg, shouting.

'You idiot,' Ginger said, moving off with the others. 'Some people are being put in prison for cheeking the Germans.'

The officer hurled himself up the last step and grabbed Joe by the collar. 'Get this thing off me,' he bawled, plucking a waving tentacle off his hairy leg. 'We try to be kind to you kids. Then you repay us by stupid tricks. You should be grateful we are in your island, improving your ways.'

Joe raised an eyebrow. 'Improving us, eh?'

The officer glared at him.

'Sorry, sir,' said Joe, backing away. 'Actually, the octopus slipped out of my hands and flew off. The purple ones are terrific fliers.' He smiled politely. 'Just stick your hand in its mouth and turn it inside out. They always let go if you do that.'

'You do it,' shouted the man.

But Joe ducked out of his grasp and galloped away, diving into a hidden alleyway and zigzagging until he was safely in his new den, a shack hidden among the trees. No-one would follow him there. He shinned up a rope to the rafters, then peered through the hole in the roof. Below him on the beach, the red- faced officer was stumbling about, trying to put his hand in the mouth of the octopus.

Thursday August 22nd 6.30pm

A few days later, Joe and Spinner sat at her kitchen table in the evening. They were counting their earnings from picking tomatoes. 'It's a pity Mr. Percheron has to pay us in German money,' said Spinner, frowning. 'I haven't got the hang of it.'

'Flipping German Occupation marks.' Joe glared at his pile of cash. 'I hate them. Blimming...' But he broke off, staring out of the window with an open mouth.

'Blimey. Clem and Ginger just flew past like bats out of hell.'

Spinner hurried to the door, then ducked back inside. 'There's an officer pointing his finger and shouting. Good job the adults have gone to Town.' She peered through a crack in the door. 'Gosh, the officer's got muck all over his trousers.'

'Let's have a look.' Joe peered through the crack. 'Oh heck. It's Octopus Man. He's giving Clem and Ginger a right telling off. Next thing, he'll flipping arrest me.'

'What?' Spinner went white. 'He can't arrest children.'

'Oh no? That's not what I heard,' said Joe.

A minute later, they heard jackboots stamping away. Then Ginger and Clem turned up. 'What a temper,' said

Ginger. 'That was a nasty chap, don't you think, Clem?'

'Friend of Viktor's.' Clem gave a shaky laugh.

'Viktor?'

'You know. Percy's mum's boyfriend. They've been watching us all summer. Making lists. This one knows about the flags and petrol tanks and bees and everything else and the octopus of course.'

Joe grinned. 'I felt sorry for the octopus. Fancy being that close to such a hairy leg.'

'So, he's on to us?' Spinner bit her lip.

Clem shrugged. 'Well, he's ever so cross, talking about arresting me and Ginger just because we were moving some pig muck, and he…'

'…happened to be in the way,' said Ginger.

'Really, really in the way,' Clem said. 'But it might teach him not to stare.'

'Pig muck?' Joe's voice was full of joy. 'You can never get rid of that smell.'

'Ginger helped,' said Clem. 'I let him drive the tractor and trailer, but I forgot he doesn't know how.' He started to laugh. 'I tried to tell him, but did Ginger listen? Did he heck. He kept reversing into the road and then everything just tipped over.'

'You must have told me wrong,' said Ginger, looking serious. 'What a silly boy I am.'

'Octopus man doesn't know everything though,' said Clem. 'He never mentioned our pigs, even though he was covered in muck.'

'Why would he? We haven't trained them yet.' said Joe.

'How about starting now?' Spinner held up a bottle of pig oil. 'I told Dad I'd oil them while he was out. If they escape, we can just make up a story about them slipping out of our hands.'

'Oiling pigs? Why do you oil them?' Joe frowned. 'I don't get it.'

Ginger said, 'They're war machines, Joe. Remember? Machines must be oiled.'

'Pigs must be too or their skin gets flaky.'

Spinner looked at the clock. 'Dad and the others won't be back for half an hour and I've got a few stale biscuits.' She took a little package out of the cupboard and headed out. 'Let's go.'

When they were clustered round the pig sty, each boy held a piglet as Spinner oiled their backs. 'Good piggies,' she said, putting the bottle of oil out of their way. 'Reward time now.' She dropped half a biscuit into the trough and Peggy grabbed it. 'She's smiling,' said Spinner. 'Look.' She threw Peggy another, and the pig edged her brother and sister out of the way and got it first, stamping her feet impatiently.

Joe tried next. He held the biscuit high and backed away. Peggy leaped out of the sty, chasing him round the farmyard, snapping her teeth. 'Stop it,' he yelped. 'I'm all bones, you hairy twit.'

'Got an idea,' said Clem. He slung a rope round the pig's neck, tied her to a post and disappeared into his kitchen. A moment later, he returned, flourishing a pot of his mother's precious jam. He dipped a biscuit in it and ran down the lane. 'Untie her,' he yelled. Joe untied the knot and Peggy ripped the rope from his hands and galloped after Clem. There was a thump and a curse.

A few minutes later, Clem reappeared, a bruise flowering on his forehead. 'Brilliant. She'll do anything for biscuit and jam. Good old Peggy. You've got mileage, girl.' He put Peggy back into the sty and scooped some pig nuts into the trough. 'I'll put more boards round the sty tonight.'

'I'll help,' said Ginger. Then he cocked his ear. 'I can hear the grown-ups – they're coming home.'

'That officer,' said Joe. 'Octopus man. Did he mention catapults?'

'Not once.' Clem gave his slow, easy laugh. 'Not one teeny mention.'

'We'll let him get over the pig muck,' said Ginger. 'That's only fair. Then…'

'Then what?' Spinner bit her lip.

'We've got a plan,' said Clem and Ginger together. 'For Sunday evening. Bring your best catapult.'

Sunday August 25th 7pm

They met at The Trotter Club after supper.

Joe kept watch at the door. Ginger kept his voice low. 'You know how the patrol passes the graveyard at nine?'

'Every night,' Spinner said.

Clem leaned forward. 'So we'll probably see them, because we're going to lay roses on the graves at sunset. We have to fulfil the old Jersey tradition. You know. We *always* do it on the last Sunday of the school holidays. So we...'

'No, we don't,' Joe interrupted from the door. 'I've never done it, ever.'

Clem looked astonished. 'You've forgotten, Joe. Too much sunshine. We always do it, don't we, gang? At sunset, like I said.' He twirled his catapult. 'And we always take our catapults with us to scare off the seagulls in case they mess on the roses. Don't we?'

Joe banged his forehead with his fist. 'Silly me. 'Course we do.'

'When the clock strikes nine,' Ginger said, 'it's rather noisy. No-one would hear anyone creeping about in the graveyard. It's getting darker, this time of year.'

'It's the custom to wear dark clothes to lay roses,' said Spinner. 'Isn't it?'

The others nodded. 'Wise girl, remembering about the traditional clothes,' said Clem. 'Very wise indeed. Well, we'd better get ready to do our duty. It's a bit of a bore, this roses thing, but… there we are.'

'Nice Jersey kids,' said Joe.

'Always doing our duty,' agreed Clem.

8pm

Half an hour later, they crept through the fields in black clothes. When they reached the graveyard, Ginger held out a box of pebbles and shells and they filled their pockets. Clem handed out roses from his father's garden.

Ginger checked the church clock. 'We've got fifteen minutes.'

Spinner's voice was anxious as they slunk into the graveyard, looking for big gravestones to hide behind. 'Suppose they catch us?'

'Why should they?' said Clem. 'They won't know where the stones have come from, because of…'

'…ace triple bouncers,' finished Ginger.

'Anyhow, I told them about stone throwing seagulls,' said Joe. 'They can't say they haven't been warned.'

Ginger said, 'When I give an owl hoot, fire. OK?'

'Also,' murmured Clem, 'show respect. It's a gravcyard.' He glanced at the house opposite the church. 'I know the people there.'

Spinner watched him run off, silent in his school gym shoes. He knocked softly at the front door and whispered to the woman who opened it. She nodded, glancing up the road, adding something in Jersey French.

'She can see them coming,' he said, joining them again. 'Everything's arranged. Get into position, gang.'

He touched Spinner's shoulder. 'Nothing to worry about, Spinner.'

'I'm not worried,' hissed Spinner. 'Not at all.' She hummed a little tune as Joe dragged her to a grave and left her behind it. After fitting some gravel in her sling and trying a few shots, her hands steadied.

By the graveyard fence, she could see Clem and Ginger with a pile of stones beside them, roses laid on nearby graves. Joe sat on the church roof beating off inquisitive seagulls. The steady tramp of jackboots advanced towards the churchyard.

As the clock struck, Ginger hooted. Spinner pulled back her elastic and fired. She could see Ginger and Clem's arms working like pistons as stones zipped through the air, flicked off the walls and gravestones and hit helmets over and over again, rattling and bouncing from all directions like hailstones.

'Pas auf, pas auf,' shouted the patrol sergeant, crouching and looking wildly about.

Immediately, the children stopped.

On the last strike of the clock, Joe yelled from the roof, 'Get off, you blasted seagulls. Them Germans aren't used to stone-throwing gulls. Shoooooo.'

The sergeant aimed his gun. 'Hande hoch, hande hoch. Hands up.'

Joe waggled his hands at him. 'I can't, officer. I need me hands for shooin' off the gulls.'

At that, the sergeant tore into the graveyard. Spinner saw him trip over Clem and Ginger's feet as they knelt by a grave. He pointed his gun at them and shouted something furious. The window of the house flung open and the owner shouted a torrent of Jersey French, jabbing her finger at the patrol. 'You! Yes, you. What do you think you're doing, shouting at praying children, pointing guns?'

Spinner giggled nervously as the sergeant stopped in his tracks. She sneaked away to the higher part of the graveyard as he shouted, 'Madam, they've been throwing stones. There is a boy up there.' He pointed at the church roof, then frowned. The church roof was empty, apart from a seagull pacing up and down on the ridge… 'But he has gone.' He took off his helmet and scratched his head.

'They are laying roses on the graves of strangers. It's a Jersey custom this night. Look, you *pehon*.' The woman pointed at Spinner. 'That girl at the top of the graveyard's carrying roses. Over there,' she indicated Joe, 'is a boy. They are religious children doing their duty on an important day for Jersey.'

'As we are, Madam,' said the sergeant, 'doing our duty. My men are covered in cuts for their trouble.'

'You're damn lucky,' said the woman. 'It could have been worse if that boy hadn't scared away the seagulls. Bah, they're a problem in our island, the stone-throwing birds. Now,' she pulled the window catch, 'I'm off to bed. I suggest you do the same.'

The sergeant shouted to his men to assemble. Suddenly he lurched forwards and grabbed Ginger's arm digging his nails so they bit through his jumper. With his face so close to Ginger's, he growled, 'You aren't a real Jersey boy, are you? Half and half, not a pure islander.'

Ginger tried to tug away, but the sergeant dug his nails in further.

Clem moved forward, bunching his fists. 'Ginger's as good as anyone. He's the best…'

The sergeant whipped round and stared at Clem. 'You dirty peasant. Keep your mouth shut, or I'll visit your parents.' He turned to Ginger again. 'You have a mother and a sister, I hear.'

Ginger didn't answer, biting his lip to stop himself crying as the sergeant went on, 'We are watching you, little trumpeter, and your peasant friend the sousa player. We are not as stupid as that woman thinks.'

He glanced up at the roof. 'And that boy up there. Tell him to watch his step and the girl with short hair. The girl with the bees.'

He spat on the ground, then turned back to find his patrol.

When the soldiers had marched away, Spinner and Joe ran down to join the other two.

'That's Percy's mother's boyfriend. Name of Viktor. Nasty bit of work, isn't he? Filthy breath too, like bad eggs,' Joe said. He flicked Spinner on the arm. 'I'm off. Well done girl.'

'I'm going home. I bet they know where I live. I don't want my sister hurt because of me.'

'They know where *I* live too,' said Joe. 'But they'll be too frightened of Dad to do anything.'

10.30pm

When the others had left, Joe raced down the road under the stars to the shack into the trees. He loved sleeping in his den when he wasn't looking after his family.

He liked staring at the sky through the bomb hole in the roof from his bed of folded German flags, stolen from all over the island. He'd sketched boats on the walls, using charcoal he'd made himself.

However, as he closed his eyes, a vision came into his head. He remembered Ginger's words earlier and suddenly had a vision of him trembling in front of Viktor, his glasses askew, trying to defend his mother and little sister with his father's gun. The picture in his head seemed almost real and he sat bolt upright, yelling, 'Don't hurt him, don't hurt him.'

He tossed and turned but sleep wouldn't come.

So he got up, muttering, 'You'd better move away from that house, Ginger. You and your family and your gun,' as though his words would sail through the hole in the roof to the other side of the island.

Sitting at his makeshift table, he lit a candle stub and drew a picture for his mother. He drew the sunset on the beach, crayoning it carefully. At the bottom, he wrote a verse of her favourite poem, copying the words from her poetry book which he'd borrowed. He checked every letter in case he made a stupid mistake. After that, he began to yawn. As soon as he lay on his bed again, he sank into sleep.

When he woke, the sun was beaming through the roof hole onto his picture. He decided he'd take it home after he'd made a cup of tea on his primus stove. But as he filled his tin kettle, there was a bang like a thunderclap outside. 'Ruddy hell,' he shouted, racing across the room. There was another explosion and pieces of ceiling crashed to the floor, splattering him with dust and rubble. He leapt out of the way, shielding his head with his hands. He grabbed a tin potty and shoved it on his head.

The next explosion was nearer and the ground trembled. 'Crikey,' he muttered, 'it's like the end of the world.' Reaching for his stolen Zeiss binoculars, he hung them round his neck. Then he tucked a catapult into his belt and shinned up the rope on to the rafters. He felt the edges of the roof hole, pulling away shards of plaster and tile. Then he climbed out, crawling to the bullet-riddled chimney for shelter.

Feeling in his pocket for ammunition, he checked the grass below, then across the beach through the binoculars, listening for a German order. However, when he fired his catapult through the trees, no-one shrieked or shouted. Beyond the rim of sea, France lay swathed in smoke as usual, but the island was clear and sunny.

After a while he let himself down, deciding to nip up to Spinner's place instead of going home, in case they were in trouble up there. He tucked his picture under the flags and yanked open the door to brilliant sunshine and a shining sea.

A dazzling fountain exploded out of the water. The bike bell he'd hung outside the door rang, although there was no-one outside to press it. Joe ripped it off, slammed the door shut, jabbed in the key and twisted it. As the lock clicked into place, another piece of roof crashed to the floor inside. 'Jesus,' he yelled, before racing up the lane.

Monday August 26th 8am

'Depth charges,' explained Clem calmly, when Joe arrived into the farmyard. 'The Royal Navy's trying to blow up German communications at sea.' He glanced at Joe. 'No need to wear that potty on your head. You look like the enemy.'

'It's my hard hat,' explained Joe. He took it off, looking at the pig sty. 'What's *that* noise then?'

'They're nervous.' Clem passed the swill bucket. 'Give them their breakfast.'

The pigs were staggering around like drunks. Hotspur foamed at the mouth and even Patch was squealing. Peggy hurtled from wall to wall, crashing into the others and Joe had to push her down as she tried to leap over the wall. 'It's only a few depth-charges, piggies. Here, have your brekky and shut up.' The pigs skidded to a halt and lined up as he poured feed into their trough.

Spinner pushed open the gate. Although she was six years older than Diddie, she reminded him of his little sister today, trailing her mother's blue cardigan round her waist and clutching the cat. 'Lizzie's cat,' she announced with a catch in her voice, 'is frightened. Peggy was too. She jumped out of the pen and I only just caught her and she had the runs down my pyjamas.' She waved at the washing line, where her pyjamas flapped in the morning breeze.

Before Joe could say anything, she wailed, 'The hens haven't laid a single egg. Dad's in town. The phone keeps ringing and everyone's crying and I heard Dad telling someone that the Germans have iron fists inside velvet gloves. I'm *sure* they're taking revenge on the island because of us.'

'US?'

'Because of what we did last night and,' she shouted, 'I can't find my blue book *anywhere*. I kept a record of what we've done and if they find it...'

There was another huge explosion at sea. Spinner whimpered as a tower of potato boxes wobbled and crashed to the ground. A mouse scurried from underneath.

'*I'm* really frightened.' Spinner's mouth opened wide, like a toddler's. Out of it came a strange, high-pitched howl.

Clem raced towards her.

'Can't stop, can't stop' sobbed Spinner, cradling the cat. 'Hitler's bombing England and I'll never see Mummy again. Not, not...' she stammered, 'n... n... n... not ever again. Nor Lizzie. We don't know if they're alive or dead. *If only we had news.* If only there was some post, but they've cut us off. It's like prison living here, not knowing anything.' She wrenched herself away and fled up the ladder into the hayloft with the cat. Then the howling began again, muffled by hay.

Joe and Clem exchanged glances. 'Crikey. What'll we do?'

Clem thought. 'I know, we'll take her down to the sea and show her what's happening. It's best to know.'

'We could go to my den,' replied Joe. 'Well it's a shack really, I sometimes...'

He was about to explain about sleeping there, when Spinner emerged from the hayloft, her face blotchy. So he talked about the depth charges instead. 'Clem thinks we should check them out.'

She looked at him doubtfully. 'All right, if I can take Peggy. She'll feel safer with me. I'll oil her first because of the sun.'

They set off with the pig tugging her rope. Spinner tried to hold her, but it was no good. Peggy gave a massive grunt, heaved her hairy shoulders and pulled the rope out of Spinner's hands before galloping down the lane to the beach, her oily bottom twinkling in the sun. 'She'll get lost,' she yelled, hurtling after her. They dashed after her, jumping as another explosion suddenly rocked the island.

At the top of the slipway, they saw her on the beach. Peggy had stopped dead, gazing at a water spout in puzzlement. Then she slipped the rope off, leaped over the rocks and headed for Joe's den.

'Crumbs,' said Joe. 'She's smelled my tin of cocoa. You'll love my den, though...' Then he froze, pointing. On his shack door, someone had daubed, in thick, red paint, the word COCHON. He stared at it in disbelief.

'That's horrible,' whispered Spinner. 'Calling someone a pig's really rude.'

Joe shrugged. 'I bet Percy done it. He's always spying when he runs away from Viktor. Sleeps outside in the trees.'

Spinner's eyes widened. 'You never said he came here.'

'Didn't want to scare you.'

'I can't see him... Oh, oh dear,' Spinner gasped, 'We forgot about Peggy. The tide's coming up. She might drown.'

Clem snapped into action, pointing to the others in

turn. 'OK. You go right, you go left, and I'll go strai...'

But before he could finish, there was a squeal from the beach below. A voice yelled, 'Get off, you disgusting creature. You're all greasy.' Percy appeared, thundering across the beach. Then Peggy roared into sight, cornered him and yanked his shorts.

Percy flapped his hands at her and swore. But Peggy stuck her trotters into the sand and kept on tugging. There was a loud ripping sound and she stared at him, a large piece of material in her mouth. Percy yelled, 'Rotten beast.' He threw a stone at her and ran off, swearing.

'Crikey,' said Joe. 'That pig's got brains.'

'No she hasn't. Percy has sweets in his pocket,' said Clem.

Peggy galloped towards them and dropped the cloth at Spinner's feet. On it was a splash of red paint, crusty as blood. Joe picked it up. 'Our first scalp. Let's hang it outside The Trotter Club.' He looked at Spinner and Clem. 'Percy'll be on the warpath now and he'll definitely tell Viktor.'

September 1940

Thursday September 5th 7.30am

Dearest Mummy,

I wonder if my last letter reached you? Here's another. Fingers crossed you get it.

The pigs are growing and we're training them to help us with various things. Peggy likes to chase the soldiers and take off bits of their trousers. We always say sorry but we've hung them up like scalps. There are so many eggs to share, and we have a LOT of rabbit stew.

Auntie Vi has let down my school skirt with a strip of brown and orange curtain. It looks strange with grey flannel, but she says I will be decent and warm. It's boiling weather and the material's very scratchy. I lost my blue book but found it again so that's good.

We are allowed to listen to the BBC again after two months because the Germans want us to know about the Blitz. This is Propaganda, Ginger says.

It was still early, so Spinner decided to add to her blue

book. She drew Big Ben with flames round it, then wrote: *The Blitz sounds horrible.*

Downstairs, Mr. Braye put on a record, full volume, so Spinner put her book under her pillow and slid down the banisters.

Her father looked pale, as if he'd been up all night. 'That was Beethoven,' he said, 'His fifth symphony. Dit dit dit dah. It's on the wireless a lot.'

'Dit dit dit dah?' Spinner looked at him questioningly.

'The first four beats are the same as V in Morse Code. V for Victory. They're playing it on the BBC all the time and that's a kind of code too.'

'It's funny that we use German music as our code,' said Spinner. She took a piece of toast. 'What are you doing today while I'm at school?'

'This and that.' He looked away for a moment, then went on, 'I'm going to clear junk from the flat above the garage. Maybe whitewash the walls.'

'Why? Do the Germans want our house? They're doing that everywhere, Lily Le Brocq said. They just take...'

'No, no. It's not for us. I've invited the Martin family here for the winter. It's too far for Ginger to cycle in the dark. and anyway...'

'Ginger's no good at shooting.'

'Shooting? Why would he shoot?' Mr. Braye looked puzzled. 'And what with?'

'Defending his family,' Spinner said airily. 'He's excellent with his catapult.'

Her father frowned. 'I hope he won't have to do that. Some of the soldiers are all right, Spin. I met one the other day who plays the flute.'

'But there are soldiers like Viktor...'

'Hardly any, thank goodness,' said Mr. Braye. 'No, it's just that it'll be a dark winter out there in the west. Electricity will be rationed more, as time goes on. If they move here, we can pool our resources.'

'They have a horrible neighbour.'

'Gaston. He's...' Mr. Braye rolled his eyes and changed the subject. 'Have a good time at school.' He looked out of the window. 'Sometimes I wish we hadn't hidden the car in the woodpile. It's going to rain and I don't fancy a long bike ride in a downpour.'

'Cars are banned anyhow,' said Spinner. 'So it doesn't make any difference, does it? They took our boat, so I don't see why they should have the car as well.'

She picked up her paper bag of sandwiches. 'Good luck sorting the flat.' Then she went out to hitch a lift to school with Clem. He was wearing his senior school uniform, black and yellow. 'Hey, you look so grown up.'

'It's Bill's old blazer,' he said. 'C'mon, hop on the luggage rack.' As they cycled, he said over his shoulder, 'Dad said if I fight or I'm caught doing anything stupid against the enemy, I'm out.'

'Out?'

'Out of school and working on the farm,' said Clem.

'Oh,' replied Spinner. 'So The Trotter Club's over?'

Clem braked at the school gates and she got off. 'It's not over. We just need new tactics. Anyhow, winter's coming, so we won't have much chance.' He waved goodbye and set off to his new school in Town.

'We signed in blood,' muttered Spinner.

'What?' Lily Le Brocq turned up. 'What did you say about blood? Clem hasn't been fighting again has he?'

'No. He's given up all that,' said Spinner. She put her arm through Lily's and they walked into the top class.

But even though she had Lily, she suddenly she felt alone. Clem had always been at the same school as her, ever since she was five. Now he was with Ginger and everything was changing.

'It's funny we're in the top class, isn't it?'

Lily nodded. 'It's so grown up' She looked round. 'Where's Joe? I can't see him, or Diddie?'

9.15am

Mrs. Le Carin was ill again. This time it was more serious and Mr. Le Carin was working away still. At seven in the morning, she'd staggered into the kitchen and collapsed on the floor. 'Mum,' Joe had whispered, shaking her shoulder. 'Mum, wake up.' But his mother lay like a doll on the ground, her legs bent awkwardly and her skin pale and sweaty.

By the time the ambulance had taken her to hospital, it was too late for school. So he took Diddie and Arthur to Mr. Braye, his breath coming in gasps. Then he hitched a lift to the hospital and ran up its grey steps, along the corridors to his mother's ward.

'I'm staying, Miss,' he said to the nurse. 'You can't take me away.'

The nurse patted his shoulder. 'All right Joe. Just this once.'

'Thanks, Miss.' Joe sniffed and wiped his nose on his cuff, so the nurse gave him a clean hanky and drew curtains round one side of the bed so they could be private. All morning, he sat beside his mother, holding her hand. 'You're lucky you got the window bed, aren't you Mum?'

His mother nodded weakly, following his gaze. 'It's

a rough day,' she muttered. 'Good job your dad's not fishing any more, now he's working on the new road.'

'He wouldn't catch much this weather.'

Fierce autumn squalls scribbled the sea and flailed the leaves in the hospital garden. Rain poured out of a broken gutter on to the windows and his mother lay still, listening to it all. She opened her eyes when he told her about the sea patterns. 'Good old Joe. You know your weather like a proper fisherman's son.'

'I learned a poem for you from your poetry book. It took ages to learn, but Spinner helped.'

She squeezed his hand. 'Let's hear it.'

'*I must down to the seas again…*' said Joe. As he recited, he realised with a pang that she was different. Her hair didn't look right and she wore a funny washed-out nightie with a bow at the back, like a baby.

A different nurse came through the curtains. 'That's a lovely poem. But go home now, my love.' She took him by the hand as though he was eight. Joe didn't mind. She smelled nice, of soap and disinfectant. 'Joe, are you all right?'

Joe kicked the door open. 'Yeah. I'm always all right thanks, Miss.'

Outside, rain speared through his shirt and a German motorbike splashed him, roaring past importantly. Joe shook his fist, cursing like his father, but by the time he reached home, the storm was over and the sun shining again. Someone had tidied the kitchen and there were flowers on the table in a jam jar. Joe pulled off his sodden shirt and picked up a note beside it.

Dad took the kids to your gran's place like you asked him. They are all right. You can stay with us or Mrs.

P. says sleep at the farm if you like. We'll cheer you up.
Love Spinner xxxxxxx

Joe read it again, puzzling over a couple of words. Then he went outside and hung his shirt on the line. As it flapped in the sunshine, he sat in a corner of the garden against a lobster pot and thumped a sheet of corrugated iron with his fist. Then he hit it again, using both fists, faster and faster and harder and harder, battering so hard that it bounced and echoed against the wall. Even then he didn't stop until he saw that his knees were splattered in blood from his knuckles.

Then he clasped his hands round his legs and rocked to and fro, his head on his bloody knees, sobbing as though his heart was breaking.

Friday September 13th 8.30am

The next day, Joe borrowed Clem's bike and rode to the North find his father.

'I can't come,' said Mr. Le Carin. 'Too much work.'

'You can't face Mum not being well, you mean.' Joe glared at him. 'She wants to see you, so I reckon you'd better miss a few days' work.' He jumped back on Clem's bike. 'And you do want to see her, whatever you say.'

On the way home, the rain hammered down again and once more he was soaked, running up the grey hospital steps dripping. The nurse said, 'Your mum's a tiny bit better, dear. She just needed good food.'

He dripped into the ward and his mother smiled when she saw him. 'You naughty boy, getting so wet.' Then she looked at his knuckles and touched them gently. 'You been in the wars?'

'Just knocked into something,' Joe shrugged, then looked at his mother. 'You feeling better, Mum?'

Mrs. le Carin touched his knuckles gently again, and after a few minutes' chat she told him to go home and change.

Instead, he cycled to the farmhouse to give back the bike. Mrs. Percheron gave him a towel and some of Clem's clothes. When he was dry he sat at the farmhouse table and bit into a soft, hot bun, straight from the oven. 'Seaweed buns, aren't they? Mum used to make these before she got weak.'

Mrs. Percheron handed him a pot of jam and a large spoon. 'Pile it on, my love.' She poured more tea. When he'd eaten his fill, she showed him Bill's old room, patting the high bed. 'Stay any time.'

Joe smiled at last, because he'd noticed the potty under the bed, with its flowery decoration. 'Blimey, Mrs. P. That's a fancy one. Thank you for the offer.'

As he left the farmhouse, he saw Spinner feeding the pigs. Her feet were in a puddle beside the pigsty and her tufty hair was soaked.

'Come and see my den,' he said, helping fill the trough.

'Only if Percy's not about.'

'I haven't seen him since Peggy had a go at him.' Joe rinsed the buckets under the farmyard pump then suddenly slammed the buckets down. Spinner dashed after him as he muttered, 'If Mum dies, I'm going to take revenge on the enemy and it isn't going to be with catapults.' He lowered his voice. 'I flamin' mean it, Spin.'

'It's not the Germans' fault she's ill.' Spinner touched his arm, but he shook it off. 'She needs something called insulin. The hospital can't get it because the Germans are here. So it *is* their flamin' fault. The doctors would have sent Mum to England to sort it if it wasn't for bloody Hitler turning Jersey *into a flaming colony.*'

'A colony?' Spinner looked puzzled.

'Yeah. Ginger said they think we're a colony of ants for them to stamp on. Anyhow. *About Mum.* We all have to die sometime and Mum's lived a lot longer than Bill Percheron. That's what she said today.'

He kicked aside a rusty tin and stomped to the door

of his shack, unlocking the door with an angry wrench. 'It's the enemy's fault, because there isn't enough food in the island. The soldiers eat like kings. Mum needs the right food. And we can't get it!'

'She could have one of my rabbits. Roast, with parsley.'

Joe shook his head. 'You love your rabbits, Spin. It's all right. I can fish for her.' He looked round his den. 'I'm staying here till Mum comes out of hospital. Dad says he hasn't touched a drink for a month but I don't believe it and he might come home for a few days.'

Spinner shivered, remembering the time when she'd seen Mr. Le Carin rolling out of the pub, fighting, his flat fisherman's cap whirling off his head down the slipway. 'I'm glad you've got this place, Joe.' She looked at his drawings on the walls, the soft-looking bed on orange boxes, a row of metal cups and the little spirit cooker and even a flowers in a jam jar.

'The flowers are for Mum and the stuff's nicked from the barracks. They've stolen our island,' said Joe. 'So I don't reckon it's theft taking things from them. Sit down. Make yourself at home.'

She sat on a box with *ACHTUNG* stamped liberally all over it. 'Ammo box,' he explained. 'Nice and strong.'

'*Ammo!*'

'Course it's not ammo. They don't leave it lying around for us to pinch, you know.'

'Why would we pinch it? We don't really want to use...' She broke off and stared at the floor, putting her hand to her mouth. 'Joe,' she whispered, pointing, 'Blood.'

'What? I haven't cut meself.' Joe leaned down to sniff a small red puddle behind the cooker. 'No. It's not blood.' He poked it with his finger. 'Same red paint as last time. Still wet. I reckon Perce has broke in.'

Spinner's heart raced. 'We must've just missed him.'

'If he's blimmin' mucked about with my things, I'll kill him.' He riffled through his mother's poetry book. A note fluttered out, scrawled with Percy's handwriting. At the bottom of the paper, there was a thumb-print in red paint. Joe handed it to Spinner.

She read out loud: '*Hello poetry boy. How's your girlfriend Spinner? Funny name, like an egg whisk.*'

'Don't take any notice, Spin. He'll know you're reading it to me. He's probably drilled a hole in the wall to spy on us.'

Spinner looked round wildly, but Joe shook his head and said, 'There aren't any holes really Spin. Only in the roof and he wouldn't dare risk the climb.'

Spinner read on: '*My real dad taught me to pick locks. Isn't that a shame? I have another dad now and he's an important German called Viktor. One day, I'll show him everything you've stole, even the German flags on your bed. Ten, Joe. That's a lot of stealing and I got something you lot signed in blood. Be very afraid.*

'*Tell Spinner I'll tell my mum's boyfriend about her pig.*

'*Your enemy, Percival Du Brin.*'

'He's taken The Trotter Club certificate.' Spinner leaped off the ammo box. 'He'll show it to Viktor. Then we'll end up in prison. We wrote about using weapons. *WEAPONS*, Joe. We could be in terrible trouble.'

'Quit fussing.' Joe handed her a biscuit, stamped with a German name. 'Percy's a flamin' nuisance. Viktor won't take any notice. He'll think he's made the certificate himself.'

Saturday September 21st 2pm

Spinner ran upstairs to the flat above the garage. Her father was screwing a bookshelf to the wall. 'Good news,' she said, panting. 'I've just come from Joe's place and his mother's home.'

'Wonderful news,' said Mr. Braye. 'That's marvellous.'

'I think they fed her well at hospital. A nurse is going to visit her at home.' Spinner looked round the flat with its bright blue curtains and red cushions. 'I'd be happy living here.' She opened the little skylight in the kitchen, then shut it quickly. 'Still raining.'

'It's like Noah's flood,' said Mr. Braye. 'I've never seen so much water. Awful for the farmers.' He changed the subject. 'You know, I think we'll have to take the car out of the woodpile. People know about the Austin Ruby.'

'But won't the Germans take it?'

'They might, but there'd be big trouble if they found it. I'll ask Clem to help us then ask him to come with us to visit Ginger. We could fetch some of their things for the flat in the sousa cart, tow it behind our bikes.'

They stepped outside and Spinner put out her hand. 'It's stopped. I'll fetch some eggs and radishes for them.'

It didn't take long to move the car out of the woodpile and dust it down and soon they were bowling along through Town, Spinner on the back of Clem's bike and Mr. Braye pulling the sousa cart behind his. Spinner clutched a bag with some honey, Mrs. Percheron's seaweed cakes, scarlet radishes and six eggs. Clem had a skinned rabbit in his bike basket.

'Hope no-one stops us,' said Spinner as they cycled up the dark valley.

But there was hardly a soldier in sight. 'It must be changeover day,' said Mr. Braye. 'Some leaving the island and new ones arriving.'

When they arrived, Ginger was in his father's shed, stacking furniture. He cheered when they cycled up his drive, panting and puffing after the long climb up the valley. His little sister Rosie rushed out, waving a painting. 'For you, Uncle Hedley,' she yelled.

'Wow. A yellow octopus,' said Mr. Braye.

'Not octopus,' said Rosie. 'It's SUN.'

'Hello, Edie,' said Mr. Braye to his sister as the others went into the shed.

'I'm stacking everything tightly,' Ginger said. 'Then I'll lock up. They want our house for their sergeants.'

'I hope it's not Viktor!' said Spinner. 'But you're coming to stay with us, that makes it bearable, maybe? What can we carry home for you?'

'Our books. The Germans are burning books.' Ginger wiped his glasses. 'I hate that.'

Clem and Spinner helped him to stack books into the sousa cart until it sank on its chassis, then Spinner went indoors to see her aunt Edie and Rosie. Clem murmured, 'What are you going to do about the gun?'

Ginger lowered his voice. 'I'm getting nightmares about it.'

'I'll work something out.' Clem thought for a moment.

'What we'll do, is…'

But Mr. Braye came out of the house and said, 'Time to go. There's more rain coming.' He pointed at a black cloud. 'See?'

Soon they were rolling down St. Peter's Valley, but just as the first drops began to fall, a soldier stepped out into the road in front of them. He stuck his hand out to stop them.

Mr. Braye said, 'Just keep quiet, kids. We haven't done anything wrong.'

The soldier's face gave nothing away. He looked at the bikes, then shouted to a mate who ran over to join him, rattling off a few words in German. The other one gave a short bark of laughter. Then he got hold of the sousa cart and tipped it over, so that all the books fell into the mud.

'Ruddy b…' began Clem, but Mr. Braye gave him a warning look.

The two soldiers poked among the books with their bayonets, then one nodded at Mr. Braye. 'You may pick them up now.' They stood back and watched, nudging each other as they all began to stack the books back in the cart.

As Mr. Braye set off, Spinner noticed that his knuckles were white on the handlebars. For once, she held tightly to Clem as he pounded the pedals along the sea front and through Town.

When they got home, the Austin Ruby had gone. Mr. Percheron told them a couple of soldiers had taken it, under orders, they said. 'They said you'll get some money for it.'

'Who cares about money,' cried Spinner. 'That was Mummy's car. She loved it and I loved it and Dad loved it. It's not fair.'

But Mr. Braye said nothing. He patted Spinner gently on the shoulder, then walked into their house in silence.

Wednesday September 25th 8.45am

On the Wednesday, Mr. Hinguette made four announcements in assembly.

'Children, please do not pick up leaflets dropped by our Royal Air Force. There are many on the island. You are not allowed to read them or keep them.'

Joe rolled his eyes at Spinner and tapped his pocket. She could see a piece of paper sticking out of it.

Mr. Hinguette went on. 'There will be parish lunches for children. Your parents may apply for them. Next, a woman has been imprisoned for insulting an officer.' He looked over his glasses at Joe. 'I am confident no-one in this school would do such a silly thing.'

Joe smirked, his fingers crossed as usual.

'Lastly,' and here Mr. Hinguette cleared his throat, 'the German language is on the curriculum from today.'

'I'm out of it,' said Joe at playtime. 'It's bad enough with all them rules. But learning their ruddy language is off limits.' He jumped over the playground wall. 'I'm off. I've got a haybox to make.'

Spinner watched him run along the beach and wondered if he'd ever come back to school. Learning the enemy's language was the last thing Joe needed.

Later, she found him on the beach. He was forking

seaweed into piles for Mr. Percheron. 'I'm more use collecting seaweed than learning Jerry,' he muttered. 'At least it helps the crops. Learning German is just...'

'Collusion, Ginger says. I think that means...'

'Whatever. I don't care. I'm not doing it.'

'My father speaks German,' she said. 'It could be useful to know what they're saying. We could spy on them.'

Joe looked at her and his face was tired. 'I never even learned to read properly at school. So what's the flipping point of being there at all? I'll never learn another language.'

'You speak Jersey French and French.'

'I grew up with it. Everyone did. It's like breathing.' He shovelled another pile of seaweed as Mr. Percheron reversed his tractor trailer down the beach. 'Mr. Percheron hasn't anyone to help him these days, so I'm going to do that instead.' He pointed at the sky. 'Seen them?'

Spinner nodded. 'Bombers.'

'There's going to be a big push by the enemy. They're setting off from our airport. Guess who they're fighting?'

'Our boys?' Spinner bit her lip. 'That's horrible, as if Jersey's helping the Germans.'

'Yeah. But our boys will win.'

October 1940

Saturday October 12th 9am

Suitcases were crammed and the house swept clean and Ginger's mother said,

'We'll have a picnic today then leave first thing tomorrow. How about that?'

'A picnic, a picnic,' yelled Rosie.

Ginger locked up as Mrs. Martin set off, her red skirt like a poppy. As she strode towards the sea, he could hear her and Rosie singing. Overhead, German planes roared from the airport nearby. He raced down the hill on his bike, overtaking his mother. In no time, he was in the sea, gliding under the breakers in a silent, green world where the fish swam in ignorance of Hitler.

Then he ran up the beach, splashing through puddles. As he dragged on his clothes, tugging them over his goose-pimpled body and shaking with cold, he felt suddenly crazily happy because everything seemed the same as it always used to be – cold water, egg sandwiches and a picnic in a freezing wind.

Mrs. Martin sat on a rug, unwrapping little cloaks of

greaseproof paper from the sandwiches and arranging them on a plate. 'For what we about to receive,' she said, 'may we be truly thankful.'

Above them, seagulls wheeled and the bombardment in France could have been a breaker, thundering on the rocks, nothing else. But all of a sudden, mid-way through her second sandwich, Rosie stopped eating. Open mouthed, she pointed at the slipway, a hundred yards along the beach. 'Soldiers and horses,' she shouted, spitting egg crumbs.

Ginger said, 'Don't stare.' He shivered and he put his arm round Rosie, but she pulled away from him, staring resolutely at the glorious sight of horse after magnificent horse trotting confidently down the slipway for their daily exercise on the sand, ridden by soldiers in perfect uniform.

Rosie loved men in uniform, whoever they were. 'Daddies,' she said, her fat, pink hand waving a sandwich crust.

Ginger said, 'Rosie, we don't like those soldiers.'

'Do,' said Rosie.

'Rosie dear,' said Mrs. Martin. 'Try not to look.'

But as the troop cantered closer, heading for the sea, it was impossible not to watch. Soon, they were only fifty yards away. The thud of hooves grew louder as the men urged their horses through the edge of the water, spray like frills round the horses' flanks.

Between the horses and the family, an oyster-catcher stalked in its black and white suit, pecking for worms, its beak a blaze of orange.

The soldier's stirrups glinted. One wore spurs and his uniform was black. 'Daddy,' said Rosie, clapping her hands.

All of a sudden, the soldier with spurs tapped another with his whip, indicating the family on their tartan rug. Their two horses broke away from the group, spearing through sun-warmed puddles. As they trotted closer, fine, white sand blew sideways from their hooves.

The oyster-catcher took flight.

Soon, the family could see the shine on the bridles and boots. Mrs. Martin passed cakes and Ginger squeezed his sister's small, plump shoulders, his heart racing at the sight of the man in black uniform. He bit his lip, noticing the anxious expression on the other soldier's face.

Rosie licked the icing on her cake, but Ginger whispered to his mother, 'Mother, that one in black's nasty. I think he's SS or Gestapo. Really horrible.'

'Take no notice.' Mrs. Martin's voice was tight. 'Just smile politely.'

Ginger couldn't smile. He put down his cake, tightening his grip on Rosie. The horses reached a line of pebbles near the family, who ate on. Rosie laughed, cake balanced on her small, starfish hand. 'Daddy,' she shouted again.

Unhurriedly, the horses danced nearer, so close that the family smelled the horses' sweet, grassy breath. No-one spoke. Then, as though a conductor had flicked his hands in the air in front of them, the horses stopped dead.

Against the sunlight, the horses looked enormous.

Mrs. Martin held out her arms for Rosie. As Ginger passed his little sister, he noticed the pressed black shirt, the fiercely groomed hair, the pistol butt that shone from constant handling. 'SS,' he murmured. 'You bet.'

The oyster-catcher landed, gliding over the pebble barrier towards Rosie who held out her cake to it.

The Black-Shirt picked up his whip.

Mrs. Martin pulled Rosie tight, but the little girl pulled away from her mother. Still she held out the cake to the bird. 'Nice cake, nice cake,' she said, over and over again.

Commander Martin always told his son to stand for adults, even for Old Gaston. Shakily, Ginger pulled himself to his feet, but the man in black slid his foot out of its stirrup. Sunlight glinted on his spur as his boot lashed out, glancing Ginger in the face and knocking off his glasses so that he collapsed backwards.

As his glasses crumpled beneath him, the man spoke. His voice was icy. 'I have heard about you, Trumpet Boy. You play silly games with your friends. It is well known at the barracks.'

The other officer looked embarrassed, muttering at the Black-Shirt, who waved him away and looked down at Rosie and her outstretched hand with its little cake.

Then he sneered and lashed at the cake with his whip.

Rosie let out a thin, wretched wail. Mrs. Martin folded her arms round her little daughter and Ginger saw that her eyes had filled with tears.

At that, he found his strength. He knew he'd have to tell about the hidden shotgun, still buried under the bricks. So he yelled, 'I'll give it you Sir, I will.'

The Black-Shirt gazed at him through gold-rimmed glasses, then stared at Mrs. Martin as she rasped, 'Ginger, be quiet.'

Almost in slow motion, the Black-Shirt's horse reared up, flailing its hooves and missing their heads by inches, whish, whish, whish. Ginger stared at the horse above him, its belly glistening with sweat. Then suddenly the horse's hooves smashed to the ground, flattening the little cake.

The Black-Shirt laughed, then cut his horse savagely with his whip and cantered away. He was still smiling as he reached his companion, who looked back, apologetically.

Rosie pulled away from her mother's arms and began to shake. Then she held out her hand and sobbed. As Ginger took it gently in his, he saw there was a cruel, red whip-line across her palm.

Ginger knew then that he'd use his father's gun if anyone ever tried to hurt her again. It wouldn't bother him at all.

Sunday October 13th 9.30am

The next day, Ginger and Clem lifted the pram on to the farm trailer. They tied it down, together with a few of Mrs. Martin's favourite possessions and packing cases full of photographs and blankets.

Gaston wandered up to watch. 'Did you take your father's guns to the Parish room, Master Martin? The German authorities are taking an interest in you, I hear.'

Clem growled, 'Cut it out, Mr. Gaston. Go away.' He glared at Gaston, bunching his fists.

Ginger said, 'You've got green sugar in your beard. Did you know that the Germans leave green sweets on window sills to poison us?'

The old man spat, then hurried away. They heard him spitting all the way home.

'Good riddance,' said Clem. He turned to Ginger. 'What bad things? What sweets?'

Ginger shrugged. 'I'll tell you about it later.'

He helped his sister and mother on to the bus, saying, 'See you in a bit.'

When the bus had gone, Clem said, 'The gun. Let's do it now, quick. I'll keep watch.' He jumped on a gate post, watching Gaston digging in his fields, far enough away. Then he looked up and down the hill behind them, and listened for German trucks.

Ginger raced off and came back, struggling with the weight of the gun. 'I did take Father's other rifles to the Parish room, but I'm worried stiff about this one.'

'No need.' Clem took the oilskin package in one hand. 'You keep watch now, while I sort this out.' Soon the gun was strapped in a wooden box underneath the trailer that looked like part of it. 'Is that everything?'

Ginger nodded and took a last look at his home. Clem turned the tractor key and they trundled between the fields, down the valley and through Town. 'Just smile,' said Clem. 'No-one will stop us. Nothing's covered, so they can see everything on the trailer.'

'Except You Know What...' Ginger waved at every soldier, but each time he said, 'I'm not enjoying this.'

And each time, Clem grinned, and said, 'I ruddy am.'

7pm

Later, the Percherons and Lizzie's cat joined them for a house warming party. Rosie stayed up until her eyelids drooped and she had to be carried to her cot, where she fell instantly asleep. When Mrs. Martin was sure the little girl couldn't hear, she and Ginger explained what had happened on the beach.

'Oh, for God's sake,' said Mr.Braye, clenching his fists. 'What a terrible thing. You poor things.'

'I thought you said there were rules...' began Spinner.

Ginger interrupted, 'The other officer came to see us afterwards, in the evening, Captain Von Pernet. We were scared stiff.' He pushed his glasses into place, then went on. 'But he was quite nice. He said sorry and told us the Black-Shirt belonged to an organisation his country's ashamed of.'

'This Von Pernet. Why didn't he stop him then?' muttered Clem, his eyes blackening.

'Don't be hasty in judgment, son,' said Mr. Percheron, but there was a heaviness in his voice.

'He couldn't. I reckon. Anyhow, he said the Black-Shirt was only visiting for the day.' Ginger swallowed. 'Thank ruddy goodness. Von Pernet brought us sweets, but we refused. He left them on the window sill. In the morning, they were gone.'

'Oh,' Spinner's eyes were large. 'That's horrible. No-one steals in Jersey.'

'Gaston took them,' Ginger explained. 'His beard was full of green sugar, so I told him the sweets were poisoned.'

'He spat all the way home,' said Clem, as everyone laughed.

November 1940

Saturday November 2nd 8am

The Red Cross Messages arrived all at once, a sheaf of them. 'Mum's all right!' shouted Spinner. 'Living in Devon away from the bombs.'

'Training to be a nurse and playing music to the troops. Sends us lots of love,' said Mr. Braye.

When Spinner had read the Red Cross message again and again, she rushed up to the flat to see the Martin family. 'Father's all right,' said Ginger, waving another message.

'Cake?' said Mrs. Martin.

'*JAVOL*,' said Spinner. '*BITTE SCHON*.'

Ginger looked at her disdainfully. 'I see your German's coming on.'

'That's about it, and *PAS AUF* and *HANDE HOCH*,' Spinner scattered crumbs as she raced off to the farmhouse. But the Percherons hadn't received a message from England.

'No dear,' said Mrs. Percheron. 'We haven't heard from George yet but I am sure we will soon.' She poured from the tea pot, her hand shaking slightly. 'Tea? We must celebrate your lovely news.'

Mr. Percheron took off his cap and wiped his head. 'Yes, my dear. It's wonderful for you and your father. And we will have our own news too, one day.'

'Real tea and cake,' said Spinner later. 'A red-letter day. A Red Cross letter day.'

Mr. Braye looked up from his number games. 'It's amazing what twenty-five words can do to cheer us all up.'

'The wonderful thing is,' said Spinner, 'the messages are in their own handwriting. You'd have thought they'd be typed, like telegrams.'

'We'll keep writing them,' said Mr. Braye. 'But never tell her anything bad.'

'Like about losing the Austin Ruby,' said Spinner. 'It really makes me spit, seeing those officers driving about it in it like royalty.'

Mr. Braye nodded. 'It makes me mad too.'

'You? You're never cross.'

'Aren't I?' He looked at her over his glasses. Anyway, I heard some terrific news today. There are more messages coming through for us. On the wireless! Imagine that! The BBC has organised it.' He turned on the wireless, putting his head to the speaker... 'Oh, this is wonderful. They've asked for Channel Islanders in England to speak to their families. Listen.'

They sat together at the table, listening through crackling sound waves. Then Spinner sat bolt upright. 'That's Lizzie speaking.'

'This is a message for Spinner Braye,' said Lizzie, loud and clear. 'We and your mother are safe in England and we are thinking of you. Over and out.'

Mr. Braye reached for his daughter's hand. Then a voice spoke in Jersey French. '*Salut, salut Jerrias. A betot, et Dieu vous garde.*'

Spinner blinked back tears and pulled the cat towards her. 'They said, 'Hello, hello, people of Jersey. Until we meet again, God keep you.'

Friday November 15th 4pm

Clem was kept busy after school building a false wall in the barn. 'It's for the animals,' he explained to his friends. 'We might not use it for ages, months even.'

'What's the flipping point then?' asked Joe.

'We could hide things in there, or hide ourselves if we had to. Anyway, they've started taking animals. If we kill a pig, we have to give most of it to feed the troops. Damn cheek.'

'It looks as if it's always been there,' said Spinner, running her hands over the wall, 'except it's a bit clean.'

'I'm throwing dirt at it,' said Clem. 'Join me.' He picked up a shovel full of muck and hurled it at the wall, so Spinner did the same, shouting with laughter as muck flew everywhere.

Joe came to help on the farm when he could, trying to keep out of the way of the truancy officer. 'Mum says I've got to go back to school,' he said. 'Anyhow, I have to take Diddie. She can't go on her own. She gets up to mischief, putting sand in soldiers' boots with her friends.'

'Bad as you,' said Clem. 'Done anything wicked lately?'

'Turned a few signposts the wrong direction. More sea water in fuel tanks, a few toy pistol caps on railway tracks, that new railway they're building. Talking of building...'

'They're sticking concrete everywhere. Bunkers, the lot.

'Auntie Vi's been forced to have a bunker in her garden. She shouts about it all the time.'

'Blimey. She must scared them stiff,' said Clem.

Ginger came downstairs from the flat, his face pale. 'I've just been listening to the wireless. Bad news. Coventry's been bombed to bits It's terrible. They...' He looked at Spinner and stopped talking. 'Everything's gone. Even the cathedral.'

'I heard.' Clem shovelled cement. 'Want to use my punch bag?'

December 1940

Saturday December 7th 9am

A few weeks later, when frost coated the fields, Ginger and Clem went off to The Trotter Club yet again. 'Punching,' explained Ginger. 'Makes me feel better.'

'Won't it stop you playing your trumpet?' asked Spinner.

Ginger shook his head and she and Joe watched them walk away, noticing them whispering together. 'They're up to something,' she said. 'Clem and Ginger think we're kids, now they're at senior school. They haven't time for us.'

'Kids?' Joe laughed, '*They're the kids.* Those two wouldn't last five minutes with a father like mine. Don't take any notice. They're just letting off steam. Come on, let's feed Peggy. They're like machines them pigs, eat eat eat.'

'Mr. Percheron's turnip pile's getting lower and lower. And by the way, turnips turn pigs into…' Spinner hesitated.

'Giant farters,' finished Joe. 'Jolly useful if we could store the gas.'

The two older boys spent the rest of the day in The Trotter Club. Spinner saw them running up and down the hill, carrying tools and pieces of wood. When she asked if she could help, they looked mysterious. 'No. You look after Rosie.'

She loved Rosie. But she wouldn't look after her just because they told her to. So she went into the secret pig sty behind the wall, cleaned out the pigs, angrily shovelling manure and jumping out of Hotspur's way. That afternoon, she turned to a blank page in her blue book and drew the older boys, giving Ginger clown glasses and Clem tombstone teeth.

She showed Lizzie's cat. 'What do you think, puss?'

During evening band practice, The Hot Trotters learned a new tune. Ginger and Clem whispered together as Mr. Braye demonstrated, singing as he played the piano. 'It's rude to whisper,' hissed Spinner, kicking Ginger's ankle. He didn't answer, so she kicked him again.

Afterwards, Ginger said he'd go with Clem to give the cows their evening feed. 'Too dark for you in the yard, Spinner,' he said. 'Best you get some sleep. Sleep deprivation is comparative with starvation, you know.'

Spinner tried to push past, but Clem stopped her. 'We aren't leaving you out. Ginger's right. It's really dark and it's going to rain.'

'I'm not afraid of the dark, I don't mind getting wet and of course you're leaving me out. What do you *think* it looks like?' Spinner shouted. She stormed upstairs and threw herself into bed.

Monday December 9th 4pm

No matter how many times Spinner asked, Clem wouldn't tell her what he and Ginger were up to. Joe was back at school and said he didn't care. After the last lesson was over, she, Joe and Lily walked home together. Half way, Lily said, 'They say that if you're a Girl Guide, you could go to prison.'

'*What?*' Spinner found herself shouting. '*Prison for kids? Why?*'

'Daddy says,' Lily lowered her voice, 'the Germans think Guides and Scouts are a cover because they learn map reading and knots. All societies are banned, not just Guides. Clubs and everything, gangs, everything.'

'Well,' replied Spinner, her face red, 'Father'll tell them it's a stupid rule.' With that, she tore home, saw her father in the garden and charged towards him, dropping her satchel on the doorstep. 'They're banning Guides, Daddy. Why? I LOVE being a Guide.'

Spinner kicked at a cabbage stalk as Mr. Braye said, 'If we make a fuss, they've won. Actually,' he paused and patted her shoulder, gently, 'I'm having to obey another rule right now and I don't want to one bit. I'm very sorry.'

He took a pigeon from the dovecote, murmuring gently to it. Then he said, his face crumpling, 'All pigeons are to be destroyed.' Spinner stared at him, open mouthed. Then she pulled his arm, trying to let the pigeon escape. But Mr. Braye held the pigeon high.

She hunched her shoulders, wrapping her arms round herself as he put the birds in a cardboard box. Then she burst out, '*What have the pigeons done?*'

'I'm so sorry.' Mr. Braye lifted down the last. 'The German authorities think we'll send messages.'

Spinner brushed away tears. 'I tried to send one to Mummy, but the pigeon just flew back. The enemy shouldn't tell us what to do all the time.' She stamped back to the house, not daring to look back at the soft eyes of the pigeons in case she cried. 'And I'm not eating pigeon pie.'

She leaned out of the window, feeling winter on her face. Clem and Ginger were still in The Trotter Club. She could hear them, hammering and sawing. Then they began to play their instruments in turn, the sousa very loud. Someone was playing percussion, a bang, bang, bang, almost like gunshot.

Guns.

Guns.

Spinner stamped downstairs, her mouth dry. So that's why they were whispering. They had some guns and they didn't want her to know. They didn't want her to join in their secret.

Mr. Percheron was in their kitchen, raging about an order to give his best cow to the German authorities. Spinner tore past into the blinding rain, splashing up the hill to The Trotter Club.

Clem opened it an inch and Spinner was sure she could smell cider. He muttered, 'Sorry Spinner. Can't let you in. Go home and keep dry.' Then he closed the door and she heard it lock from inside.

'Clubs are banned,' she shouted. 'Take that notice off the door. Stupid Trotter Club.'

Cider as well as guns, she thought. Serves them right if they get drunk and shoot themselves. She stormed home. Mr. Percheron and her father had gone, but there was a note on the table.

Have gone to Town. German authorities want me to translate again. See you later.

At this, she made herself stop scowling. 'Poor Dad,' she said to Lizzie's cat. 'They're making use of him and he hates it.'

The house felt lonely, so Spinner splashed across the yard to the farm. Mrs. Percheron's kitchen was sweet-scented and friendly. There were packets of dried fruit to open and taste, saved specially for Christmas and Auntie Vi was helping, stirring and measuring. Spinner helped, peeling apples. Now and then, Mrs. Percheron tumbled something delicious in a trace of sugar and gave it to her. 'Try this,' she said, smiling.

Spinner dashed away tears as she glanced up the hill. Mrs. Percheron handed her more treats, saying, 'They don't mean to be unkind. Clem thinks the world of you, my dear.'

Mr. Percheron was sitting in front of the fire, painting fir cones gold. 'I'm cheering myself up by using Bill's paint. He always painted fir-cones at Christmas.'

Spinner picked up one and smelled it. The scent brought Bill right back into the room, as though he was with them, broad and handsome like Clem and George, wearing his Royal Navy uniform. 'I bet George'll be here next Christmas. Ginger's father will be back too, and Mum.'

By the cooker, Auntie Vi suddenly boomed, 'The news from England's so bad I'm glad I'm in Jersey, even with that lot,' she raised her voice to a shout in case there were soldiers listening. *'Not that I listen to the BBC of course.'*

Mrs. Percheron gave a sad little sigh, pfff, pfff. 'Let's pray the enemy goes soon.'

Auntie Vi fanned herself with a plate, changing the subject. 'I asked the Le Carins for Christmas. They could do with a square meal. I've made a big cake too.'

Spinner said, 'That's a lovely idea.' Suddenly, she didn't mind about Ginger taking away Clem. He was angry a lot these days, punching things and glaring, his eyes going black, muttering about what he was going to do to the enemy. She knew it was really about Christmas. After all, Bill was dead and they hadn't heard from George for months.

Tuesday December 10th 6pm

The next day, the island was shrouded in sea mist. On the west of the island, it was thick, punctuated with raindrops. Percy was facing locked doors too. His mother had shoved him out of his own home into the grey day. 'For Gawd's sake,' she screamed. 'Stop hanging about.'

It was bad enough at his new school, where no-one talked to him because his mother had a German boyfriend. But home was worse. He pretended to like Viktor, who'd moved into Ginger's house up the road and hated it because the fire wouldn't light. Every time he visited Percy's house, he stared at him and his mother as though they were responsible for the faulty chimney. 'The idiots who lived there didn't sweep it.'

Percy agreed Ginger's family were idiots, but Viktor didn't race off on his motorbike to arrest them. So Percy added that Ginger's father was an English naval officer. Viktor scowled again and said his own father had been at sea in the last war and *so what?*

Pondering angrily on this, Percy trudged along, water running down his neck. There'd been a horrible argument at dinner time when he'd demanded a second helping. Viktor fixed him with his pebble-eye look, told him to be self-controlled like a German boy in the Hitler Youth.

That's why he was out here now, in the dark and mist, not having seconds. He sniffed, glad his mother gave him a clean hanky every day. 'At least I'm not like Joe, with his lazy mother,' he muttered, feeling for a hanky in his trouser pocket.

Now would be the perfect time to tell Viktor about The Trotter Club. It would serve Joe right and all his boring friends. They wouldn't laugh if Viktor caught them. As for the horrible, greasy pig, Viktor would love roast pork for Christmas.

He smiled grimly, rain dripping off his nose. He'd show Viktor their club papers signed in blood, evidence that would take the children off to prison. Well, maybe not prison, but they could have a nasty punishment. Tit for tat, thought Percy.

At this cheering thought, he set off into the wind again, glancing at the church clock. An hour to go. He dawdled along, squinting through the gloom until he suddenly bumped into Ginger's old neighbour,

'Crumbs, talk about you look cold, my boy,' exclaimed Gaston. 'Come and get warm by my fire.'

Percy smiled uncertainly. He wasn't sure he liked the look of Gaston. There was food in his beard and his eyes reminded him of Viktor's. On the other hand, it would be nice to sit by a fire. 'Thank you very much.'

'I've sweets to share and I'll tell you about the Martins. Bah, they think they're so damn posh.' He gave a cracked laugh. 'English father, what do you expect?'

For a strange, unexpected moment, Percy felt a twinge of uncertainty.

Gaston gave another cracked laugh and Percy followed him into his house. The kitchen smelled awful. He took a cracked cup of tea from Gaston and tried to drink, his stomach retching at the taste. *Mouse droppings*, he thought.

Gaston scratched his beard and gulped his tea, sucking it through broken teeth.

So Percy said, 'I got a new bike yesterday.' He leaned forward and whispered, 'I reckon they killed a pig at the Percheron's farm, for Christmas. I saw them yesterday, Ginger and Clem, taking pieces to all their neighbours. That's against the German laws. So I took his bike. It was only right.'

'You're a clever lad,' said Gaston. He gave a nasty chuckle, then added, 'That Ginger's wicked. He plays music the Germans don't like. Jazz, they call it. And national anthems...'

'Poland, Norway,' said Percy. 'Ginger disguises them. But the soldiers aren't stupid. They know what he's doing. I told them.'

There was a long silence. Percy warmed his legs beside the glowing coals. 'I'm going to paint the bike black.' He spread out his hands, showing Gaston a streak of black paint between his fingers. 'I've started already.'

Old Gaston picked up a filthy piece of tobacco and began to chew. He spat on the floor, just missing Percy. 'Ginger's father might be angry if he thinks someone stole it from his boy.'

'His ship will probably go down, so it doesn't matter.' Percy bit his lip. 'Anyhow, I'll make Ginger take it back. He'll like it better when I've painted it.'

Wednesday December 25th 11am

Christmas Day! Percy hadn't believed it would come. He'd made paper chains but there was no sign of lunch. His mother wasn't even wearing an apron.

'Lunch?' Mrs. Du Brin gave a tinkling laugh. 'You won't go hungry my dear. Viktor's bringing us everything from the barracks.'

Percy plodded to church alone. Everyone there was with their families, but when he tried to sit near anyone, they edged away. One woman tried to smile at him, but he looked down. He knew what they thought of his mother.

'*Where a Mother laid her baby,*' sang the choir.

He pushed his way out of church, away from all the happiness and kindness and togetherness. 'They won't bloody see me crying.'

At his house, he found Viktor in the kitchen with his mother. They were laughing in a way that cut him out, but there was a smell of roast beef. Percy's mouth watered.

'Sit down, Percy,' said Mrs. Du Brin. She took a tiny joint of beef from the oven and laid it on a dish. 'Jingle Bells,' she sang, straining cabbage and potatoes and arranging them round the beef.

There was a thin slice each, one potato and a pile of

cabbage. No gravy. Percy was not allowed more, though he asked politely. No-one mentioned pudding. His mother and Viktor drank wine, their faces flushed. After lunch, Percy offered to wash up so they could get on with party games. But Viktor fixed him with his pebble eyes, saying, 'That bicycle your friend gave you? *Hein?* The one you've been painting?'

Percy nodded and Mrs. Du Brin smiled uneasily. 'Ride round the island and say "Happy Christmas" to everyone.'

'On Christmas Day? We usually play party games.'

His mother interrupted, 'Viktor's going away soon.' She opened the door, handing Percy his new balaclava. 'Don't whine. You've had plenty of presents.'

Percy stumbled outside, climbed on to the bike and pedalled down the valley towards town. It was his first free-wheel ever and the air whistled through his hair. For a moment, he felt strangely happy.

He was out of breath by the time he'd cycled up the lane to Spinner's house. He leaned the bike against the hedge, then dashed across the garden to crouch under a window. Craning up, he caught a glimpse of a tall girl in a red dress. He had no idea who she was. Then he gasped, 'Spinner Braye.'

She'd grown tall, her hair long enough for curls. A small girl bobbed up at the window, her hair in party bows. Then she shouted, 'Man! Funny man in the garden.'

Percy ducked and crawled away, feeling the child's eyes staring at his back. The front door opened. A man's voice said, 'No-one here.' Percy held his breath as Mr. Braye flicked on a torch, beaming it over the garden. Then he shrugged and turned back indoors. Percy crept back to the window and put his ear to the glass, because someone had pulled the curtains.

There was a shout of delight. 'Flippin' heck. Mr. Braye's given me a drum,' There was a rumbling reply. A drum, thought Percy, angrily, thinking of his own Christmas presents, every one of them grey, woolly and too big.

The moon had emerged from the clouds and shone brilliantly on everything. Stretching his stiff legs, Percy wandered into the farmyard to the pig sty but it was empty. He peered into the hole in the wall where he knew they slept, because he'd nipped into the yard plenty of times to look at them.

'Bet they killed them for Christmas and sold them. Made loads of money on the Black Market,' he muttered. Then he grinned, 'I'd better tell Viktor they're breaking the rules.'

He went back into Spinner's garden and waited in the shadows, watching the Brayes' house. The back door opened and shut, letting out a glorious smell of Christmas dinner. Without a second thought, he hurried to the house and crept into the kitchen.

A pudding boiled over the fire. On the table sat an oval blue and white plate, dwarfed by a joint of pork, half eaten. Percy grabbed a knife and sliced, then gathered the warm meat in his hands and scuttled to the hall, turning upstairs and racing on tip toe to the top floor. Sitting on the landing, he listened to the party downstairs, cramming meat into his mouth.

'Blimmin' flippin' wonderful,' he breathed, chewing the last morsel. He wiped his greasy hands on his trousers and pulled himself upright by the banisters, deciding to explore. He sneaked into Spinner's room, yanked back the curtains to let the moon do its work. His eyes took in the large room with its sloping ceiling. Spinner's plaits still hung on their hook.

He pulled them down and held them to his head, smirking as he looked in the mirror. He wondered why she'd cut them off. Then he remembered teasing her and just for a moment, he felt guilty that he'd taunted her so much.

But he quickly shook off the feeling and crept to Spinner's bed. Just as he'd thought, there was something under the pillow. 'Girls always do that,' he muttered.

Laughing softly, he carried her blue book to the window and flicked through it by moonlight. 'I will smile and sing under all difficulties,' he read, repeating it in a mock girl's voice and adding, 'Ha ha, try singing in prison.' He read on. 'Wireless in the outhouse... Secret club... War Machines...'

He kept sniggering to himself until he came across a picture of himself. The picture wasn't very handsome. For a moment he wasn't sure who it was, except his name was underneath it. Fury bubbled up inside him. 'So,' he muttered. 'I really do frighten you.'

After a while, he tore out a page, picked up a pencil and scribbled: *Soon you will have the smile wiped off your face.*

He placed this message on the table, shut the book and returned it to its hiding place. 'Well, your club isn't secret now, Spinner Braye.'

He took the plaits and went to explore Mr. Braye's study in the next room. On the desk were two instruction manuals and a coil of wire. One was entitled '*How to Make a Crystal Radio,*' the other, '*Find Success in Forgery.*' He pocketed the radio book and wound the plaits round his neck like a scarf, then scuttled downstairs.

Someone shouted, 'Let's play sardines.'

The hall doorway burst open as Percy shot outside into the dark and sprinted for cover by the pig sty. Suddenly, from nowhere, a huge, white greasy form thundered towards him out of the dark and whacked him on the back.

Percy fell to the ground, swearing. When he'd picked himself up, he looked over the pig sty wall. Peggy was sitting calmly in the corner, as though she'd been there all evening and he could have sworn she winked at him.

'You wait,' threatened Percy. He leaned over and yanked off the red Christmas ribbon tied around her neck, then grabbed his bike. He put the book and the plaits into the bike basket and set off into the dark.

January 1941

Saturday January 11th 8am

Mr. Braye cooked bacon for breakfast on Spinner's birthday, though the pieces were small. 'It's a pity Patch had to go,' he said to Spinner. 'But at least we've kept Hotspur and …'

'…lovely, lovely Peggy,' finished Spinner. 'Clem wants to put them back in the pig sty. They don't like being indoors. It's too boring for them, and he thinks they'll fight.'

'Pigs eat each other when they're bored,' said Joe, suddenly pushing open the kitchen door, a grin on his face

'That's horrible,' said Spinner .

Mr. Braye gave Joe the rest of his own helping. 'Good job you're here. I'm not a bit hungry today.'

Joe's eyes lit up. 'Thanks, Mr. Braye.' Picking up his knife and fork, he said, 'Hey, Spin, a little bird told me you was thirteen today.'

A pile of parcels lay beside Spinner's plate, carefully wrapped in brown paper. 'Dad has to go to work. Poor

Dad.' She made a face at her father, who smiled wryly. 'I'll open my presents when you're back. Coming to my birthday tea, Joe?'

'You bet,' said Joe, polishing off bacon.

'How's your mother?' asked Mr. Braye. 'She looked so much better at Christmas.'

'Not bad,' said Joe. 'The nurse comes every day now.'

'I'm glad she has help.' Mr. Braye tucked his scarf into his coat and left the house.

Joe held out his fists to Spinner. 'Left or right?' Spinner tapped the left. Joe shook his head, wincing. 'Mind my chilblains, Spinner. Try the other one.'

She tapped his right fist, avoiding his sore knuckles. Joe slowly uncurled his fingers. In his palm lay a tiny carved pig, exactly like Peggy. It had a curly tail, whiskers and even Peggy's wicked smile. 'Happy Birthday, Spin.'

Spinner turned it over and over, beaming. 'That's the best present I've ever had. Oh, thank you. It's beautiful. Where did you get it?'

'Blimey Spinner, don't go over the top. I made it.'

'You *made* it? I didn't know you could carve.' She stroked the pig's head. 'I'll keep it in my pocket for luck.'

Joe washed his plate and cutlery. 'Coat on, girl. It's flippin' freezing outside.'

10am

When Spinner was swathed in layers, they set off.

'I reckon it's going to snow.' said Joe glancing at the sky. His tackety boots echoed on the hard earth and Spinner's cheeks flamed in the wind. It was colder still on the *cotil*. Joe pushed open the club door, his bare hands purple with cold. Spinner followed him inside, and gasped.

The cottage had been knocked into one big room and one of the walls was covered with charcoal drawings. She knew at once that Joe was the artist. He'd drawn her father's boat so well she could almost hear the sails flapping. Mr. Braye was sketched at the helm, his hair wild. 'Wow,' she exclaimed, her eyes like saucers.

Peggy was pictured with a piece of cloth in her mouth. There were musical notes dotted in the sky and seagulls dropping stones. Clem's cows stared over the milking parlour door. At the top flew Spitfires, Hurricanes and Lancaster bombers. 'I could look at that all day,' Spinner said. 'Did you really do all this, Joe?'

Joe scowled. 'Don't go on.'

Ginger and Clem suddenly appeared, carrying a big parcel wrapped in brown paper. 'Happy Birthday,' they said together. Clem went on, 'Sorry you thought we were leaving you out, but we were doing this. The band was your idea, so we made a concert room.'

Ginger went on, 'We'll give concerts and raise money to help people.'

'Dad says that's a better way of fighting,' explained Clem.

Spinner stared round the enormous room. 'We could fit a big audience in here, and there's a fire.'

'Not much of one,' said Clem. 'We aren't meant to light them in the day. But we can tell them we're burning out an old bird's nest or something.

Spinner moved nearer the fire and warmed her hands. 'We brought the instruments with us to try out the sound,' Clem said, waving towards the sousa, the trumpet and Joe's new set of drums. 'But even with the fire, it's too cold to practice.' He flapped his arms about to warm them.

'Let Spinner open her flippin' parcel,' said Joe.

Ginger handed her the parcel and Spinner peeled off paper. Her eyes widened as she uncovered a brass instrument. 'Crikey, is this for me?'

'It's Father's saxophone,' said Ginger. 'Fifty times bigger than your recorder. The best. Mother says you can borrow it.'

'Made of brass, not wood,' said Clem, helpfully, as though she might not realise.

Spinner blew into the mouthpiece, but nothing happened. She blew again, her face scarlet. 'I'll never manage.'

'Haven't you got lungs? You're thirteen not six. Blow harder, Braye. You can make a sound like an elephant fart on that.'

'Shut up, Joe.' Spinner blew again, then again and finally again.

'*Elephants!*' yelled Ginger.

'You must practise hard,' said Clem.

'Get farting,' added Joe.

'Cut it out Joe,' said Clem. Then he added, 'We need you to make a hell of a racket...'

'...to cover any noise we make with them.' finished Ginger. He pulled oilskin-wrapped bundles from behind a potato barrel.

'Remember what we swore in blood?' Clem grinned. '*Other weapons may be employed. Remember?*' Spinner stared at him, her mouth open, and he laughed in his friendly way. '*Guns*, Spinner. We've found some lovely guns for your birthday.'

'Four guns actually,' said Ginger. Not bad. But we have to keep stum.'

'*Four?*' Spinner nearly dropped the saxophone.

'GUNS? *And what do you mean? STUM?*'

'*Stum* means keep your mouth shut in German.' Joe leaned against the door post. 'You should do your German homework.'

Ginger laid the bundles on the floor and unwrapped one. He held up a small black pistol. 'This one's a Great War souvenir, a Luger. But the trigger's broken.'

'We haven't got any ammo yet, but I'm working on it,' said Joe.

'This is Dad's shotgun,' Ginger went on. 'I don't want to use this one until we must.'

'*Must?*' Spinner's eyes were huge. 'What on earth do you mean, Ginger? The enemy hasn't hurt anyone yet. The Germans tell us what to do, but they haven't...'

'Killed anyone?' Joe's voice was sharp. 'Only our lorry drivers in Town, Clem's brother, and a few million more. All over the world.'

'That's different. That's war.'

'This is war too, on our own island, Spinner. Brace up.'

Ginger laid two smaller guns on the floor. '*I* don't want to shoot anyone, either, but I would if Rosie was in danger.' He looked at Spinner over his spectacles. 'Bloody War, Spinner. Remember?'

Spinner gulped, 'But we don't want to make it worse. I mean...'

Ginger ignored her and picked up one of the pistols. 'Now, this is the Walther PP the Black Shirt dropped on my birthday. Soldiers don't like to be parted from their weapons, so I shoved it under some seaweed, then took it home when they'd gone.' He smiled. 'He must have been flipping furious with himself. It's a topping little pistol.'

At that, Joe fell about laughing. 'It isn't a topping

little pistol, you idiot. It's an SS pistol, flippin' bonkers to have on our hands. Heck, Ginger, I wonder what they teach you at that posh school. *Topping.*'

Ginger looked earnest. 'If they find it, there'll be trouble.'

'Give it back,' said Spinner, her eyes wide. 'Something awful might happen. Get rid of the guns.'

'They're not loaded.' Joe flicked a sweet paper at her. 'Not yet.'

'It's perfectly all right. We'll keep them in the hidden pig sty in the barn but,' Clem leaned forward, 'we've nearly finished digging pretend pets' graves to hide them properly. They're in the orchard near the pig wallow.' He grinned. 'Joe's carved names on stones. Florrie and Dolly, the names of dead pets.'

'I don't remember Florrie and Dolly,' said Spinner, frowning.

'Wake up, Spinner. There won't be dead pets, just guns,' explained Joe.

'Gosh. That's actually a clever idea,' Spinner flicked the sweet paper back.

'Gosh. Isn't it?'

Clem rolled his eyes. He took the saxophone from Spinner, exchanging it for the Holland and Holland. She held the shotgun to her shoulder and squinted down the barrel. 'It's jolly heavy.'

'You'd be better off with a pistol,' he replied. 'Try the Walther. It's not loaded, either. Just get the feel of it.'

Spinner cradled the pistol in her hands, wondering what it had done in its dark, metallic life. She held it high to aim, then clutched it to her chest, because Joe suddenly gave a yelp and charged out of the door like a startled deer.

Within seconds he was back. 'A soldier is coming up the hill!

12pm

Spinner began to shake so much she couldn't let go of the pistol and she was still clutching it as Joe raced back in again, his shoulders covered with thick snowflakes.

'There's a blizzard out there,' he yelled. 'Start a snowball fight and keep him talking whilst we get rid of the guns.'

'I'll take the guns to the barn, the rest of you do what Joe said,' Clem whispered.

They fell out of the door. Spinner forced herself to sing and the others joined in, with Joe bashing a rhythm with a couple of stones. 'Tra la,' belted out Spinner. 'Lovely, lovely snow.'

'Tra la,' sang Ginger and Joe.

As the man drew nearer, Spinner called out, 'We *never* have snow in Jersey. It's so exciting.' Ginger and Joe kept on singing, moving beside her, one each side, Ginger's red hair speckled with flakes and Joe's long yellow jumper flapping round his knees.

'Good singing,' said the soldier as he reached them, red-nosed.

'It's my birthday,' Spinner announced loudly. 'Snow's the best present!'

'Mine too. Happy Birthday to us both!' The soldier smiled.

'Happy Birthday to you, Happy Birthday to you,' sang Spinner. Ginger and Joe joined in at the tops of their voices.

'Happy Birthday to me, Josef!' the soldier sang. 'Ach,

we have so much snow where I live in the Black Forest.' He sighed again, looking at the sea. 'We make music there too. My sister plays well, like you.'

'I've got a sister too,' said Joe. 'But she don't play anything yet.'

'You'd do anything for her, wouldn't you?' The soldier tipped his cap at them then looked longingly eastwards. His voice was almost a shout, as if his sister could hear him, all the way from Germany. He said, 'Look what I'm doing for mine.'

There was silence from inside The Trotter Club, just the crackle of the fire. Ginger said he had a sister too. He added, with at tremor in his voice, 'What's your instrument?'

'I play flute for the city orchestra. Ach, I miss that too. This evening, I play a concert in your town.' He checked his watch. 'May I see your music room? I have heard your band often.' He took a step closer.

'Er,' said Ginger, 'we were keeping it secret, because we're giving a concert in the summer. We don't want...'

'...the whole island to know,' finished Spinner. 'The concert's going to be a surprise.'

The soldier laughed. 'You are like my family. They are always preparing surprises.' He craned his head, trying to look through the door. 'I promise not to tell.'

Spinner tugged his sleeve. 'Father played in Berlin when he was a music student. Mother was in the same orchestra. That's how they...'

At the same time, Joe said, 'Do your whole family play music?'

Ginger chimed in, 'What sort of surprises?'

As the soldier tried to answer them all at once, Clem emerged from The Trotter Club, staggering under the weight of his sousa. He nodded at everybody. 'Sorry, Sir. Nice to meet you, but I have to go. Got my lesson. Can't be late.'

He set off down to the farm, slipping and sliding on the snow, so Joe said, 'Come and look then. It's nice and cosy inside.'

Spinner gulped, and followed them indoors. She picked up her saxophone. 'This is my birthday present. We're trying to improve our band.'

'Very good.' The soldier gave her a kindly look, then he said to Ginger, 'Do you have your trumpet here? You are a good trumpeter, I remember.' He admired the drawings, exclaiming happily about the pigs, and saying he kept pigs at home too.

'Oh gosh,' said Joe. 'What a coincidence.'

Then Spinner gave a sharp gasp of horror, her eyes wide. The soldier was staring at the floor, his face rigid with shock. Joe looked down too and gasped as loudly as Spinner. 'A blimmin' gun,' he exclaimed, glancing up as though the gun had dropped from nowhere. 'Where's that from?

Very slowly, the soldier leaned down and picked up a small black pistol, weighed it in his hands, his eyes narrowing.

'This looks so like a Luger Pistol. It is lucky that it is just a water pistol, yah?' He looked at them one by one. Spinner thought she might be sick.

'Real guns are so dangerous are they not?'

Nobody spoke.

'I think I will take this gun away because if other soldiers find this "water pistol" they might not find it so funny.' He smiled suddenly.

Oh ha, ha,' said Joe, faintly. 'That's one of Clem's old

ones he played with when he was little. Belonged to his uncle in the Great War.'

Josef looked steadily at him, then said, 'I must go now. I must get to town for my concert. We will say nothing more about this.'

The snow whirled round The Trotter Club, gathering on its stone window-sills and against the door. The three of them stood in the shelter of the door way and watched nervously as the soldier vanished through the blizzard.

'Maybe some of them soldiers are human after all?' said Spinner.

'Spinner, you can't trust any of them,' Joe said.

'We'll have to warn Clem,' said Spinner.

'I don't think we should worry about him too much,' said Ginger. 'He had a Tokarev TT-33 pistol. So he's Wehrmacht – an ordinary soldier not a Nazi spy.'

Saturday January 11th 5.30pm

As darkness fell, snow drifted up walls and doors, over steps, up windows. Still, the sky shook out more. The pigs tucked together in the outside pig sty with their eyes tight shut. The guns were tucked together in the hidden pig sty and the snow whirled over the barn door and the pig sty, smothering them both so that even the pigs' bottoms were covered and no-one could see the entrance to the barn.

While they waited for her birthday tea, Spinner and her friends played snap in front of the fire, enjoying the rare smell of sugar drifting from the kitchen.

Mr. Percheron sat with Rosie on the floor, building a house of cards. As they were getting into their game, there was a thunderous knock at the door. Mr. Percheron leaped to his feet and Ginger jumped up too, knocking the cards to the floor and dropping his glasses.

Clem's eyes darkened. 'That soldier. Joe *told* you Spinner. Just because he spoke such good English and talked about his sister. Don't trust *any* of them, and now he's got that ruddy gun. I'm such a bloody twit, dropping it.'

She bit her lip, handing Ginger his glasses as Joe pushed a half-eaten box of chocolates under the sofa.

'They were the last chocs in the shop and Auntie Vi'll kill us if that lot get their teeth into them.'

Mr. Braye looked in from the kitchen, his face very serious. 'Keep playing.' A blast of icy air streamed into the house, blowing over Rosie's card house so that she yelled.

A German voice shouted, 'There is illegal activity in these houses and we will search. There are weapons. There are war machines here, too.'

'Crikey,' breathed Joe, 'It's our mate Viktor. He knows how to spoil a peaceful afternoon, don't he?'

Mr. Braye stood to one side as Viktor and two steely-eyed soldiers barged past him, snow on their shoulders. Mr. Braye said, 'There are no weapons here, Sir, nor war machines, whatever they might be.' He touched Spinner's arm and added gently, 'Please don't frighten the children. It's my daughter's birthday.'

His voice, she thought, sounded tight. She sat on her hands, trying to stop herself shaking.

Viktor glared through rimless glasses. 'We do not frighten children.'

Mr. Braye smiled again, not a real smile. 'Ah, I'm so glad to hear it. But I shall accompany you round our house.'

'Carry on playing, like Mr. Braye said,' hissed Clem. He scooped up the cards and shuffled them as Viktor and his cronies bundled out of the room. The only sound was the slip, slip, slip of shiny cards as he dealt. Brushing Spinner's arm with the back of his hand, he murmured, 'We aren't scared, are we?'

'Course not,' she muttered, clutching her stomach. 'Not a bit.' She hummed a little tune and tried to smile.

'Nasty mans,' screamed Rosie.

Viktor shot back into the room and pointed at Rosie. 'Shut that child up.'

Then he followed his men, thundering upstairs, slamming cupboards and smashing furniture. Something fell in the study above them with thump and there was a sound of splintering wood and books being ripped apart. Then the jackboots raced down again and into the cellar then stamped upstairs again.

Viktor barged into the room, bristly hair flecked with dust from the cellar roof and spider webs on his shoulders. He whipped a paper from his pocket and shouted in Ginger's face, 'What is this *Trotter Lub? Hein?*'

Rosie burst into tears. 'Nasty mans.'

Viktor whirled round at her, his fists tight. 'I said, *SHUT THAT CHILD UP.*'

Ginger pulled her close, stroking his sister's curls. 'Shh, Rosie.' Over the noise of Rosie's weeping, Ginger asked, 'May I see it sir? That piece of paper?' He held out his free hand, snatching it.

Viktor bellowed, grabbing at Ginger's collar and spitting, his eyes icy behind his rimless glasses. But Ginger stepped calmly back, dodging the sergeant's thick fingers. Spinner noticed his legs shaking, but he stuck his chin up. Then he held up The Trotter Club Certificate, his face the picture of innocence. 'Golly,' he scratched his head in bewilderment. 'I think this is blood at the bottom. It's crusty.'

Viktor swore, grabbing at the paper. 'Give that to me. Now, boy.'

'Why Sir? It's only an old poster for a kids' club. You don't need to waste your time with it.' Ginger tore the certificate into tiny shreds and dropped them in the fire.

At this, Viktor lunged at Ginger. 'You will come with me.'

Mr. Percheron squared up to him, putting himself in

front of Ginger. 'The boy is being very polite.'

Viktor narrowed his eyes, then pulled his fists backwards as though he was going to punch Mr. Percheron, but Clem jumped between them and the soldier, his huge fists at the ready. 'Don't hurt my father. He's old.'

'Your father's a peasant..' said Viktor, '...like you. A person who keeps company with pigs and cows.' At that, he began to laugh, a horrible, cold laugh. 'Yes. A silly old man.'

Mr. Percheron's eyes were fixed on Clem, and he mouthed, 'Don't do anything.'

Then Joe spoke, 'Excuse me Sir, but where did you find that certificate? I guess Percy gave it to you.' He sighed and picked up his cards. 'Percy's known for his lies, unfortunately.'

The sergeant bent down. 'I know exactly where you live, and I'm watching you'

Then he tramped out of the room, through the kitchen and into the yard, his footsteps muffled by the snow. They could hear him wrenching back the garden gate and shouting. Then there was a THUMP, as though he'd fallen over, followed by another shout and a muffled thunder of trotters on snowy cobbles.

Clem's face lit up. 'Who let Peggy out? She was fast asleep, enjoying being back in the pig sty.'

Joe laughed. 'She's a cunning pig, old Peggy.'

Mr. Percheron hurried off to sort out Peggy. Spinner said, 'I'll watch what's happening from my bedroom window. She raced upstairs and began to shout straight away. 'The pigs are back in their sty. Oh, no! Viktor's in your house, Clem.'

After a while, she said, 'They're looking round the fields, up to their knees in snow. Oh, gosh! They're going to The Trotter Club.' Then she hurried down to announce,

'They've stopped. Too snowy. Heading to the barn.'

'Oh my God,' said Clem. 'The gu… Erm, the cows.' He rushed out.

'It's all right,' called Spinner. 'There's too much snow at the barn door. They aren't going in. They're going to your place now, Ginger.'

Ginger rushed off as well.

Spinner galloped upstairs to see Viktor emerge from the flat, scowling and empty-handed.

Clem and Ginger returned with Mr. Percheron, their faces red from anger and cold.

Everyone settled back in front of the fire and carried on with their cards. At last, Mr. Braye looked in. His face was angry. 'They've gone. I tried to stop them going into your house, Joe, but they wouldn't listen. Your mother was upset, but now she and your father are laughing because Viktor was so furious finding nothing, not even the salted pork from Christmas.'

'Ha ha,' said Joe. 'Except he'll be even crosser with us now. That's what happens with Dad. He can be full of hate.'

Mr. Braye looked over his glasses. 'Viktor and his friends aren't at all like your father, Joe. I've seen…' Then he stopped and took a deep breath, as if he suddenly remembered that it was Spinner's birthday. 'Look, everyone, it's time for tea.'

February 1941

Wednesday February 5th 2pm

The snow came back, over and over again. After a while, everyone got tired of snowballs, so they trained Peggy inside the barn to keep themselves warm, until she was used to wearing a harness.

'Let's take her to the beach,' said Spinner one afternoon. 'She needs to get out.'

Joe agreed, but Clem said, 'Got too much to do.'

Ginger nodded. 'Music lesson. Sorry.'

Soon Peggy was in her harness, up to her belly in snow. Spinner and Joe kicked their way knee-deep down the lane under a dazzling sky.

The pig snuffled ahead, flicking snow into the air on her snout. Joe was wearing the sweater Auntie Vi had knitted for his Christmas present, and it dangled below his knees, a strange mustard colour. He did a twirl as they set off for his den. 'Good frock, isn't it?'

Spinner smiled at that, but Peggy was dragging her and she was hanging on with all her strength. 'Clem oiled her yesterday morning...' she began. But suddenly, the pig gave her a mean look and bit savagely through her harness. With a mighty wriggle, she shrugged it off and hurtled in the direction of the shack, black trotters flicking snow.

'Oh, bother,' said Spinner. 'We'll never catch her now. She's as slippery as...'

'Viktor,' finished Joe, grinning and flapping his long jersey about in the wind. Then he stopped dead. 'Talk of the devil.'

'*What?* VIKTOR? Where is he?' Spinner froze, ducking down behind a stone gatepost.

'That's him, shouting his head off round the corner. Keep stum. I'll do a rekky.' He padded off silently, peered over a wall and raced back. 'Oh heck, he's coming out of my den, must've broke in. Percy's with him.'

As they shrank into the hedge, snow tumbling on their heads from the brambles, they heard Percy shriek, 'I never stole anything. Let go, Viktor. Find Joe. *He's* the thief, not me and those other kids.'

Spinner gasped. 'Gosh, that's horrible.'

Viktor bellowed, 'Percy, you are lying. I found nothing in their houses, whatever you said. Just a few books with numbers in where that silly man plays games.'

Spinner and Joe stared at each other. 'I *knew* the soldier didn't tell on us. Percy's the tell-tale,' she whispered. 'To think, he's one of us. A Jersey boy.'

Viktor went on, 'Percival, you made me look foolish when I did the search.' There was a sound of scuffling, then he said, 'Look, your name is on this door. '*Percy lives here*' it says. Not, '*Joe Le Carin lives here*.'

'I wrote that,' Joe murmured. 'I knew he'd been sniffing around.'

'It's a horrible trick,' yelled Percy. 'Ow!'

There was such a terrific thump and squeal that Spinner flinched. 'He's hit Percy.'

Joe shook his head. 'I don't think so. It was something else.'

Viktor laughed again, a cold chuckle. 'Ach. Look what knocked you over, the big white pig. I do not think she likes you, *ja*? She's taken a piece of your jacket. Your mother will be angry.' Then he bellowed with laughter.

'You disgusting creature,' yelled Percy. 'Horrible, big, fat, oily beast.'

'Do not call me names,' said Viktor. There was another thump.

'I'm not talking to *you*,' Percy whimpered. 'GET AWAY YOU HORRIBLE PIG… You're not having my sweets as well as my jacket.' There was a scuffle and a flurry of snow. Percy whimpered again. 'You're laughing at me, Viktor. Get the pig off me.'

'Yes. You are a funny boy and you make me laugh. But you are stupid to carry sweets in your pocket when there are wild pigs about. All right, Percy. I shall make the pig go away, but next time I shall make you do it yourself.'

Something clicked, and Joe whispered, 'That's the trigger.'

'He wouldn't shoot her. No…' Spinner jumped up, but Joe yanked her down by the hem of her coat.

Suddenly, there was a crack, like a whip. Then Peggy screamed.

'He *did*. He shot her. The horrible beast,' said Spinner, her eyes huge with horror. But within moments the pig rushed back to them through the snow and when Spinner hugged her she saw there wasn't a speck of blood on her.

'Keep her quiet,' whispered Joe, handing crumbs from his pocket.

But Viktor wasn't interested in the pig. He said loudly, 'I shall take you to prison. Percy. It is not permissible to steal German things. There are flags and cups and boxes, all marked with German names.'

'*PRISON?*' gasped Percy. 'But I'm *only* thirteen and JOE STOLE THEM, not me. You can't put boys in prison. Anyhow, what will Mum do without me?'

'I will look after her,' said Viktor. 'You are nearly fourteen and wear long trousers. In Germany, that is a man. You should go to prison, or maybe a special school in France. I will think about it. Then, when you return, you will restore the German articles to the Kommandant himself.'

'I never took them,' yelled Percy, his voice growing fainter as he was marched away.

When Percy and Viktor were out of sight, Spinner and Joe ran to the den. He opened the door and gaped. 'Blimmin' heck, look at that.' Across the floor stretched a stinking puddle. 'Percy's been here a lot,' said Joe. 'So in a way, Viktor's right.'

Above their heads, thick, golden ropes hung from the beam, swishing backwards and forwards in the chilly breeze. Spinner shrieked, '*My plaits.* I've been searching ever since Christmas. She looked wildly at Joe, then pointed at the wall. '*WHAT FRIGHTENS SPINNER BRAYE.* Underneath was written, in crude capitals. *PERCY.* 'Why does he hate me?' she wailed.

'Take no notice, Spin. He hates everyone. Look.'

A photo of Clem was stuck to the wall, cut from the paper. The caption read, 'Clement Percheron with his pedigree cow, Samares Star Suzanne.' The paper was riddled with cigarette burns. Next to it, there was a photo of Ginger playing his trumpet, also covered in burns.

'He's messed up your pictures,' whispered Spinner, as she looked at Joe's drawings on the wall. 'He's smeared muck on them.' She looked away. 'Or something.'

Joe shinned up to the narrow little beam that held the shack together. He unhooked the plaits and as they dropped to Spinner's feet, he said, 'Never mind. I'll draw more pictures. Ginger can still play the trumpet and Clem'll go on winning cups for his cows for ever. It's a lot of rot, isn't it?' He jumped down and lit a cigarette, saying through a cloud of disgusting smoke, 'Your hair's growing back so who cares?'

Spinner pulled down the spoiled pictures of Ginger and Clem with shaking hands. 'For a moment, I felt sorry for him.' She took a deep breath and wiped her eyes.

Then she jumped. Peggy suddenly shot through the door draped in seaweed like a curly wig. She clattered over the floor, sidled up to Spinner and tossed her head so the seaweed flung itself in all directions. Then she smiled at Spinner and Joe and dropped a large piece of thick flannel.

'Oooh,' said Joe. 'It's part of a soldier's trousers. They must have been hanging out to dry.'

'Poor Percy,' Mr. Braye said, when they got back to Spinner's house. 'How dreadful. Fetch Ginger and Clem, please.'

When they were round the table, Mr. Braye looked over his glasses. 'Percy's in trouble. I know he's a bully, but he's one of us, from Jersey.'

'That's what I said to Joe,' began Spinner. She looked at her father.

He said, 'His mother was an unhappy little girl that no-one wanted. She's still like that, just like Percy. She has to fight the world. We need to understand that. Who knows what Percy puts up with?'

'Excuse me, Uncle Hedley,' interrupted Ginger. 'Joe fights the world too.'

Joe had been quiet, but he spoke up. 'It's different for me. My mum loves me and the kids, and my dad has shell-shock, that's all. He's all right inside, like seaside rock. He's got *TOUGH* written all the way through, not *NASTY*.'

'No-one loves Percy, just like no-one loved his mother,' Mr. Braye said. 'Try to remember that. Also,' he thumped the table, 'there are a few bad apples among the enemy.'

'Quite a lot,' chipped in Joe.

Mr. Braye gave him a look. 'Yes. A few. But otherwise we're darn lucky they've not caused much trouble so far. So, make sure,' he said heavily, 'that you only aim your catapults at clouds.'

They nodded unwillingly, but Spinner noticed Joe's fingers were crossed again.

Mr. Braye put on his coat, saying, 'Joe told me what he wants to do when he grows up. So, what about you? Your plans?'

Ginger said he wanted to be a musician and Spinner thought being a doctor would be lovely. Clem said he'd escape and join the RAF instead of breeding cows.

Mr. Braye listened carefully. Then he said, his face fierce, 'If you're caught doing stupid things, all your hopes will be cut short. You'll be sent away and might never come back. It would be a ruddy waste and break your families' hearts. This could be happening to Percy right now. I'll try to rescue him, because I wonder what his hopes are for his life and if he'll ever achieve them.'

Clem offered his bike because Mr. Braye's was punctured. He pedalled off into the evening, the bike tyres crunching on the snow.

After he'd gone, no-one spoke, until Joe said, 'That's the end of the guns. Your dad won't like it if he finds out what we put in the pets' graves last week.'

Later, Mr. Braye told them there were plenty of footprints in the snow leading out of Percy's front door. The lights were out. No-one appeared to be at home but a neighbour said she saw them leave. 'With that soldier,' she'd added, raising an eyebrow.

March 1941

Sunday March 16th 6.30pm

One evening, while Ginger's mother was cooking in the kitchen and Spinner was doing her homework in the sitting room, the back door opened.

'You heard about the prisoners?' Auntie Vi called out.

Mrs. Martin clattered spoons and Spinner heard her murmuring, 'Yes. It's terrible.'

Auntie Vi stomped across the kitchen floor and peered into the sitting room at Spinner, nodded grimly and slammed the door firmly shut between them. Spinner jumped up and put her ear to the keyhole.

Auntie Vi said, 'Them prisoners was just boys.'

'French, I heard,' said Mrs. Martin.

'Yes.' Auntie Vi was whispering. 'They was French boys landed in Guernsey, caught and brought over here. They say the Germans are going to make an example of the leader.'

'An example?' Tea cups rattled in the kitchen, as though Mrs. Martin's hands were shaking.

Auntie Vi suddenly barked, 'He's only twenty-one.

Twenty-one. Somebody's son and he's going to be...'
There was a strange, long silence, then Auntie Vi
whispered for a long time. Her voice rose and Spinner
heard her say, 'Shot. Firing squad.'

Spinner froze with horror. The tea cups on the other
side of the door rattled again. So she pushed open the
door to ask for a cup.

'Surely not?' gasped Mrs. Martin, waving Spinner
back to her homework.

Auntie Vi burst into tears. 'To think of it, in our
Jersey. How could they?'

'Wicked,' said Mrs. Martin, mouthing at Spinner,
'Go away.'

Spinner tiptoed through the other door and outside,
heading for the flat where Ginger was scratching his
head over Latin verbs. 'Shh,' he said. 'Rosie's just gone
to bed.'

'They're going to execute a prisoner.' Spinner's eyes
filled with tears. 'They're going to drive him through
the town so everyone can see him' She gulped, trying to
find the words.

Ginger's eyes were wide. He whispered, 'The
bastards. I knew they would, one day. I knew it would
come to this, Spinner. That's why Clem and I want to
keep guns.'

Spinner sat down, her legs suddenly weak. 'Auntie
Vi heard they're going to put his coffin in the lorry and
drive him right along the beach and take him up near
Percy's at St Ouen. They're going to use a firing squad.'
Then she began to weep. 'What shall we do to help
him?'

Her cousin's face was pale. 'I don't think we can do
anything.'

Spinner found she couldn't stop crying until Rosie came into the room in her nightie. 'It's all right,' she said. 'Don't worry, Rosie. I choked on a piece of bread and it made my eyes water.'

But Rosie looked puzzled. 'I don't cry if I have bread,' she said. She took a quick look at Ginger to see if he was crying too. Then she hurried to Spinner, sat on her knee and hugged her, smelling of soap and talcum powder, and Spinner could hardly bear it because Rosie was so small and innocent and knew nothing of what was happening.

When she looked at Ginger, she could see he felt exactly the same. He was cleaning his glasses, which had misted over. She wiped her tears away and took Rosie back to bed, singing her a lullaby.

When Rosie was asleep she said to Ginger, 'That's the one Mum sang to me when I was little. I miss her.'

'I bet you do. I miss Father. He'd know what to do.'

Monday March 17th 7am

The next morning, Ginger told his mother he had to be early at school. He hurried into Town, trumpet strapped to his back, racing to the sea front, tasting salty drizzle. A few people were about, hunched in raincoats and staring at sullen grey sea as if spring had suddenly vanished just as it had nearly arrived.

He stood in a bus shelter, pulled his cap low and took his trumpet from its case and fitted it together. 'The Trumpet Player,' said an old man. 'I've heard you plenty of times on the beach.'

Ginger nodded, but his hands were shaking and he could hardly assemble the instrument. 'Glad you liked it,' he said. Then he pushed into a knot of people who'd gathered to see what was going on.

A woman muttered, 'He's on his way, poor fellow.'

Ginger stood on tiptoe as soldiers marched out of town in front of a lorry. They stared straight ahead. One was very familiar. 'Viktor,' Ginger gasped, ducking down.

As the vehicle drew near, the prisoner came into view, young and very thin, his face defiant. The old man shouted, 'Shame, shame.'

Keeping low, Ginger began to play, quietly at first, then louder, swelling into a crescendo, ignoring icy looks from the soldiers who usually cheered his playing. As the lorry drew close, the prisoner locked eyes with Ginger.

Ginger lifted his trumpet high and the notes poured across the crowd, a tune everyone knew. All round him, people gasped. 'That's the French national anthem,' whispered one. '*The Marseilliase*, he's playing *The Marseilliase*.'

The prisoner blinked in recognition and mouthed, '*Vive La France*,' at Ginger, before staring straight ahead once more, averting his eyes from the coffin that his captors had placed beside him.

Ginger played on, sticking to his own composed variations on the French anthem until eventually the prisoner was out of sight. When he stopped, his whole body began to shake so that he could hardly stand up, let alone fit his trumpet back into its case. The crowd closed tightly round him as he recovered, a woman slipping a sweet into his trembling fingers and a man helping him to put his trumpet back into its case. As Ginger began to recover, he said, 'Well done, young man. We're all proud of you.'

Slowly, he set off to school. Just as he was about to cross the road, a German officer walked up to him, a tall, blond man, and in his holster a Steyr M1912 pistol, the sign of a Wehrmacht Officer. His grey eyes were not unkind as he said urgently, 'Go quickly, before you are recognised. Pull your school cap over your face.'

Ginger did as he was told and hurried away, his heart still racing in terror. Moving through town, Ginger remembered who he was. 'Von Pernet,' he breathed. 'The officer from the beach, and the one with the sweets.'

By the evening, news had spread that the Frenchman had been tied to an Ash tree and faced a firing squad.

Nearby as people heard the shots, they also heard him shouting '*Vive La France*,' before he died.

Francois Scornet.

That was the Frenchman's name.

April 1941

Sunday April 20th 9am

The ingredients lay on the dresser and she'd been eying them as she wrote, wrinkling her nose at the smell – a grim collection of butchery, a mouldy onion and a pile of grey bread crumbs. On a saucer, an egg took pride of place, newly laid.

Spinner put her letter to one side, then took the ingredients to the table. She peeled the onion and chopped it, then she took a deep breath. She'd have to tackle the meat. The mixer was screwed to the table and she put a bowl on the chair seat underneath it and got to work. First, she picked up a greenish lump of liver with tubes sticking out of it, screwing up her face at its slippery feel. She shoved it in the mincer and turned the handle, watching worms of meat fall into the bowl, where they lay in a horrible heap.

'*Rinse kidney before using,*' read Auntie Vi's recipe. Then, in capital letters. '*REMOVE ALL URINE.*'

'Urine?' muttered Spinner. Then she realised what Auntie Vi meant. She rinsed the kidney over and over again, then minced it. There was another lump of meat to deal with, bubbly and white with little veins. Spinner poked it and pulled a face. 'Ugh, disgusting.'

'Those are brains,' announced Joe, standing at the door. 'Lovely. Come on Spinner, stop being so wet.' He reached for a knife, sliced the brains into pieces and pushed them through the mincer, whirling the handle so fast that gobs of brain whizzed about, dotting the table. He swept them up and chucked them in the bowl. 'Blimey, this is going to taste good.'

He dealt with the remains of the gristly meat, then cracked the egg and tossed it into the bowl along with the breadcrumbs. 'Fetch us some parsley,' he ordered, snapping his grubby fingers and laughing.

Lizzie's cat screeched under the table, and Joe muttered, 'Watch it, puss.'

Spinner chopped up parsley and threw it into the mixture. As they shaped it into little grey and red balls, she heard drums and a brass band.

'It's Hitler's birthday,' he said. 'Shall we go into Town and celebrate? Watch the bands?'

Spinner cleaned gristle and slime from her fingers and carried the rissoles to the meat safe. 'I don't want to celebrate Hitler's birthday. Why would we?'

'We aren't really going to celebrate, silly.' Joe swiped the table roughly with a dishcloth and unscrewed the mincer. He dumped it in the sink, scraped off a few scraps of raw brain and ate them. 'Seeing as everything's getting so serious, I reckon we'll act like we're kids for the last time.' He patted his back pocket. 'I've got my catapult.'

Spinner looked down at her old jumper and dungarees, both of them darned and tight. 'If we go into Town, I'll have to change. Auntie Vi makes me put on my dress for that.'

'Auntie Vi won't be watching the soldiers. She'd rather slit her throat. Come *on*, Braye.' He held out his hand.

.Soon they were racing through Town, past the bus station, where only a year ago, holidaymakers queued for island tours. Ahead of them, German bands were belting out OOM PAH OOM PAH OOM PAH.

'Rubbish, aren't they, compared with The Hot Trotters?'

There were soldiers everywhere, uniforms immaculate, toe-caps reflecting the blue spring sky as they goose-stepped down King Street under rank after rank of fluttering flags. Joe copied them for a while, marching cockily behind a platoon, flicking stones at the back row until a German guard told him to clear off, chasing him into the crowd.

Soon they were in the Royal Square, standing outside the pub. All round them, islanders tried to ignore the band, yet found themselves watching. Joe hissed, 'Look at them potty-head medals, Spinner. Blimmin' clanking.'

'I wonder what they got them for. They look smart, don't you think?'

'Very pretty,' agreed Joe, 'for murderers.'

Spinner jumped onto a bench for a better view. 'There are hundreds of soldiers. *Thousands*. Where have they come from?' She glanced at Joe for an answer, noticing a bearded old man who was shoving between the crowds and hurrying towards them. She'd seen him somewhere before, but he hadn't been wearing a tie and a clean collar.

No. Surely it wasn't Old Gaston, Ginger's horrible neighbour? Not dressed like that? She'd seen him at

Ginger's place, where he sported a disgusting shirt and filthy braces to hold up baggy, muck-splattered trousers.

The man waved frantically. Spinner hopped down from the bench as he rushed to Joe and grabbed his arm, wafting an unwashed smell over them both, despite his Sunday best. He wheezed, 'You're friends of Ginger Martin, aren't you? That posh boy who plays those bad tunes?' He lowered his voice. 'I hear he even played when they shot the Frenchman, the traitor. That's against the rules, you know.'

'He's the best trumpeter in the island. What's wrong with that? I don't know nothing about the Frenchman.' Joe lit up a foul-smelling cigarette. 'You a Nazi or something? You aren't speaking about our friend very nicely. At Sunday school they tell us Love our Neighbours.'

'Well, you should know about Ginger Martin and his family,' said Old Gaston. 'The things I saw and heard, you wouldn't believe.'

'Actually,' Spinner interrupted. 'Ginger's my cousin.'

'And my mate,' added Joe.

'*Your* mate, *p'lo*? What would a posh boy like Ginger want with someone like you? A scabby bit of lobster-bait? Someone who don't even bother to dress for Town?' The old man stared nastily at Joe's ripped shirt and Spinner's outgrown clothes. 'Don't say I didn't warn you about that family. And Miss Braye, your friend here's been mucking about, turning signposts the wrong way.'

Spinner looked at Joe, who blew a smoke ring and shrugged. '*Me?* Do that? What for?' He gave an innocent smile.

The old man spat again. 'I have an important friend in the German army. He's a good man.' He coughed up something disgusting, spat it out then turned on his heel.

Before he disappeared down an alleyway, he shouted, 'That's a German fag, you little thief.'

'Flamin' heck, Spinner, he's a nasty bit of work?'

Spinner folded her arms tightly so Joe wouldn't see she was shaking. 'Ugh, forget about him. I can't think what he's doing this side of the island when it's potato time. He should be working on his land.'

Joe blew another smoke ring and told her his cigarettes weren't German at all. He'd made them from tobacco he'd grown and dried. 'Mixed it with some dried lettuce leaves. Lovely. Makes you sleepy though.'

'Smoking's disgusting. You'll never get a girlfriend.' Spinner flapped away the fumes. 'What about the signposts? You be careful. Someone's been telling on you. People are doing that, Daddy says. Telling, for money.'

'Well, it's not Percy. He's gone.'

Spinner winced. 'I hope he's all right.'

'He'll look after himself, you can count on that. Anyway, I'm not so stupid, I wear my balaclava when I get up to things.' He whispered in her ear, very close so she could feel his warm, smoky breath. 'We got to resist the troops a bit, girl, whatever Clem and Ginger say.' He handed Spinner a catapult, then shouted, 'Help, HELP. Watch out for stone-throwing seagulls. Help everyone, they'll ruin the parade.'

He fitted a stone to the sling and let it go.

The stone ricocheted off the walls of the Major Pierson Inn and onto a soldier's helmet. There was a short, angry shout. *WAS IST DAS?*

After a moment's hesitation, Spinner did the same, yelling all the time, 'Look out for the gulls,' as stones bounced off shop doors and roofs, pinging on helmets and gleaming jackboots so the soldiers lost concentration and marched out of order. The watching crowds hid their smiles, closing in on Joe and Spinner whenever a soldier tried to find them, but then Spinner saw Old Gaston watching them, his face vicious, scribbling notes in a grubby little notebook, spitting on his pencil lead and her heart sank. She bit her lip and touched Joe's arm. 'Let's go home Joe. We've tried everything. Everything, Joe. But we can't stand up to the enemy. I love Peggy and Daddy and Rosie too much to do anything stupid. So that's it, Joe. We must just keep our heads down, get our band so good it's practically a...'

'Blimmin' orchestra,' interrupted Joe. 'OK, Braye. I give in. But I tell you what, if Viktor comes back, we'll get rid of him and it won't be catapults, I tell you.'

May 1941

Saturday May 10th 7am

At last, Mr. Le Carin's fishing boat was back in the water. The old sailor, Mr. Jument, had spent the winter mending her. He'd plugged her bullet holes, waterproofed the hull, varnished her and painted her name in gold on the stern.

'*Star of the Deep*,' read Mr. Braye, turning up. 'Excellent name, Mr. Jument. Ready for it?' Mr. Jument nodded, so Mr. Braye slipped him an oil-skin package. 'Maybe let Joe do it? He's a good swimmer, silent too.'

'We have to take a soldier out with us,' said Mr. Jument. 'Because we're going out more than a mile.'

'If the soldier starts asking questions, tell him the boy's cleaning the anchor, or checking lobster pots. Lie, lie, lie. Keep Joe safe. If you have to, throw the package to the crabs.'

Mr. Jument winked. 'Crumbs. It's like being in a film.'

'A dangerous film, remember.'

Half an hour later the guard arrived, a young soldier, his face nervous as he noticed the churning tide at the harbour mouth. 'I am to go with you to the fishing place,' he said, his face pale.

'Hop in,' said Mr. Jument. 'One hand on the boat at all times, if you please.' He turned on the engine and shouted, 'Cast off.' In no time the boat was bucketing over the rough water at the harbour mouth. Mr. Le Carin was at the helm and Joe stood in the bows, waving ashore in case his mother could see him.

'Do not give signals,' shouted the young soldier, his voice shrill with hysteria at the sight of heavy seas ahead.

'Righto, matey,' yelled Joe, his fingers in a V behind his back.

Mr. Le Carin's hard face softened as the boat danced over glittering waves, salt water spattering the deck. The engine was sweet, he told Mr. Jument, revving so that a cloud of diesel billowed behind them, blowing back on to the guard. Half a mile out, he nudged Joe, pointing east.

'Dolphins,' shouted Joe. 'I haven't seen them for ages.' He leaned over the bow as the animals dived beneath, swooping through the green water and calling to each other as Joe began to sing, quietly at first, then louder. The creatures swam nearer, singing back. When he'd sung a few songs, Joe shouted to the guard. 'Come on, sir, sing them a nice German sea shanty. They'll love that.'

But the German stared back hollowly, reaching for the rail as another gust of diesel smoke smacked him in the face.

Joe nudged his father. 'The dolphins have brought us luck already. Look. He's going to throw up.' His father smiled grimly at the guard's tense expression and green face. Lighting up a cigarette, he blew smoke in his direction.

That did it.

As the boat slopped crabwise over the waves, their unwanted guest lost his breakfast, the smell of his own sick bringing up more retches. Mr. Le Carin winked at Joe. 'I'd give you a bacon sandwich, sir, if I had one. But there isn't much bacon about these days. Nice bit of bacon fat always helps seasickness.'

The German blanched and threw up again, his head hanging over the side into breaking waves. He was covered in sick and sea water, and a small slick of weed dangled from his ear like an ear ring. All the time, Mr. Jument sang his jolly little tune as though nothing was happening and Mr. Le Carin pulled on his home-made cigarette, revving the engine now and then to create more fumes.

The soldier lost more breakfast, so Joe said, 'Go down below, matey, into the cabin. I'll fix up a nice blanket and I've got a bucket, a bit smelly, but it'll do.'

The German edged miserably towards the cabin. Then he caught a whiff of rotten fish and threw up again.

'Blimey,' said Joe. 'You must've had a huge breakfast, sicking all that up. Have dry toast next time.' He checked his bucket. 'Oh drat, I didn't notice them old fish-heads in here.' He tipped the bucket upside down over the side and banged it. 'They've gone off. You can always tell gone-off fish, they stick to things.' He banged again and a fish-head flew sideways, catching the soldier in the face so that he retched again.

Joe remarked, 'I've never seen flying fish round here before. Only octopus fly in Jersey.' He scooped water from over the side, sloshed out the bucket and showed the German. 'It's much cleaner now. Only a few bits and bobs left now, mate.'

The man looked away, wiping sick from his uniform, oblivious to the seaweed on his ear. He whispered, 'I must lie down. I am very ill.' Joe led him below, dashing nimbly ahead while the soldier clung to the stanchion by the companionway step, his head lolling with each bang of the bows on the waves.

Joe cleared a pile of ropes from the bunk, offered him a blanket stiff with salt and moved the stinking bucket close. Then he left him to his misery, saying, 'It takes years to get used to the sea, mate. Our Admiral Lord Nelson was seasick, all the time. Don't make you less of a man, I reckon.' The German closed his eyes and turned away as mackerel lines rattled out on deck.

For a couple of hours, the lines did their work until Mr. Jument suggested they check lobster pots near the tower which stood a mile away from the island, and was one of the best areas for fishing, nice and sheltered at low tide. The soldier groaned and pulled the blanket further over his head.

Soon, the boat was nosing between rocks dried out by the low tide, then settled in a deep, calm pool behind the tower. Mr. Le Carin lowered the anchor and Mr. Jument passed Mr. Braye's package to Joe, who slipped silently into the clear waters. Clutching the package above his head, he swam to dry sand. Soon he was climbing over boulders and up steps to the tower. The wooden door stood open.

Joe used the code Mr. Braye had taught him. 'Any conger eels out here today?'

'Plenty. Look south,' came the reply. A man in a balaclava and dark clothes appeared, and stretched out his hand, adding, 'Then look north.'

Joe said, 'The north is still too rough.' Then checking that the German guard wasn't up on deck watching, he handed the package to the waiting hand before returning over the boulders, over a stony beach and back into the water. He swam to the boat and climbed on board, giving a thumbs-up to his father and Mr. Jument, whispering, 'Correct passwords. AOK.'

After giving a thumbs up to the man in the tower, he nipped below to wake the guard. 'Best come on deck, matey. I cleared weed off the anchor and I could have been up to flippin'anything. I wouldn't like you to be in trouble.'

But the man groaned and turned over, weed still pressed to his cheek. So Joe said, 'OK then. You stay here, nice and cosy.' He tucked a fish-head beside him. 'Better clear that weed off your face before you go back to the barracks. It's not smart.'

The boat headed out to sea again. Again, Mr. Le Carin steered over the roughest waters as they chugged home on the rising tide. As soon as they'd docked, Joe leaped ashore and left his father and Mr. Jument to have smoke and clear the boat.

He raced home to tell his mother about the dolphins, but she wasn't at home.

There was a note on the table from the doctor. It read, 'Have taken Mrs Le Carin to hospital again.'

3pm

'I asked the dolphins to look after you,' said Joe when he got to the ward. 'But they didn't flipping bother.' He gave his mother a smile. 'Flipping dolphins.'

'Don't give up on them,' said Mrs. Le Carin. She smiled, though her voice was weak. 'I fainted, Joe. But I'm all right now.'

Joe gave a sigh of relief. 'Good Mum. I was worried.' He told her about the German guard and how sick he'd been. 'I felt sorry for him in the end. He'd never seen the sea before he came to Jersey. He was frightened of the waves, the fish, everything. Sick over and over again, worse than Admiral Nelson.'

'It's best to think of the soldiers like that.' His mother's voice was gentle. 'You know, as human beings. But it's not easy, is it?'

'Hitler isn't a human being. He got spat straight out of hell, Clem says.'

'But the German lads are all someone's sons, like you're ours.' Mrs. Le Carin reached out her hand for his. 'Their mothers and fathers love them.'

'Can't think why,' said Joe.

'I'll tell you something wonderful. This very morning, a soldier walked into the hospital and handed in some insulin. That's the medicine I need, that we can't get hold of any more. He said, 'I got this for my mother. But she's dead, bombed in Germany.' He looked very sad, then he said, 'There's a lady here who needs this medicine. Insulin. Her son is the brave boy who plays the spoons and the drum.'

Joe's eyes widened. 'Blimey. Is that why you're better so quickly, just after a few hours? Anyhow, how does he know who I am?'

Mrs. Le Carin said she had no idea. 'You see, I've still got that same illness your grandfather had. It doesn't go away.'

'I thought you could cure it with good food, even if you don't have the medicine.' Joe squeezed her hand.

'Sometimes,' said Mrs. Le Carin 'They tried that, but we're a bit short of good food these days, aren't we?'

Joe nodded. 'You're telling me. But Mum, what was the man like?'

'I hardly noticed. The nurses offered him a cup of tea, but he rushed off. It was kind, wasn't it? He gave me this, too.' She handed him a small block of soap. 'Smells of roses. Have a sniff.'

Joe took the soap, fingering its smooth curves and sniffing the flowery scent. 'How did he get hold of the medicine, if we can't?'

'His friend's a doctor and he'd begged some for his mother because she had diabetes too and he was going home to Germany, on leave. Then she was killed in a bombing raid, so he didn't go home after all and he brought it for me. The funny thing was that his name's like yours. Josef, spelled the German way I suppose.'

'Ah. I *do* know him. He plays the flute with Spinner's dad,' Joe replied. 'Mr. Braye gets on with him, but I don't want to be too matey with any of them.'

'Joe,' his mother interrupted gently, her eyes closed, '*P'tit crabin*. There's something I want to say. Don't hurt anyone, Joe, not ever. Put yourself in their shoes. Bullying and hating and fighting, they leave a stain on people.'

'I haven't got a stain on my body,' said Joe, grinning. 'Pure as the driven snow, me.'

Mrs. Le Carin gave a faint laugh. 'And stop stealing cigarettes, you bad boy. They stopping you smelling things, and the bluebells are out and there's blossom still.' She shut her eyes. 'Bring me some, please, dear, if you could. I'd love to smell them again.'

For a terrible moment, Joe wondered if these were her last words. 'Mum?' Then he said it again louder. 'Mum?'

His mother opened her eyes again.

Joe said urgently, 'I'll get you some blossom. The orchard's loaded.' He grabbed her thin hand, thinking it was like a bird, so light and soft, the bones like tiny ribs.

She smiled. 'That would be lovely, dear. But don't upset Mr. Percheron. Tell me about this concert you're planning. Mr. Braye tells me it's going to be soon.'

Joe let go her hand, relieved, and told her the band was good enough for people to enjoy because they played on the beach in the evenings and drew in quite a crowd. 'Germans too,' he said, trying to be nice about them for her sake. 'Mrs. Percheron's promised cider for the concert. And we're going to have it exactly a year after the enemy landed to show we aren't afraid. Everyone's doing something. Even Auntie Vi's playing.'

'Playing what? I can't see Auntie Vi doing that.'

'She's plays the washboard with a wooden spoon. It's blimmin' brilliant.'

At that, his mother laughed. 'I look forward to it. Come on Joe, let's sing.' She began a song she loved, so Joe took out his spoons and accompanied her, until the nurse asked them to be quiet because the other patients were trying to sleep.

As he left, his father walked in, still in his work clothes with fish scales in his hair. Joe noticed that his eyes were full of tears as he walked towards his wife, held both her hands and said, '*Ma chiethe*. My dear.'

Monday May 12th 9am

Joe borrowed Clem's bike to go to the hospital, its basket filled with apple blossom. He said to Spinner, 'I'm not going to school. I don't care about truant officers or no-one.'

'I'll tell Mr. Hinguette. He'll understand.'

'I'm scared to hell. I can feel it here.' He thumped his chest. 'Something's happened to Mum.'

As he rode through the streets, the fear about his mother grew inside him. He pounded the pedals, muttering, 'If I spit each time I see a soldier, she'll get better. Seven for luck.' He rode as fast as he could, spitting on the ground. The seventh spit splattered on a soldier's back.

'Extra luck,' said Joe, dropping the bike and racing up the hospital steps before the soldier could catch him. He skipped every other step, scattering petals, jumping two at a time. That always brought luck too. Everyone knew that.

By the time he was at the right floor, fear was raging through him. When he saw a cluster of nurses by his mother's bed, he thought the very worst had happened. 'Mum,' he called, pushing them out of the way.

'Stop,' said the nurse. She put her arm. 'Please don't

push. We've been trying to find your father.'

'He's fishing,' said Joe, briefly, peering round her. 'I'm here instead. Let me see her.'

The nurse's arm was strong, but he shoved it away. 'Mum,' he whispered.

Diddie had sent a picture for their mother. He moved it from hand to hand, trying to dodge the nurse, juggling with the blossom.

She said, 'I'll give it to Mummy. Go home Joe. This isn't for children.'

'We don't call her Mummy,' shouted Joe. 'She's called Mavis Le Carin, or Mum to us.' He snatched the picture out of her reach. 'You can't stop me seeing her. Leave us alone.'

'Of course not, my love.' The nurse spoke gently. 'But I don't want you upset.'

Joe ducked under her arm and raced through the curtains to his mother's bed. He laid the blossom on the pillow beside his mother's head and turned to the nurse. 'I'm not upset. Please, please, Miss, leave us be and go away.'

The nurse blinked, but one of the others said, 'Let him. He's like his father. He'll go wild if we keep him from her.' The nurse nodded, her face anxious, backing behind the curtains.

However, when Joe saw her feet hovering underneath them, he knew she was listening and he hissed, 'I said, *Go away*. Please.'

Mrs. Le Carin was sweating and breathing oddly, dragging air into her lungs as if she couldn't get enough of it. Rushing to the window Joe threw it open, letting in a gust of cool salt breeze. His mother fluttered her hand in thanks, little birds with wings. Then her breathing stopped, then started, then stopped and started again, like a stalling car. She muttered, '*Man p'tit crabin.*'

'*My little crab,*' said Joe. 'You always call me that, Mum. Can you smell the blossom? It's apple, from Mr. Percheron's orchard.' He captured her fluttering hands, his voice urgent, 'Diddie's sent a picture.'

Mrs. Le Carin didn't react, but Joe was sure she could hear. So he carried on, as if he could pull her out of her strange, stumbling state. Holding up the picture, he said, 'Diddie's drawn dolphins to bring you luck and Arthur's drawn on her picture too, something with lots of legs. So many legs, it's funny.'

His mother's breathing changed again. It was as if she was grabbing at the lovely salt sea air pouring through the window. She wriggled on the pillow, her face beaded with sweat.

'Can you smell the sea, Mum? It's from our beach, isn't it?' He squeezed her hands gently. 'Dad's out at Icho Tower today. He'll get a good catch.' For a wonderful moment, he thought she was going to open her eyes, because she squeezed his hand back, very weakly.

She'd always loved the beach. 'Can you smell it? And the blossom?'

He began to sing her the rude song she loved about Hitler because it always made her laugh. But she didn't even smile. All of a sudden, he found himself saying, 'Mum, I'll grow up so you can be proud of me, I promise, oh Mum, I promise I'll look after the children, if only you'll get better.' Then he closed his eyes too and prayed, 'Dolphins, dolphins, bring her your luck.'

Keeping his eyes shut, he recited her poem. '*I must down to the seas again, to the lonely sea and the sky.*' He'd learned the whole of it now and she'd be so happy.

But when he opened his eyes, she'd stopped breathing altogether.

'Mum,' he whispered, 'you've forgotten to breathe. Wake up, do it, please do it for us. Please, please.' He flung himself at her and hugged her, smelling her sweet scent.

But she didn't hug him back. She didn't even move. Joe shook her hand, but it was cold. Frantic, he tried to turn her head, his hands gentle. But her eyes looked far away even though they stared at him. His voice rose to a yell. 'Look, Mum. Look at me. It's your boy, Joe. Don't you know who I am?'

Suddenly he understood that she'd gone.

'Mum,' he began, but he couldn't go on. He wrapped his arms round his skinny chest and held himself so he wouldn't cry. He took a last, long look at his beautiful mother and pushed his way through the curtains.

'Oh, my poor boy,' the nurse said, 'I'm so sorry. It's a terrible thing, the worst thing to lose your mother. I...'

Joe scowled at her and shouted, 'I'm not blubbing, Miss. So shut up and sit with her 'til my dad comes.' Then, as he left, he added, 'Sorry Miss. I don't mean to be rude.'

11am

All the way home, Joe held himself together like a hermit crab in its shell. Round and round went the bike pedals and with every turn, he whispered, '*Mum, Mum, Mum.*'

He paused outside his cottage, where his mother would never put flowers on the table again. Still, he held together, tight, pushing tears away. Then he cycled on, his pedals beating out, '*Mum, Mum, Mum.*'

Soon he was at the harbour. *Star of the Deep* was chugging round the pier-head. On deck, his father sorted the day's catch as Mr. Jument steered the boat to the quay. Briefly they looked at him. Mr. Le Carin dropped his nets. Then Mr. Jument revved the boat towards the quay.

Joe shook with the burden of his terrible news.

He stumbled off Clem's bike and let it drop. As its wheels whirred, he watched the men as they drew nearer, kneading his hands together, wondering how to tell his father.

But he didn't have to say anything. The news must have been written on his face in capital letters, because Mr. Jument brought the boat alongside quickly and his father jumped out. He gave a huge groan and ran towards his son.

'She's gone, isn't she? '

Joe nodded, mute.

'I knew when I saw you.' Tears poured down his face as he said, 'I thought she'd have more time.'

'Well. She didn't.' Joe stood still as stone. But when his father tried to give him a clumsy hug, he suffered it. Then he rushed away, choking with sobs.

As Mr. Jument drove his father to the hospital, Joe sat on the end of the harbour until sunset, staring out to sea and bouncing pebbles on the water. When he was quite sure that no-one could hear him, long after curfew, he began to sob again as if he'd never stop for the rest of his life. Tears ripped out of his chest like an animal's howls, though he tried his best to control himself.

When he was calmer, he said out loud, 'If them damn Nazis hadn't landed, Mum would be all right. It's their fault. I'll do something to them, I flaming will.' Standing up, he shouted, 'RESISTANCE.'

Who cared if there were soldiers listening, or Old Gaston?

'RESISTANCE,' he yelled again and again.

But his echoing voice made him feel lonelier than he'd been in his whole life. He knew, there and then, that resistance was pointless. It wouldn't bring his mother back and no-one would ever call him *my little crab* again.

As the moon rose, he went home, glancing upwards. The stars were already out. He'd know his mother's star straight away. It would be green and bright and sparkling, or even a whole spray of stars, like apple blossom.

June 1941

Saturday June 14h 11am

'So,' said Mr. Braye after band practice a few weeks later. 'We'll give the concert in two weeks.' He looked at the calendar on the wall. 'It'll be exactly a year since we were invaded. You up for that Joe?'

Joe nodded 'Course I am. Just because of Mum and everything...' he swallowed, '...it don't mean we give up on a single flipping thing.'

'We could have a collection afterwards,' said Clem, 'for the hospital.'

'They need all sorts,' said Joe. He went to the door. 'Auntie Vi's moving in tonight and I'd best clean up Diddie and Arthur.'

Spinner caught her breath. 'Auntie Vi? Why?'

'They're taking over her house. She's been moving into our place for days.'

'Crikey,' said Ginger. 'What about her marigolds? She loves them.'

'She's brought a whole lot round already.' Joe grinned. 'There's a tub of them by the back door. She's scrubbed out the house again, moving into my room with Diddie and Arthur, I'm in the corridor and she's in a temper all the time.'

Mr. Braye patted him on the shoulder. 'I could offer a room at our house.'

'Thank you, but we don't mind. It's a squash, but she can cook a meal from a couple of cockles and a piece of seaweed.'

After he'd gone, Spinner said, 'I've made some posters already. I'll just write the date on them, then I'll go and pin them up round the parish.'

Soon she was walking down the lane with a roll of posters, pinning them to trees and telegraph posts. She'd put one on the parish notice board, too. Even though she was sad for Joe, she couldn't help humming. It was such a perfect day. Then she froze.

Something rustled behind the hedge.

Then there was silence and a waft of cheap cigarette smoke, followed by a terrible, raw sob. Spinner stood still, hardly liking to breathe in case she was in the way of someone's unhappiness.

Then a single word flew up into the air. '*Mum.*'

She hesitated, then hurried quietly away. Now and then she looked back, in case she could help, but all she could see was a curl of smoke on the other side of the hedge.

When all the posters were pinned, she wandered down the slipway. There might be limpets for Lizzie's cat, now the tide was on the turn, or even cockles to put in soup for supper. She began to search among the rocks, her skirt tucked into her knickers as she paddled through deeper water. Suddenly someone yelled, 'Oi, Spinner Braye. Don't take all the cockles.'

Joe was walking down the steps, carrying Arthur and

followed by Diddie. Auntie Vi loomed over the sea wall and shouted after them, 'Keep them out of my way until the clock strikes six.'

Spinner splashed out of the water and went to help. When Arthur was settled on the sand, banging the sand with a little spade, Diddie rushed off and began hitting the wall.

'Auntie Vi said she could have an ice cream when the war's over,' said Joe. 'But Diddie thought she said, 'When the *wall's* over. She's been hitting it for days with her friends.'

'I don't think she's got a hope,' said Spinner. 'Hey, look at all those ships coming in from France.' She pointed at the horizon.

'They're bringing workers in to build bunkers.' Joe sighed. 'Like the one they're building in Auntie Vi's garden.'

'What sort of workers? German builders?'

Joe shook his head. 'Prisoners. I saw some down the harbour. They're in a bad way, hungry.' He suddenly looked fierce. 'I'm not feeling sorry for myself, Spinner. They're much worse off then any of us. You should see them, they're skinny like starved almost to death…'

'Joe,' shouted Diddie, rushing over the sand. 'I got a bit of wall off.' She held out her hand to show a tiny piece of cement.'

'Blimey,' said Joe. 'You'll have it down in no time.'

'Ice cream,' shouted Diddie, racing off again.

Spinner laughed, then she said, 'I keep thinking about Percy. I hope he's all right. People keep saying things about prison camps and…'

'Yeah,' said Joe. 'I've been thinking about him too, ever since I saw them prisoners.'

Saturday June 21st 9am

On the other side of the island, Percy's mother, Mrs. Du Brin, was putting on her lipstick. She liked to do this very carefully, making her lips a nice shape. As she concentrated, she suddenly jumped and drew scarlet across her chin.

There was someone at the door, reflected in the mirror, tall and thin.

Mrs. Du Brin whipped round. 'For crying out loud, who do you think you are, walking into my house?' She stood up, tall in scarlet high heels, staring at him insolently.

'I'm *Percy*, your son. Don't you know me?'

Mrs. Du Brin's face crumpled. She took a step forward. 'Percy? Is it really you? You smell awful. Why's your hair so short?' She tried to stroke his head. '*Darling.*'

He held his hands in front of himself like a shield. 'Stop it, Mum. They shaved my head and I'm not your darling.'

'Of course you are. My boy.'

'If I was your darling, you'd have rescued me.' Percy glared at her. 'But instead, you came to France with Viktor to see me. You took me out to lunch, like having a day out from a boarding school...'

'It was a lovely place. All those pretty trees.'

'*Trees?*' Percy spoke louder, and his mother put her finger to her scarlet lips, in case the neighbours heard. But Percy continued, 'Viktor wouldn't let me speak to you. I tried to pass you a note, but you left me...'

'Viktor was right to send you away. You broke the rules and now you're lying.' Mrs. du Brin shook her head. 'Why are you wearing those awful clothes? It's important to keep yourself clean, you know, even if it's difficult. There's always the sea.'

Percy blinked back tears. 'Leave Viktor. He doesn't love you, Mother. He thinks you're stupid. I was hiding on the boat coming back and I heard him telling his friends. He was laughing about you.'

Mrs. Du Brin raised her eyebrows. 'You're too young to understand. He wants to marry me when the war's over.'

Percy grabbed the lipstick and hurled it out of the window. 'I'm old enough to know a great deal, especially about him.' He glanced at the clock. 'He'll be here soon. I heard him say he had a job to do, then he was coming to see you. He *laughed* when he told his mates.'

'I tell you, I love him.' His mother's face suddenly looked pinched and thin. 'But I'm sorry if you had a bad time. I thought, I really thought...'

'No you aren't sorry. You never cared. What kind of mother would...'

But he didn't finish. Outside, a motorbike roared up the road and came to halt outside his mother's house. Percy glanced from behind the curtain. 'Don't tell Viktor I'm here. Don't tell him I escaped. Don't tell him I ran all the way from that terrible place, whatever you do, because he'll make things bad for you, I promise.' He looked at her fiercely, his face white. 'Please, Mum, for God's sake, don't tell him I'm back, do you hear me?'

Then he shot down the stairs into the back garden and found Ginger's bike in the shed where he'd left it. He waited until Viktor was indoors. When the front door slammed, he wheeled the bike silently onto the road, keeping low until he was out of sight, racing down the valley, powered by fear.

In no time he was whizzing along the sea front, weaving his way in and out of lorries and cyclists and keeping to the right so no-one would stop him. Soon he was the other side of Town, pedalling up the lane to the Brayes'.

He pushed the bike for the last stretch, clutching the handlebars to keep himself steady. Then he staggered, exhausted. The bike fell as his legs gave way and he collapsed, bumping his head on the gatepost as the world went black, then blazed white, then black again.

As he swam in and out of consciousness, he heard a bucket clanking and footsteps. There was a reek of fish and someone called, 'Spinner, fetch your dad. There's a body here that's almost flipping dead. Nearly bald, too, poor devil.'

There was a gasp, then a girl's voice. 'What on earth's happened to him?'

'Go on, girl, get your dad, for God's sake,' said the person with the bucket. Light footsteps raced away, as he went on, 'It's Percy, isn't it? You poor old bloke. Come on, wake up, or I'll smack your face with a wet sand-eel. Come on mate. Don't give up on us.'

'Joe,' Percy muttered, giving a weak smile. '*Bonjour* and all that.'

Then he sank into unconsciousness again as Joe

touched his shoulder. 'Blimey, Perce. You don't half stink.'

12.30pm

When Percy opened his eyes again, he found himself lying on the kitchen sofa in Spinner's house. Mr. Braye gave him sips of hot, sweet tea and Spinner spooned jam into his mouth. After a while, he opened his eyes properly.

'Can you tell us what happened then, Percy?'

'Viktor pretended I was fifteen. He took me to a training camp.' He blinked back tears, so everyone looked away while he recovered. 'It was miles from anywhere, in the woods where no-one could see us.'

Mr. Braye gave him another sip of tea. 'Take your time, Percy.'

'Horrible things happened.'

Spinner offered him another spoon of jam. Percy nodded his thanks. 'Viktor told them I was his adopted son. They tried to force me think the sort of stuff Hitler says about people like Lizzie.'

Ginger looked away and Spinner dug into the jar again. 'Mr. Hitler's cruel to them,' she said, fiercely spooning jam.

'But I wouldn't.' Percy blinked then rubbed his eyes with his fists. 'I wouldn't think the way they did, so they sent me to a camp. People were taken away from it in cattle trucks. I knew I'd be next.'

'How terrible,' said Mr. Braye. 'How dreadful for you. Poor boy.'

Percy drank tea, holding the cup with trembling fingers. 'I was lucky. A friend helped me escape. He drew map for me on the ground in the dust and said where his friends lived, who'd help me. I had to trust him. He risked his life for me.'

The others leaned forward as Percy fought back tears. 'But how did you get out of the camp?' asked Ginger. 'There must have been guards everywhere.'

Percy closed his eyes at the memory. 'My friend hid me when we went to work in the forest. It was horrible work. We were treated like slaves.'

Clem's eyes darkened. 'There are prisoners on the island being treated like that too.'

'It's happening everywhere,' said Percy. He went on, 'I hid behind the trees. As I ran for it, he said, 'Keep the sun on your back and you'll find your way home.' Tears trickled down Percy's face as he whispered, 'I wish it was him who escaped, not me. He was better than I am.' He rubbed away the tears again, and closed his eyes.

'Blimming war,' said Joe. 'And there we were, thinking it was going to be a laugh. Poor old Perce.' He rattled his bucket. 'Want a sand-eel, Perce? Make you feel at home?'

Percy gave a weak nod, so Joe moved to the cooker. As he fried, a wonderful smell rose from the pan. 'We got barbed wire all over the place,' he told Percy. 'So we're not allowed to fish at low water. This lot did the high jump over the wire, lucky for you.'

'Joe's crazy,' said Ginger. 'He dodges through the mines and breaks the curfew.'

'Here,' said Joe, handing him a sand-eel. 'Try this and don't believe Ginger. I never break the rules.'

'It's too dangerous to go against anything they say,' said Percy. He managed to smile as he ate the last scrap, 'But maybe it's worth it.'

Mr. Braye ran his fingers through his hair. 'Your friend sounds a good man.'

Percy gulped tea. 'He shared his food and his blanket and he said there's always been evil in the world but I must let it bounce off me, otherwise it'll soak in and take me over.' He gulped some more. 'He said I have a choice of what I want to be. I knew right then I'd been half-way to being like Old Gaston or Viktor and his Nazi mates and that I must get back to the island and sort everything out, even Mum.'

After this long speech, no-one could look at each other, because they'd never seen this side of Percy and it was almost like looking at a person with no clothes on.

Ginger pushed his glasses back into place and said, 'It's all right about the bike. You paid for what you did, a lot more than you should have.'

'Sorry I called you Freaky. Sorry I painted it,' Percy replied, 'It was better red.'

'Black's OK. Grown up.'

Joe plonked the rest of the sand-eels in front of Percy smoking hot, and he tucked in. Afterwards, he had a long, hot bath and slept, dressed in old clothes of Bill's.

Saturday June 28th 10am

'She's huge,' said Spinner a week later, trying to force Peggy out of the sty. For once, the pig didn't want to leave her home and braced herself against the wall, snapping at Spinner. 'I can't think how she got so big without me noticing.'

'Try a biscuit,' advised Clem, holding out a crumby morsel, 'but break them up. These are the last of them. There's not enough sugar in the rations for baking.'

Spinner edged round Peggy, holding half a biscuit high. The pig's eyes followed it and she jumped out of the sty, gobbled it and headed for Clem's pocket. But he was too quick for her, looping a halter over her head.

'Here,' he said, holding the pig with his knees, 'push the sousa cart so she's between the shafts.' Like magic, Peggy reversed, her eyes on Clem as he held up a scrap of toast and jam.

Spinner climbed into the cart and gripped the sides.

'Hold tight,' said Clem, fastening ropes from the halter to the shafts, 'The trouble these days,' he added, prodding Peggy with a stick, 'is everyone's too thin. She needs to get used to pulling heavy weights if she's going to be useful.'

'Rosie could sit on my lap for extra weight,' said Spinner.

'Then Viktor would arrive,' said Clem, 'and say *SHUT THAT CHILD UP.*'

'The beast,' said Spinner as Peggy pulled them out of the yard and into the lane. Soon they were trotting along happily, except Spinner kept yelling, 'Ouch, that bit was bumpy. Slow down.' But the pig charged on regardless.

However, on the corner near Joe's den, she skidded to such an abrupt halt that Spinner flew out of the cart smack into Percy, who was wandering about in a daze.

'Percy,' she shouted, dusting herself down. 'Percy! We've been worried about you. Where have you been the last week? Are you all right?'

'He isn't,' muttered Clem. 'We should have gone over to his place and checked up.' He yanked the pig's reins. 'Stand still, you damn pig. What's up, Percy? You're shaking.'

'I've just seen Viktor.' He swallowed and added, 'He's brought prisoners here from France.'

'Prisoners? Like those ones Joe saw at the harbour a couple of weeks ago?'

'I don't know about them' said Percy. 'But I think those ones were Spanish. This lot is Russian. We had some in the camp and they were treated worse than anyone else.'

Spinner flinched. 'Why? Poor things.'

'Hitler has a grudge against Russians,' Percy said, 'The prisoners just passed this way, being marched along. I hid behind Joe's den, but I saw them. They looked terrible, even worse than the ones in camp. Starving. Feet in rags, stinking.' He swallowed, pointed down the road. 'They went that way.'

Spinner clutched her stomach. 'Can we help them? I can fetch some apples.'

Percy shook his head. 'I reckon it'll be dangerous to feed them.'

'But we can't just stand by,' said Clem. 'We'll have to help.'

Percy didn't seem to hear. He went on, 'The soldiers beat them with rifle butts and I didn't stop them. I didn't dare, and that makes me a flipping coward.' He caught his breath, a sob tearing out of his chest.

Clem's face darkened. 'That's filthy, beating people. But you couldn't have done anything, Perce.'

Percy stammered, 'Viktor told Mum the prisoners are going to build forts and work in the quarry. They're bringing loads of them and they'll work them to death. I saw that in the camp.'

Percy looked over his shoulder again. 'There's something else. I saw Gaston chatting to Viktor. He spies all over the place, and I'm worried Viktor's watching you.'

'Into the truck with you, Perce,' said Clem, helping him. 'Don't worry. Everything'll be all right.' When Percy was in the truck and Clem was pulling him, Spinner suddenly noticed Clem doing something she'd never seen before. He was holding the truck handle with one hand and crossing himself with the other, like Auntie Vi did in church.

11am

When they arrived home, they heard Ginger playing his trumpet in the flat, loud and clear. Peggy plonked down in the shafts to listen, her ears forward like saucers.

Percy gasped, clutching his chest. 'Ginger's playing the Russian national anthem.'

'So?' Clem looked puzzled. 'He likes to play the

anthem of every country as it's invaded. Only he does his own version. So that's all right.'

'You *know* anthems are banned.' Percy pulled himself out of the truck.

'Ginger doesn't take any notice of rules. He always...' Spinner stopped, because Percy suddenly froze. His eyes glittered with terror, like a rabbit's in the glare of the poacher's lamp.

'*Motorbike*,' he whispered. 'Make Ginger stop. Listen.' He looked frantically up at the flat, then at Spinner and Clem, then into the direction of a distant motorbike. '*Viktor.*'

Spinner could see his chest thumping up and down. She took his arm, 'We'll sort him out.'

Percy whispered fearfully, 'You won't. No-one can.'

'We're really good at tricks,' said Spinner, though her chest felt as though it was beating as hard as Percy's. She dragged up the hill and into The Trotter Club, saying, 'We'll blow three blasts on Ginger's trumpet if Viktor heads your way. Then you can slip out of the back window and hide in the fields.'

'But how can you get rid of Viktor?'

'We've got Peggy on our side. She's a war machine.' Spinner patted Percy's shoulder, adding, 'Chin up Percy. Everything will be all right.'

She ran back to the yard.

Clem had taken Peggy out of her shafts and was holding on to her collar as she munched on toast, her eyes swivelling in the direction of the sound of the motorbike.

'She loves chasing soldiers,' said Spinner. 'I think she's taken the backs off three pairs of trousers.'

'She'll get caught if she goes on,' Clem said. He gave the pig more toast and whispered in her ear, smoothing and stroking the folds behind them so that she gave a little croon of delight just as Viktor's bike roared into the yard, scattering chickens and skidding to a halt in front of the pig sty.

Spinner glanced up the hill. The Trotter Club door was closed.

'Good morning,' she said, clutching Joe's carved pig in her pocket. 'Can we help?'

Viktor ignored her, took off black leather gloves and placed them on his handlebars.

Peggy snorted and Spinner said, 'Don't go near the pig.'

The man gave her an icy look. 'I can deal with pigs.' He kicked Peggy so hard with his jackboot that she squealed. He ran forward to try again, but Clem shot between him and the pig. So the jackboot thumped him in the stomach, *thwack*.

Clem gasped, bent double and Viktor laughed.

Spinner dashed forward to help, but Clem stood up without her, grabbing for breath as Viktor gave him a contemptuous look and turned on his heel, storming towards the flat, where Ginger played on. Battering the door, Viktor yelled, '*Raus, Raus.*'

The music stopped.

Viktor yelled again. '*Raus, Raus.* Come out or I will break the door.'

Footsteps ran down the flat stairs and the door opened. Ginger peered out, trumpet in hand. 'Is there an emergency?'

Spinner clutched the carved pig again and Clem grabbed Peggy's collar again, panting.

Viktor's face turned scarlet. 'National anthems are against the rules. It is a deliberate insult to the Fuhrer to play them in public.'

~ 224 ~

upside down where Dad forgot to put them back.'

'How do you know that? He was probably dancing and knocking things over.' Clem's face was scarlet. 'You're just sticking up for him.'

'It's *not* that.' Spinner lowered her voice. 'Look, I saw Dad's diary. He wrote something like this: *'Another search. What does V want? Today, he brought more men and they were everywhere. Left a hell of a mess. But not too much of the rough stuff yet.'*

Ginger took off his glasses and wiped them. 'That *is* a bit worrying. Are you sure he means Viktor?'

'Who else?' Spinner scuffed the dust with her toes. 'I shouldn't have looked at his diary, but it was open on the table and he was asleep beside it. He had a big bruise on his arm. Huge.' She swallowed. 'It was bleeding a bit, too.'

'Prove it,' Clem was sneering. 'Viktor probably visits to get a free cup of tea.'

Spinner flew at him, grabbing his black curls and Clem shoved her off so she fell over. 'It's true. Do you want me to get him? To prove it? Show his bruise?'

At that, Clem shook himself, as though sloughing off a skin. He put out his hand to Spinner, his eyes full of tears. 'I didn't mean...'

Suddenly, the door flew open and everyone jumped. But it was only Joe, his hair sticking up. 'I just seen Viktor. He was in a hell of a rage, face like a tomato. Where's Percy? We better warn him.'

'*Percy?*' Everyone was talking at once.

'Oh ruddy hell,' said Clem. 'We forgot all about him, me yelling at Spinner and everything happening.' He ran outside and searched round the outside of the building. Then he came in again. 'No sign of him.'

Joe said, 'We got to find him.'

'I'll keep watch,' Spinner offered, as the boys scattered up and down the *cotil* and into the next fields.

At last Clem shouted, 'Found him. Come and help.'

Percy was pressed flat under the hedge, hands over his head.

Spinner touched his shoulder and he flinched, so Joe shook open a grubby packet of German cigarettes and held it out. 'Come on Perce. You're safe with us.'

After a while, Percy crawled out, keeping low, his eyes like a hunted animal. He tried to speak, but all that came out was, 'You don't know what you're playing with. Viktor's worse than fire. He's worse than...' There was a pause.

The other four looked at each other in consternation. Clem put his hand under his shoulder, 'Stand up Percy. You'll be safer inside.'

Percy uncurled himself and they saw his shirt was soaked with sweat and mud. He pulled it off, crunched it into a ball and hurled it into the hedge as though he was throwing away his terror. Spinner gasped, because his ribs stuck out like sticks and across his back was a long, jagged scar.

Clem wriggled out of his shirt. 'Put that on, Percy.' The shirt billowed round Percy and Clem asked, 'What did they do to you?'

Percy looked round anxiously, as though it wasn't just walls that had ears, but hedges and fences and trees also and maybe even the sky.

'A guard in the camp was annoyed with me,' said Percy. He shrugged. 'It was nothing.'

'*Nothing?* He did that to you?' gasped Spinner. 'How's that nothing?'

'There are worse men out there than Viktor. Much worse.' Percy gave her a weary look. No-one knew what to say. Then Percy went on, 'My friend said we must keep our dreams. He asked about mine and I didn't know.'

'You mean, like I want to be a doctor?' asked Spinner.

Percy nodded. 'I thought and thought, then decided I'd be a cook. One day, I'd open a wonderful shop where you could buy delicious things, cream buns, slathered in chocolate. Rich stews, full of beans. Coffee, spices. Giant meringues.'

'Stop, stop,' cried Joe, holding his stomach.

Percy gave a proper smile. 'My friend had been a cook before they took him. I promised I'd remember in case he...' there was a pause... 'didn't make it.'

Ginger wiped his glasses. 'I could play jazz in this wonderful shop.'

'I'd like that,' replied Percy, his face lighting up. Then he added, 'If anyone's hungry and hasn't any money, I'll give them food. *Just give it them.*'

He stood up. 'Best if I go home now and check up on mum. Viktor might take it out on her.'

'Where do you watch from?' asked Ginger.

'Next door's shed,' said Percy. 'The old lady stays indoors most of the time, scared of the enemy. It's a good shed, close to Mum's fence.'

'Be careful,' said Spinner, touching his arm.

For a moment, everyone thought Percy was going to cry. But he went on, 'If anything happens to Mum, I'll do something to Viktor. I don't know what, but I'll think of something.'

After he'd left, Joe said, 'Blimey. Good old Perce.'

Spinner was about to speak when she spotted her father, treading wearily up the hill. When he reached them, he said in a heavy voice, 'I imagine you all think that I have lost my mind. But I asked Viktor to the concert because it's wiser to keep your enemies close.'

'The concert was for *us*.' Clem glowered, then reluctantly added, 'Sir.'

'Viktor will ruin it,' wailed Spinner.

'No he won't,' replied Mr. Braye. 'We'll give him plenty of Mrs. Percheron's cider. It's so strong, he'll fall asleep. Anyhow, we have to have a German monitor. It's the rules.' Spinner looked dubious, so he went on, 'He won't turn up. Why would he want to go to a children's concert?'

Clem was still clenching his hands as though he could hardly stop himself from lashing out.

Mr. Braye said, 'I'm sorry you feel this way, Clem, but trust me. This is the best way to deal with men like Viktor.'

'Tactics,' replied Ginger thoughtfully. 'I think I understand.'

'Well, I ruddy don't,' said Clem. 'Sir.'

'We did that before,' said Spinner thoughtfully, 'with that man called Josef. We invited him into The Trotter Club. It was a good idea.'

'Yes, but he was OK,' said Joe.

'We didn't know that,' said Ginger. 'We just hoped for the best.'

After Mr. Braye had left, Joe touched Spinner's arm. 'The good thing about your father, Spinner, is he always says sorry. Not many grown-ups do that.'

Clem suddenly gave a curt laugh. 'Actually, he's a *complete* genius. He's giving us the chance to get rid of Viktor.'

'How? said Joe.

Clem grinned. 'I've been dreaming about this for ages. We'll make sure Viktor's drink knocks him out, then cart him out to the tower at low water, using Peggy and the truck. What do you think?'

'Excellent idea, church boy,' replied Joe.

'So,' said Spinner, folding her arms. 'What exactly will we do with him when he's out there?'

'Well,' said Clem. He leaned forward, and whispered.

July 1941

Saturday July 4th 8am

As Joe and Clem walked along the beach below Joe's cottage, Clem said, 'I took the cows and Hotspur over the hill to the Le Brocqs' place. The animals wouldn't like the concert. If I put them in the hiding place, they'll kick up, make a row. Even if Viktor didn't mean it about taking them away, I'm not risking it.'

'Flipping right,' said Joe, splashing through a puddle.

Clem held out a package. '*I* don't know what it is, but Mr. Braye says *you* will.'

Joe lowered his voice. 'You've got to really keep *stum*. It's for the War Office in England. Photos and maps. Everything's in code. We take them to the tower when we fish the big tides. There's always someone there to take it. Man in black. Never seen his face.'

'*Bloody hell*,' whispered Clem. 'So Mr. Braye's a spy?'

Joe nodded, tucking the package in his pocket. 'God help him if the Germans find out, so keep your gob shut.'

They walked up the slipway to the coast road and Clem said. 'I guess Viktor's suspicious, searching Mr.

Braye all the time,' He shook his head. 'I was wrong about him.'

As they walked, constantly checking for patrols, Clem spoke quietly. 'I've taken the headstones off the pets' graves, ready. Let's get the pistol later, when everyone's out of the way. Just for defence, mind.'

Joe nodded. 'Yeah. Right. And remember, keep that flipping gob shut, Clem, whatever happens, eh?'

Clem wiped sweat off the back of his neck. 'Everything's ready. It's going to work, You and me doing the hard stuff and Ginger and Spinner running the tricks.' He grinned, then said, 'I'm going to oil the cart. Don't want the wheels squeaking.'

He set off to the farm and Joe hurried home. He nipped indoors to scribble a quick note: *WE WILL BRING HIM AFTER MIDNIGHT*. Then he slid it into the package, taped it shut and hurried off to the harbour. When he saw his father on *Star of the Deep*, he handed it over. 'I'm not coming fishing today, Dad. You deliver it. I got things to do for the concert.'

'Son, I have to talk to you.'

Joe squared up to him. '*Talk?* Blimey. You never done that before.'

There was a horrible moment as Mr. Le Carin clenched his fist, then unclenched it again. He said through his teeth, 'I'm sorry. I tried to be a good father.'

'You certainly been a father,' replied Joe. 'Three of us.'

'But I need to go away.' His father's mouth was a thin line. 'I have to fight, Joe. That's what I know. Fighting and fishing. I wanted to bring the kids back from gran's, but as I said, I can't look after them and earn a living.' He lowered his voice. 'I'm thinking of joining the French Resistance.'

'Oh yeah? What about Jersey Resistance? And what's going to happen to us? Auntie Vi won't want to stay with us for ever.'

'I've arranged everything. If I go, you'll all be cared for.'

'That's another first then,' replied Joe. He stared at the French coast.

Mr. Le Carin opened his mouth to answer, but the guard arrived, his expression cheerful. '*Guten Morgen.* Today, I am not going to be sick,' he vowed, taking a seat. 'It is a lovely day. *Hein?*'

Mr. Le Carin gave the guard a furious glance and said, 'See you at the concert, Son, if I get back after doing your job.'

'Course you will,' muttered Joe. 'You got the luck of the devil.'

2pm

Everyone was carrying chairs. Spinner had never seen so many. Chairs from the farmhouse, chairs from the flat, chairs from bedrooms and dining rooms and kitchens. All carried to The Trotter Club. Even Auntie Vi helped.

When they were all arranged, they gathered for a dress rehearsal. They'd just begun to play when Josef turned up, the soldier they'd met in the snow, who played the flute with Mr. Braye.

'Joining us?' asked Joe.

The soldier shook his head and went out of the room with Mr. Braye. Spinner looked at Joe, who said, 'On with the music.'

After a while, Mr. Braye returned. Everyone stopped playing, except Rosie who kept whacking her triangle. He looked over his glasses so that even she became quiet. 'Josef says we must be careful which tunes we play tonight. Viktor is definitely coming, and he's on the warpath.'

Spinner's stomach did its somersault, but the boys were watching her, so she smiled at them, tossing back her hair as though she didn't care. When the rehearsal was over, Mr. Braye said, 'You'll be wonderful. We'll make lots of money to help people and we're not doing anything that breaks the rules. Everyone will love your music. Well done.'

'That's good,' said Joe. He kicked Spinner's foot, and she didn't dare look at him or Clem and Ginger. 'I hate breaking rules.'

Mr. Braye said, 'We're going to enjoy ourselves.'

'Bimmin' right.' Joe gave a final flourish on his spoons.

Mr. Braye raised an eyebrow and added, 'Two hours to go. See you later in your Sunday best. Polished shoes. The lot. Get that oil off you face, Clem. What on earth have you been doing?'

Clem gave Joe a knowing look. 'Just oiling the wheels on my sousa cart, sir.'

2.45pm

A few minutes later, Spinner slipped into the farm kitchen, carrying her mother's cardigan. She took the pestle and mortar from its shelf and, checking that she was alone, ground a couple of pills into a fine powder. Then she beat butter with her own sugar ration, whipped in two of her hens' eggs and folded in sifted potato flour. Last she mixed in the powder she'd made from the pills and spooned the lot into a tin. 'Good old Clem, finding those vet's pills,' she muttered.

She put the little cake in the bread oven. While it baked, she washed everything carefully. 'We don't want everyone falling asleep,' she muttered. Then she made another cake with the ingredients Mrs. Percheron had left out for her.

Soon the first cake was ready, brown and sweet smelling, with a trace of sugar on top. 'For you, Viktor,' she murmured. The cat jumped on to the table, mewing at the smell. Spinner pushed it off and wrote a note for Mrs. Percheron. *'Thank you for sharing your rations.'*

She left the second cake on the table to cool.

Tucking the first one under her cardigan, she hurried through the gate to her house. As she went upstairs, her father called from his study, 'Why on earth are you wearing a cardigan on a boiling day like this?'

'Helps me to think of Mum,' replied Spinner. She raced past him to her room and hid Viktor's cake in her drawer. After she'd changed into her red dress, she looked out of her window at the sea. Over the French coast, towering clouds gathered.

Spinner picked up Lizzie's stone from its place on the window-sill, her fingers running over the round granite.

She whispered, 'We're doing this for you, Lizzie, and everyone else the enemy hates. Think of us.' Then she put it in her pocket, where it hung heavy and solid, banging against her leg.

In the other pocket, she tucked the carved pig.

4pm

'I hope Old Gaston isn't nosing about,' said Clem. 'You better keep watch. He'll tell Viktor what we're up to just like that.' He snapped his fingers before kneeling down beside one of the pretend pets' graves.

'Haven't you heard?' Joe looked astonished. 'I thought everyone knew.'

'Knew what?' Clem slit a rectangle in the grass.

'About Gaston,' said Joe. 'Viktor pushed him over the cliff.'

'WHAT?' Clem looked up, open mouthed, his penknife suddenly still.

'Viktor said Gaston was trying to pull him over and it was an accident.'

'Ruddy hell. That's horrible.' Clem lifted the grass cover from the grave, felt inside and pulled out a parcel. As he brushed off dirt, he swore again and said, 'I didn't like Old Gaston, but that's crazy. He wasn't even strong enough to throw a cat, let alone a man like Viktor over a cliff.'

'Yeah. Viktor's lying like hell.' replied Joe. 'Gaston was a squealer. But he was a Jerseyman, one of us.'

'My God, that Viktor's a b...' Clem unwrapped the parcel and showed Joe the Walther PP pistol. 'Now you've told me that lovely bit of news, I'm not so worried about taking this with us. Maybe we could shoot...'

'Steady, Percheron. Remember what it says in the Bible.'

'*Thou Shalt Do No Murder.* That's the fourth commandment.' Clem gave Joe a toothy grin. 'Here's another of the Ten Commandments: *Love Your Neighbour.* Ginger was Gaston's neighbour.'

'Well, I didn't love Gaston whatever the Bible says and I don't think Ginger did,' said Joe.

'Here's one more from the Bible. *'Vengeance Shall be Mine, Said the Lord.'*

'Blimey Clem. You're getting a bit above yourself. You aren't God Almighty Himself. We're only taking this for defence.'

Clem gave a bitter laugh and replaced the grass.

Joe put back the headstone. 'Poor Florrie,' he said, tracing the name he'd carved for a pretend pet. 'She was a nice old dog.'

They hurried back to the sousa cart, which they'd hidden behind the farm wall near The Trotter Club. 'Now we're safe,' Clem murmured, slipping the pistol into a secret compartment underneath it. 'It took me ages to make this, but I think it works.'

Joe stared at the cart, his eyes narrowed. 'You can't see it at all. Blimming clever, Clem.'

Clem grinned, 'Everything's going to plan. Now we need Peggy.'

He took half a biscuit from his shorts pocket and they headed for the pig sty, where he looped the collar over Peggy's head and led her through the farmyard.

Clem patted her head. 'It's going to thunder.'

'That'll gee her up,' said Joe. 'I need to show you something.' He pointed to a bundle of wires on the ground. 'I nicked those explosives from Dad's boat.'

Clem grinned in his old way, showing his big white teeth.

'They're safety rockets really,' continued Joe, but Ginger and I clumped them up and laid a trail, fuses to go. If there's thunder, no-one'll guess what we done.' He pulled a cigarette stub from behind his ear and struck a match. Then he screeched and stamped it out, pointing at the fuses. 'Flippin' heck. I nearly blew us up. Forgot about that lot.'

'That'd ruin everything,' said Clem. 'Ginger and Spinner would never manage Viktor alone.'

6pm

As Joe and Clem locked up his den, leaving Peggy sleeping off her supper, Ginger and Spinner stood beside a table in the farmyard. Ginger was in his school suit and tie, and Spinner had squeezed her feet into the red shoes that matched her dress.

They were filling glasses with cider, waiting for the audience to arrive. 'Crikey, my hands are shaking,' said Ginger. 'Yours too.'

Spinner poured more wobbling glassfuls. 'I'm not scared.'

'Course you are,' said Ginger.

Spinner shook her head. 'I used to write down everything that scared me, Percy, bombs, potty heads, the lot. A whole book of it, page after page. You name it. But then I ripped out the pages about fear and threw them to Peggy. I just kept the good pages.'

Ginger looked at her curiously. 'Did she like them?'

'She snapped them up. That pig's so well trained she can even eat fear.'

'We aren't fighters, you and me. Not like Joe and Clem. They're made of iron.'

'Aren't we?' Spinner arranged the glasses into tidy rows.

'Maybe,' Ginger conceded. 'But in a different way. Clem's dangerous. We aren't.'

'Dangerous?'

'Joe says he's a smoking volcano, and I reckon he's right,' said Ginger.

'He used to be gentle,' replied Spinner, biting her lip. 'He was the kindest person I knew.'

'He still is,' said Ginger. 'But he wants to protect us all.' He wiped his glasses then reached into his pocket for a brown bottle. 'Father's rum. Sailors drink a tot every day to keep up their spirits, Dad said.' He made a face, sniffing. 'Crikey, it's jolly strong. It's taking the hairs out of my nostrils.'

'*We* should be drinking it if it keeps up spirits, not wasting it on Viktor,' said Spinner, picking up a large, crystal glass and admiring its sparkle. 'I chose this for Viktor's cocktail. Nice, isn't it?'

Ginger eyed the thick layer of powder at the bottom of the glass. 'Perfect. Viktor's such a delicate chap. He deserves pure crystal.' He poured in a generous dollop of rum, then whisked it with his finger until the powder had dissolved. 'Fill it up with cider and,' he looked over his glasses anxiously, 'don't give it to anyone else.'

Suddenly, Spinner felt a wave of panic. She bit her lip again. 'Ginger, we won't….?'

'*Finish him off?*' Ginger slapped his forehead. 'No, of course not. That drink will simply send him to sleep, then we'll dump him at low water. Von Pernet will have to rescue him. They'll send him away for being stupid and wasting their time and we'll never be bothered by him again.'

'I hope Clem and Joe won't do anything silly.'

Ginger whispered, 'I checked the guns' hiding place early this morning. The grass on the graves wasn't disturbed one bit, so Clem and Joe hadn't dug up the guns. I asked Joe if he had any ammo yesterday and he didn't even hear me. So there won't be any stupid goings on.'

Spinner placed Viktor's cocktail at the back. She said in a small voice, 'In Sunday School we learned that commandment. *Thou Shalt Do No Murder.* I don't want to go to hell or anything.'

'Brace up Spinner. I checked everything from my book of poisons. This powder we've got, it's only a kind of tranquilliser to keep animals calm.' He smiled. 'But we could decorate the drink with foxgloves.' He gave a cackle of laughter and said he was going to change.

Thunder rumbled, softly at first, then a little closer. Spinner went to talk to Percy, who stood by the gate, programmes in his hands. On his head was a wig topped with a bowler hat. A moustache was pencilled under his nose and he'd borrowed a striped jacket from Mr. Braye. He pulled his hat brim low. 'Don't want Viktor to recognise me.'

Spinner handed him a glass of cider. 'You look exactly like a jazz man. Perfect.' She gave him an encouraging smile, then jumped as the thunder growled again.

Percy swigged the cider. 'Thunder can't hurt you, Spinner. Only people do that.' He blinked and said, 'Mum has a black eye from Viktor.'

'Why? What for? Your poor mum.'

'She rang Mr. Percheron and told him to hide his animals. Viktor heard her and went bonkers.'

'Oh, the *poor* thing.' Spinner patted his arm. 'How horrible when she was so brave to ring the farm.'

For a moment, Percy looked proud. 'She's very brave, my mum but she isn't sensible. If she'd used Jersey French, he wouldn't have understood.'

Spinner nodded. Then she said, 'Daddy's got bruises on his arms. I'm worried stiff about them. I don't think he fell over or anything.'

Percy bit his lip. 'Viktor said your dad's a spy and he's going to get him.'

'A spy?' Spinner gasped. 'Of course he isn't. He just translates for the Bailiff.'

A motorbike engine revved in the distance and Percy froze.

Spinner noticed that his hands were trembling. At this, red hot rage began to flow through her body. 'Don't worry, Percy. Of course Dad isn't a spy. That's stupid talk. And that's probably another bike. Viktor won't come to our silly concert. He wouldn't bother.'

Percy didn't look convinced. Spinner patted his arm again, and said, 'If he does come, just hide in the milking parlour. There's lots of straw in there.'

7pm
The audience was arriving one by one, then a whole crowd including Auntie Vi and Joe's gran in their black dresses and lipstick and tight, curled hair and Mr. Jument the seafarer. As Percy handed out programmes, Spinner handed cider, her stomach churning as the motorbike drew nearer.

Mr. Braye appeared, tidy in a dark suit, hair tamed. He beamed at the crowd. 'How lovely to see you all.' He waved his hand at The Trotter Club. 'The concert's in the old potato store. Take your drinks and mind the steep path, please.' As they passed him, he whispered in each guest's ear. 'Watch what you say. Jersey French only. Awful man... Viktor...'

Spinner watched them enter The Trotter Club, and could hear their cries of delight as they saw Joe's pictures. She tried another sip of cider, then gasped and clutched the little carved pig as the motorbike roared up the lane and Percy dropped the programmes before rushing into the milking parlour. She tugged her father's sleeve. 'Daddy, he's coming. *Viktor.* I can tell by the engine.'

Mr. Braye put his arm round her and she could feel his breathing change. 'Remember, he'll find nothing here, then he'll never bother us again. That's what we're aiming at. It's a bluff, sweetie. He's such a great oaf, with all sorts of stupid ideas. Remember that.'

Spinner tried not to shake as she picked up the crystal glass and Viktor jumped off the bike. Dressed in a black leather jacket and dark trousers, white shirt gleaming and shoes polished, he swaggered across the yard to Mr. Braye where he stared at him, his pebble eyes glittering.

He put his face close to Mr. Braye, and said in a steely voice, 'Where are the animals? There are no cows in the orchard, and I see no pigs.' He peered into the sty and whirled back. 'Tell me. What has that stupid farmer done with them?

Spinner held out the glass, trembling with rage and terror. Then she noticed Percy in the shadows, so she forced herself to be still.

Mr. Braye answered Viktor in level tones. 'Mr. Percheron's animals have been moved. They don't like noise. However,' he paused and looked Viktor straight into his cold grey eyes, 'I assure you they'll be ready after the concert. We have discussed the matter, Mr. Percheron and I, if that is who you mean by saying '*that stupid farmer*'. His tone was icy.

Spinner broke in hastily. 'Good evening, Sir. May I say how smart you look?'

'You may not,' snapped Viktor. He snatched the glass, then stalked up to The Trotter Club, pushing past a knot of people. All the way, he went on about Mr. Percheron. 'The animals should be ready for me. I sent orders to the old man.'

When he'd shoved his way into The Trotter Club,

Spinner saw Percy emerge from the milking parlour, dust off straw and sit on the steps. He didn't say a thing, just sat there with his head in his hands.

7.30pm
Joe ran up the hill, followed by his sister and his father, carrying the baby. 'Sorry we're late, Mr. Braye, but at least we're all here,' he whispered, patting the marigold he'd put in his buttonhole. 'Blimey, I feel posh.' He grinned at Spinner, who rolled her eyes.

As soon as Joe had caught his breath, Mr. Braye said, 'Good luck everyone. I'm proud of you.' Then he led the band into their new concert hall, declaring, 'Please stand for the Hot Trotters, the best band in Jersey.'

As they entered The Trotter Club, Joe stared at Viktor and whistled under his breath. 'Viktor's dressed to kill, isn't he? Look at his black uniform and shiny boots. Blimey. Very Heil Hitler.'

When they'd sat down, Ginger blasted out *Roll Out the Barrel*, which made everyone laugh because half the seats were potato barrels. But Viktor sat sullenly in his large red chair from the farmhouse, sneering.

Clem muttered, 'We'll burn that damn chair after the concert.'

Then Spinner stood up. 'Woke up this morning, feeling BAAAAAD,' she sang. The audience smiled, keeping the rhythm with their feet as the rest of the band joined in.

Viktor wiped his sweating face with his hanky, trying to make out the words. Then Joe stood on a potato barrel, his face cocky as he sang in Jersey French. After he'd sung a few verses that made the audience roar, he stopped the band and spoke directly to Viktor. 'Sir, I'll just sing that again in English. We wouldn't like to leave you out.'

Then he sang again. The audience smiled again, furtively and Spinner knew why. Joe had told her that he'd sing in Jersey French and the words would be very rude indeed about the enemy. But when he sang in English, the words were all to do with fish and jolly fishermen.

Viktor scowled, spat on the floor and gulped his drink.

'That foxed him,' hissed Joe as Ginger began another tune. 'Knees up Mother Brown,' sang the audience, kicking up their legs.

After that was over, Joe beamed at the audience. 'The Hot Trotters are delighted to present our number one favourite. It was composed by the band and it's called *Farmyard Noises*.' He stood on the conductor's box. 'Take it away, the goats and the elephant.'

Soon the audience was crying with laughter, even Auntie Vi. But Viktor was fast asleep. 'Blimey,' said Joe, loudly. 'Glad you're enjoying it so much, Sir.' Then he announced the interval, adding, 'Cake for the children.'

Mr. Percheron said there was plenty of cider left and topped up Viktor's glass while Mrs. Percheron gave slices of Spinner's ordinary cake to the children. Rosie yelled, 'No cake for that man.' Viktor woke then, and gave a look that frightened her so much she hid behind Mrs. Percheron's legs.

So Spinner said brightly, 'Here's a special cake for you, Sir.' She offered him a plate. The little cake sat on it, sweet and tempting.

Viktor glared at the audience as he swept the cake off the plate. Then he nibbled it slowly, tantalising the children in the audience as he enjoyed every little scrap, careful not to spill a crumb.

'Greedy pig,' murmured Clem.

Viktor licked his fingers, one by one and sipped his refilled glass. Then he sank back into the red chair.

Mr. Braye climbed on the conductor's box. He glanced pointedly at Viktor's jackboots sprawled on the floor. Then he addressed the audience. 'You'll like this one. It's called, *Your Feet's too Big.*'

At that, the audience cackled, especially Joe's gran, whose false teeth clattered to the ground and had to be rescued by Mr. Le Carin. Viktor glanced in the old lady's direction, his expression vague and glazed while she dusted them off and fitted them back in.

By the time Mr. Braye announced the next piece, he was snoring. Mr. Braye said, 'You'll know this one, "*Beautiful Jersey*".' He handed out shells, pebbles and bells.

When everyone was quiet, Mrs. Martin pulled her bow across her violin strings, painting a picture of the island with her playing: heather covered cliffs, sandy beaches and flowery lanes. Spinner joined in with bird songs on her recorder, playing the saxophone now and then for goats. Then Ginger trumpeted winter storms and Clem played the sousa to represent cows, horses and Peggy.

Auntie Vi rapped out on the washboard while the other adults clapped shells and pebbles or rattled harness bells. Rosie whacked her triangle and Joe rattled his spoons on the bucket, on his knee and in the air.

Viktor slept on, his arms lolling backwards and legs spread-eagled. A line of marigold petals stuck to a slick of dribble on his lapel.

The clapping went on and on and the collection bowl filled to the brim. The audience smothered laughter as they squeezed past Viktor on their way out. 'Flippin' marigold petals,' said Mr. Jument. 'You wouldn't think them Gestapo blokes wore flowers.'

When everyone had gone, Mr. Braye congratulated the band. 'Who'd have thought we'd do that, a year ago?'

Viktor kicked out at something in his dreams, so Joe's father said, 'Come on Hedley, give us a hand.' The two men dragged the soldier outside then bumped him down to the farmyard to prop him against the pig sty.

'Well, isn't that the perfect place for him, near the pig sty?' said Mr. Le Carin. He turned to his children. 'Time for you to catch your beauty sleep, kids. We're going home.'

He patted Joe on the shoulder. 'Well done son.' Then he hoisted Diddie and Arthur on to Viktor's motorbike, turned the ignition and said, 'Best not have this thing cluttering up your farmyard. Someone might ask questions.' He grinned at them all and roared down the lane.

'Crikey, he just smiled,' said Joe. 'Spooky, isn't it?' Then he cocked his head. 'That thunder's back.'

Sunday July 6th just after midnight

After all the adults were asleep, the children crept to the farmyard in dark clothes. 'Percy's in Bill's old room, flat out,' said Clem.

'Let's be having him then,' said Joe, putting his arms under Viktor's legs. 'Blimey, his hair don't half pong.'

'He puts stuff on it.' Clem's voice was loud with disgust as they heaved him into the sousa cart. 'Like Hitler. My dad would kill me if I did that.'

'He'd kill you right now, if he knew what you're up to,' said Joe. 'So keep your voice down, church boy.'

Spinner giggled nervously. 'We should go.'

Ginger nodded. 'The patrol's gone back to barracks. But there could be traps.'

'I muffled the wheels,' said Clem, running his hand over the cloth he'd tied round each one.

Viktor lay in the cart, legs splayed out. Joe checked the knots round his ankles as Ginger announced softly, 'Lady and gentlemen, before we begin, I wish you well in our great effort for which we signed in blood a year ago.' He pulled a small Jersey flag from his pocket. 'Also, we are *not* murderers.'

He waited for a rumble of thunder to pass then held out the flag. Everyone grasped a corner of it over Viktor's head, then swore, silently, to stick together. Clem led the chant:

'Evil flourishes, when good people fail to act. We will not let evil win.'

Joe locked handcuffs round Viktor's wrists, glancing up at the towering clouds. 'It's freak weather, full moon and thunder.'

'Perhaps it's a sign,' said Spinner, trying to sound confident.

The air was heavy with roses. Clem nipped one off and tucked it into Viktor's buttonhole. Then he gave another to Spinner. 'Watch like a hawk. There are spies everywhere. Let's go.'

The boys dragged the cart across the moonlit yard. When they reached the lane, it rolled more easily. As it gathered pace, Spinner ran ahead, dodging from side to side, listening and watching. She checked each darkened cottage and gateway for soldiers, her heart banging so loudly she thought she might wake Viktor.

'They're hiding from the thunder,' said Joe, grunting with effort as they reached the beach. 'Mummy's boys.'

They pulled the cart behind a rock and crouched down while Clem crept to fetch Peggy from her hiding place. Ginger removed the muffles, handing them one by one to Joe, who tucked them under Viktor. 'That'll keep you comfy,' he whispered to the sergeant.

Clem returned with the pig. As he reversed her between the shafts, he said, 'Don't look so worried, Spin. Viktor won't remember a thing '

Joe looped a slip knot round Peggy's neck and handed it to Ginger. Clem muttered, 'Ruddy hell, Joe, it's dark.' He wiped his face with his cuff. 'Sweaty, too.'

'What do you expect? Street lights?' Joe gave Ginger a paper bag, saying, 'That's the last of the Auntie Vi's biscuits.'

'You stole them?' Spinner's eyes grew round.

'She lives at our place now,' said Joe. 'It's easy. Keep hold of that rope, Ginger, in case Peggy bolts for it.'

Ginger tied the rope to his belt, then coaxed the pig forward with half a biscuit. Lightning flickered as Peggy strained after him, slowly at first then in a rhythm as she raced over wet sand, trotters crunching on empty shells. Clem and Spinner pushed the cart and Joe kept pace with Ginger and his biscuits, guiding him along the route he knew blindfold, in silence. Once, he reassured them. 'There aren't any mines round here. Not one. We kept watch, Dad and I, when they were laying them.'

Each side of them, rocks towered and the gullies glittered in the lightning. Peggy squealed with excitement as she followed the sweet scent of Auntie Vi's biscuits. Now and then she stumbled in a puddle and Viktor's feet caught on rocks, then jerked back into place.

Joe shouted, 'Getting used to the dark?'

'No,' muttered Spinner, stubbing her feet. 'I don't like it out here.' She looked round her and shuddered. 'I don't know how you dare come out here alone.'

'Plenty of places to hide,' Joe said, waving at the high rocks. 'Plenty of congers to eat you.'

Spinner gave a shriek, but Clem tried to comfort her. 'Everything'll be fine. Nothing to worry about.'

'Shut up, Clem. I'm smiling inside.'

At last they arrived at the big gully, which was still half full of water. The sandbanks were in sight and the top of the tower beyond them. 'It's too deep to cross,' Joe said as the cart jerked to a juddering halt. He waded a few paces into the gully, then splashed back. 'It's not safe. We'll have to wait for the tide.'

Ginger untied the leading rope from his belt, handing

it to Clem. 'Let Peggy have a swim. She must be tired.'

Clem started to release the pig, but the harness slid in his hands and Peggy shot forward, yanking the cart so it swayed to one side. Clem let go of the harness and grabbed the cart, yelling, 'CATCH HER.'

'Peggy,' shouted Spinner. She flung her arms round the pig's neck, but Peggy was too slippery to hold.

Then Joe grabbed her tail. At that, she turned on him, snapping her teeth and glaring round to see who'd hurt her. While she was twisting her head from side to side, Ginger and Clem crept up and looped the leading rope twice round her neck.

Viktor snorted, twitching in his sleep as Spinner took a deep breath and stroked the pig's ears. 'Come on Peg. Be a good piggy,' she murmured.

Peggy put up her nose and sniffed. Then she trotted round Viktor on the end of her rope, sniffing his hair, then his uniform, then his boots. Suddenly, she bit the knots on his ankle ropes and Viktor's legs fell from their shackles.

'Jesus,' shouted Joe.

But Peggy yelped with joy, stuffed her nose into the cart and gobbled. Then she yanked the leading rope from Clem and Ginger and raced away.

'Ruddy hell,' shouted Clem, leaping up and ripping off his belt. 'Viktor must have dropped cake crumbs into his trouser turn-ups. That's what she was after.' He wrapped the belt round the soldier's ankles, pulling it tight.

Viktor reared up and fell out of the cart. Then he kicked off Clem's belt, his legs flailing in their gleaming jackboots. He shouted something terrifying in German, before tumbling head first into the edge of the gully. 'Heil Hitler,' he yelled, rolling around in the shallow water.

He stayed face down in the water for so long that the

children crept anxiously towards him, wondering if they should stop him from drowning.

Ginger pushed his glasses into place. 'He's going to trick you.'

'No he won't. He's really still,' said Spinner, hardly able to breathe. She poked Viktor's shoulders and then screamed as the man jumped up and shook himself like a dog.

Joe flung himself in front of her, yelling 'Run.'

Viktor looped his handcuffed wrists over him. But Joe dropped down, wriggling out of his clutches. As he skipped out of the way, Viktor stumbled after him, splat, splat, splat through rock pools and ribbons of seaweed.

'Heil Hitler!' shouted Spinner.

'Idiot,' hissed Clem.

'I'm diverting him.'

Viktor stopped dead and turned, his eyes glittering and his boots draped in weed. Then he barged towards Spinner, swearing as he slipped on the slimy rocks.

Spinner screamed. 'I can't move,' she yelled. 'My legs...' She looked down, as if her feet had a conger wrapped round them. 'The sand's trapping me.'

Clem leaped across the rocks and grabbed her, ramming his elbow against Viktor, then punching him. He half carried, half dragged Spinner out of harm's way as the sergeant slipped yet again, then recovered himself.

High above them, Joe was silhouetted against the moon on a rock, whirling his catapult above his head. Then he aimed.

Pebbles zipped through the air, hard as shot. As Viktor clutched his head, Joe let go again and again and again, shouting, 'That's for Mum. That's for Bill, that's for George and that's for Percy.' He jumped up and down on his rock, goading Viktor as the man tried to reach him, spinning his catapult and aiming at Viktor's eyes. '*Paisson d'cliave. Paisson. Paisson.*'

Spinner scrambled beside him and hurled Lizzie's pebble with all her strength. As it hit Viktor on the forehead, she shrieked, 'That's for searching our house, and for Lizzie, and for all her people.'

Beside her, Ginger pulled his catapult as well, bellowing, 'That's for Francois Scornet. *Vive La France.*' He sang the French National Anthem, full volume, without a single variation, just as it should be.

Lightning ripped through the clouds, lighting the blood on Viktor's face as he stumbled in and out of the shallows, blindly trying to catch them, a stream of filth pouring from his mouth as they danced away from rock to rock, flinging stones.

Then Clem roared a command. 'STOP. STAND BACK.' Even Viktor froze, wildly looking around the rocks as the moon gleamed in a sudden, starry space above. Clem shoved Spinner, pushing her back with one hand, hissing, 'For God's sake, stay there. Keep out of the way.'

Keeping his left arm outstretched across her, as if she was a child, he stepped slowly towards Viktor, his feet squeaking on the wet sand, sparks of phosphorescence flicking off his boots. Then he came to a halt, an arm's length from Viktor and pulled the Walther PP pistol from inside his shirt. '*Hande hoch,*' he spat. 'Hands up.'

1.20am

Viktor stared at the boy in disbelief, slowly raising his hands as the moon slid behind boiling clouds.

The Gestapo pistol glinted in Clem's large, capable

hand. His finger was on the trigger as he aimed at Viktor's head. Then he said, as calmly as though he was about to milk the cows, 'Say your prayers, Viktor, if you know how.'

Spinner ducked under his arm, tugging his shirt. She sobbed, 'Don't Clem. Please, please, don't. *Thou Shalt Do No Murder.*'

Clem shook her away and said through gritted teeth, 'Viktor murdered Percy's spirit and his heart and his hopes.' He glanced at her, an icy look. 'This is his DELIVERANCE.' He shouted this at the top of his voice, over the thunder and the gurgling water and the roar of a bomber flying overhead to England.

In that tiny moment, Viktor threw himself at Clem with all his weight, knocking the gun out of his hands and spewing oaths as he scratched the boy's face with his handcuffs.

Growling like an angry dog, Clem began to punch, his fists hammering Viktor's chest. Rose petals fluttered on to him from Viktor's buttonhole, sticking in a smear of blood from the scratch made by the handcuffs.

Above him, Viktor laughed, barely staggering at Clem's mighty blows.

Ginger and Joe raced into the attack, wrenching Viktor's coat so the back ripped up the middle, as Spinner pummelled him with her fists.

Viktor spun round, battering Ginger and Joe with his whirling fists and their metal cuffs, and Clem kept on punching. All the time, he laughed, then he slapped Spinner hard, so she reeled backwards and fell into a puddle.

Ginger ran to help her, clutching the side of his face as Viktor kept laughing, a terrible cold shout at the joy of hurting, and Joe thrashed at him from the back.

But suddenly, Viktor stopped, shoving Clem away

from him like a puppet. A thin scream had filled the air, whining towards them.

Out of the darkness, a pig was charging towards them, her rope flicking water from side to side as she headed for Viktor and rammed him behind the knees. He gave a final bellow and crumpled forwards, smacking his face against a rock.

As lightning forked over the gully, Ginger snatched the ankle ropes and wrapped them back in place, reef-knotting them to the cart. Clem picked up the pistol again, staring at it with crazy eyes, his black hair matted. He pointed the weapon at the stars and clicked the trigger. There was a flash and a bang and he staggered backwards, panting.

Spinner gasped as Ginger splashed towards him.

Joe said sharply, 'I'm going to fetch my dad. We need help with this man. Put that down.'

Clem waved the pistol casually in the air. 'We don't need your dad. I won't miss.'

Spinner whispered, 'Please, Clem, if you shoot him dead, you'll never get over it, even if you aren't caught. Then who'll look after the cows?'

'You,' replied Clem. He took aim. 'Vengeance *shall* be mine.'

Ginger stepped between the soldier and Clem, his voice very quiet. 'This isn't what we planned. Put it down, Clem.'

Clem glared at him, panting like an animal. 'You've never lost anyone.'

Ginger moved nearer. 'Father could be in the water right now, like Bill.' He put his hand on Clem's shoulder, but his friend pushed him away with bloody hands and lifted the pistol over him.

'Murdering won't help any of us. Put it down.'

Clem sniffed and the pistol wavered, then he aimed again.

In a gap between the clouds, stars glittered – a garland of brilliant flowers. Joe touched Spinner's arm. 'Mum's watching us.' he whispered. Then he began to sing, very softly. 'I woke up this morning.'

'Feeling baaaaaad.'

Ginger joined in, his voice croaky.

'I woke up this morning, feeling baaaad,
Percy's had a bad time, and we all feel saaaaad.'

Clem gave a half-smile. Keeping the pistol pointing at Viktor, he sang,

'The sun's going to shine one day.
But I don't know when, so I got the blues man.'

He lowered the gun.

Joe lit a cigarette. 'It's OK, Clem.' He handed the cigarette to Clem, its tip glowing in the dark, 'And I reckon Bill's looking out for you, with my mum.'

Clem gave a wry smile and took a long pull on the cigarette. 'Ruddy hell. It's filthy.' He chucked it away and looked fiercely at the unconscious soldier. 'Viktor, move one finger, and you're dead.' Then he turned to Joe. 'Go and fetch your dad.'

There was a sound of running trotters and Peggy turned up, her expression eager. Ginger said, 'I'll stay with Clem, and Peggy will stand guard. Heil Peggy.'

1.35am

As Spinner and Joe ran back to the beach, it began to rain, a sudden heavy shower.

'Good,' said Joe. 'That'll keep the patrols indoors.'

'He mustn't shoot Viktor,' Spinner said. 'They'll catch him and do what they did to the Frenchman.'

'Don't kid yourself. Clem always meant to kill Viktor. He still does. That's why I did what I did.' Joe glanced back, but Ginger and Clem were hidden among the rocks. 'I'll get my dad, you get yours and Clem's, and maybe we can save him.'

Spinner tore up the flooded lane, the rain beating into her face until she stopped dead in her tracks. Two men were running towards her and she dodged into the hedge.

'CLEM! GINGER!' shouted one man.

Then the other yelled, 'SPINNER! JOE!'

Spinner peered carefully through the leaves. Through the rain, she saw Mr. Percheron and her father running past. Shoving the branches aside, she ran after them. When she was close, she tugged at her father's sleeve so that he spun round, his face streaked with rain. She kept her voice quiet. 'Dad, don't shout. It's me.'

'Spinner! Where have you been? We've been looking everywhere.' Mr. Braye gripped her by the shoulder. 'I swear if anyone's hurt you, I'll kill them.'

'Not me dad. I'm not hurt. Not Joe either. We're OK, but...'

Mr. Percheron's voice was urgent. 'Where are Clem and Ginger? They've broken the curfew. Viktor's gone too. I hope they aren't with him?'

Spinner stamped her feet. 'We don't have much time. Please, please hurry. Clem has a gun and we're scared he's going to use it on Viktor.'

'My Clem? With a gun?' Mr. Percheron stopped dead.

'Come *on*.' Spinner set off back to the slipway, dragging her father behind her as Mr. Percheron followed.

Puffing and panting, they arrived at the beach to find

the Le Carins already there. Mr. Le Carin was shouting at Joe, shaking his shoulder. '*No*, I'm not having you kids risking your lives. You stay here.'

'You're too old for all this,' said Joe, scornfully. 'You need us.'

Spinner and the other two fathers raced up to the Le Carins. Joe tried to wriggle out of his father's grasp, but Mr. Le Carin held tight, then grabbed Spinner as well. 'You kids stay here, I tell you.'

Mr. Braye said, 'Mr. Le Carin's right. It's bloody...' He stopped. 'It's very dangerous out there, and at least he knows the route.' He put his hand firmly on Spinner's shoulder. 'Don't follow, for God's sake.'

Spinner nodded. 'All right, Dad. But you'd better go. Hurry. Clem's mad with fury.'

Mr. Braye splashed down the slipway, followed by the two other men. As headed off to the gullies, he called back, 'Keep hidden.'

As they stood together and watched the men disappear into the darkness, Spinner suddenly jumped and pointed out among the rocks. She shrieked to Joe. 'I saw a flash. It was Clem, I know it was. He's used the gun.'

'No. That was lightning again. Course it wasn't gun fire. You couldn't see it from here.'

Spinner's voice was shrill. 'That *was* the gun, I know it was. It was different.' With a catch in her voice, she stammered, 'I... I... think Clem's shot him after all.'

Joe tried to think of a reply and failed, so he said, 'Look Spin, let the men sort it out. We've a job to do.'

Spinner looked at him questioningly.

'Yep,' Joe went on. 'We're going to blow up my den. The rain's easing, so the night patrol will bob up any minute. We'll need to divert them.'

'Blow up your den? What on earth for?' Spinner brushed a strand of wet hair off her face. 'You just painted it.'

'What's more important? A den? Or Ginger and Clem? If we blow it up, the patrol won't notice what's going on with Viktor.' Joe said, 'Stop staring at me like that. Come on.'

Spinner bit her lip, then followed him through the pine trees to the shack.

Once inside, Joe struck a match, ready to light the fuse if he needed to. 'I've laid explosives in a clump to make the biggest bang, but only if a patrol turns up.'

'*Explosives?*' Spinner looked wildly round.

'Don't panic. They're just flares from Dad's boat. Ginger and I worked on them. They're only sort of bombs, not real ones.'

'I don't *want* to be blown up. You're crazy.'

'Righto.' Joe waved the match about carelessly, then picked up something. 'Look, I got a nice red lipstick from Percy's mum. Go and draw some big V for Victory signs all over the place. The Germans'll love that.'

Spinner took the lipstick. 'Don't get hurt Joe.' Then she ran out to draw a big V on the slipway and a whole row of them along the road.

1.55am

Ginger heard the men first, through the gloom. He put on his glasses, wincing as the sides touched his ears, and peered round the rocks. Then he gave a sigh of relief. 'It's all right, Clem. They're coming.'

Clem stared at him, his hair flattened by rain. 'I *had* to do it.'

'Everything will be fine,' said Ginger.

In front of them, Viktor lay face down on the sand, not moving a muscle. Water slid towards him, its foaming edge dark. Clem stuck his boot into it 'Blood,' he whispered. 'Viktor's filthy blood.'

'Leave it, Clem. You've done your...' Ginger took a deep breath. 'Your work. Just... stay quiet. Let's listen.'

Clem looked out to sea, muttering, 'I *had* to.'

'We've got this...' Ginger picked up the pistol with shaky hands, '...if we need it.' Then he glanced round at the sound of voices. He touched Clem on the shoulder. 'Look... look... I told you... they're coming.'

Mr. Percheron was splashing towards them through the gully, his face dripping with sweat and rain. He looked wildly round for Clem. 'Is Clem here? It's so dark... can't see a thing... Clem. What's that on the sand? Oh my *God*. What the hell have you kids done?'

As the other men reached them, Clem beat his fist against his forehead. 'I had to, Dad. He went for us...'

Mr. Percheron rushed to Clem and shouted, 'I said, what have you *done*, boy?'

Clem wrenched himself from his father's grasp, eyes blazing. '*NO*, Dad. I'm not a boy any more. That's all over.' Then his face crumpled. 'I'm sorry, Dad. So sorry.'

Mr. Percheron grabbed him and held on to him, groaning, 'Oh my poor, poor boy. Whatever has happened?'

Mr. Le Carin dropped to his knees beside Viktor, placing his fingers to his neck while Mr. Braye draped his sweater round Ginger's shoulders, murmuring, 'Tell us.'

'We... we... were taking Viktor to the tower because of what he did to Percy, then...'

'Don't you get it?' Clem shouted. 'Viktor's *dead*.

That's what happened. Now he won't hurt anyone again. Not Percy. Not Ginger. Not Rosie, or anyone, ever again.'

Ginger slumped back against Mr. Braye. Then he lifted his hand away from his head and one ear lobe swung loose.

'Dear God,' said Mr. Braye. 'Who did that to you?'

Mr. Le Carin swore loudly, pointing at Viktor. 'I can guess.'

'Then he shoved me over and tried to stamp on my fingers. So Clem went mad. He pulled Viktor off me and screamed that I need my ears to listen and my fingers to play... music...' He swallowed, and stammered, 'Then... he... shot him.'

Mr. Percheron turned his son to face him, shaking his arm. 'What are we going to do now?' He glanced at Viktor and his voice sank. 'You've finished off a Nazi, son. The worst thing that could happen, the very worst.'

'Wait a moment.' Mr. Le Carin held up his hand. 'I felt something move.' He put his hand under Viktor's chest, then looked up. 'He's still breathing.'

'He *isn't* breathing,' Clem shouted.

'I reckon you missed, Clem. He must have tripped and hit his head on a rock.' Mr. Le Carin wiped the sweat from his brow.

'NO,' yelled Clem. 'He *is* dead. I did it for Bill and George and for all of us.' His voice sank to a whisper, 'and Jersey too.'

'He's right.' Ginger took off his glasses and wiped off some blood. Then he put them back on and pointed at Viktor. 'Clem did shoot him. Right through the eye. He... he... said it was him or us.'

'Steady,' said Mr. Le Carin. 'Let's get Viktor the right way up before the water gets any deeper.' He turned the soldier over, grunting with effort and feeling for bullet wounds. 'There's no sign of bullet damage, boys, though he's bleeding badly from a couple of nasty cuts.' He touched Viktor's face. 'You haven't shot him through the eye. All present and correct. Both eyes. The rocks have done some damage to his head though.'

Ginger touched Mr. Le Carin's arm, his eyes pleading. 'We didn't mean this to happen. But when he turned on us, we *had* to. Then the pistol flashed as if it was full of ammo.' He shook his head, looking away from Viktor. 'But we didn't have any ammo. We never did. We were just trying to threaten him.'

'Of *course* we had it,' said Clem. 'Joe stole some and we loaded the pistol together. I'm not *stupid*. I knew we had to be ready for Viktor. Just because you're so blinking clever, you think you know everything and...'

'Calm down, both of you, so we can work out what to do,' Mr. Braye said, wrapping his hanky round Ginger's head. 'Stop that bleeding, for a start.'

As he tied it, Ginger said to Clem, 'Joe's not stupid either. He must have changed that ammo to blanks. I reckon that's what he was doing when he was late for the concert.'

'Course he didn't,' growled Clem. 'Otherwise he wouldn't have gone to fetch Dad.'

'Shut up, both of you.' Mr. Le Carin glared at them. 'They could hear you in France, let alone Jersey.' He folded his arms and said, 'I'd like to leave this idiot tied to a rock. But I guess we mustn't.' He took Viktor by the legs. 'Come on, don't just stand there. Give us a hand.'

Mr. Percheron took an anxious look at Clem, then helped lift the soldier by the armpits. 'Heavier than a pig,' he said, heaving him into the cart with Mr. Le Carin.

Mr. Braye held Viktor's head, wrinkling his nose in disgust. 'He stinks of hair oil and cider.' Then he addressed Viktor directly, his voice fierce. 'I hope you're proud of yourself, you ruddy swine?'

'It's getting lighter – anyone could see us.' Ginger looked at the sky anxiously.

Mr. Percheron went back to Clem. 'I want to get these kids home. It's not safe out here.'

Viktor's legs hung over the edge of the cart, his eyelids fluttering. Mr. Le Carin held a knife to his throat as he began to struggle. 'Don't even think of it, you drunken bully.'

But as he repeated this warning, Viktor's eyes suddenly opened as though he'd seen something. Then he gave a loud snort and fell back asleep.

Ginger gasped as a shadow fell over them all.

Mr. Le Carin spun round, his knife poised.

2.15am

A figure stood on the outcrop above them.

'PERCY,' shouted Clem. 'I *knew* you couldn't be trusted – you're a stinking liar.' He scrabbled in the sand for the pistol.

'STOP, I'm not Percy,' ordered the stranger. His voice was deep, not at all like Percy's. 'Leave this to me,' he said, firmly, glancing at Viktor. 'This is my job, not yours. Quieten down. Voices carry.'

Mr. Percheron frowned, eying the figure. 'Hush, Clem.' He stared round at the others, his eyes fearful. 'I've seen this before.' He took a step forward. 'In the trenches, when all the lads were dying. An angel, at Mons...'

The man gave a rumbling laugh. 'An angel? When I was a kid, you called me the very devil, Dad!' He climbed down on to the sand. 'You know who I am. Dad?'

Clem gasped and dropped the pistol.

Everyone backed off except for Mr. Le Carin. He gave a nod of recognition, murmured a few words, then touched Mr. Percheron's arm. 'Even if he's an angel in your eyes, he's your boy. Your George. I can promise you that. And he'll sort out this mess all right.'

Mr. Percheron reached out trembling hands. 'George?' His voice faltered and he took a step forward. '*George?*'

Mr. Le Carin steadied him as he stumbled.

'But how can *this* be?'

Clem went closer. Then he turned and said, 'Dad. It's no trick. It's bloody *true.*'

Very slowly, they all edged towards George, Mr. Percheron holding back. But George went towards them. 'My old Dad... it's the most crazy, most wonderful thing in the world to see you.' He hugged his father, then grabbed Clem too. Then he pushed him away and looked him up and down. 'You've grown so tall.'

Mr. Percheron whispered, '*My son.*' He looked down at Viktor and shook his head. 'To meet you like this... just when we need you... a miracle.'

'I'm no miracle, Dad.'

There was a long pause. The tide licked their feet while Mr. Percheron forced out his words. 'Why didn't you let us know you were well? We haven't heard since Christmas and your mother's been so... worried... so frightened. She can't get over Bill, and she thought... you were...'

'I sent messages...but you know how it is, Dad... poor Mum. I think of you all the time...'

'We've waited and waited, for months.' Then he stared back at the island, as if Mrs. Percheron was listening. His voice cracked. 'I wish she could see you now.'

'I wish that too. But you know I have to stay secret. Otherwise they might hurt you and Mum and Clem. I can't tell you why I'm here, except...' he looked again at Viktor. '...I'll help sort out this horrible fellow before he wakes up.'

'I can't believe it's you, George.' Clem rubbed his eyes. 'We've ruddy missed you.'

Mr. Percheron pulled a hanky from his pocket and mopped his face.

'I'll help George to the tower with Viktor,' said Mr. Le Carin. 'He'll take him away in his boat, won't you George?'

'To England,' said George. 'He won't trouble you again.'

'Best if I go with him,' said Mr. Le Carin. 'I know the way through the gullies.'

'Tell George what Viktor's done,' said Ginger to Clem, his voice faint.

'I know all about him,' said George. 'I've received information, you see.' He tucked the pistol into the cart with Viktor and handed Clem the belt he'd used to tie Viktor's feet. 'Your name's on it,' he said. 'Best not leave it out here.' He and Mr. Le Carin heaved the cart out of the pool where it had settled half way up its wheels. Slowly it began to move.

As he moved off with Mr. Le Carin and his prisoner, George said, 'Mr. Braye knows why I'm here. He'll tell you. But I can't return. It's too dangerous, not just for me, but for you all.' He gave a small wave, then said, 'Chins up, all of you.' Then he walked away, keeping low against the rocks in his dark clothes.

Viktor's jackboots glittered in the sunrise as they

dragged the cart towards to the gully, half lifting, half floating it, splashing through the rising tide. Then they were on the sandbanks, dark figures against the rising sun heading for Icho Tower.

'I wanted to murder him,' whispered Clem as they hurried back through the rocks.

'But you didn't… Ginger said softly, pulling him by the sleeve through a shallow pool. 'You were trying to look after everyone out there. And if it wasn't for you, your dad and you would never have seen George.'

Clem stopped and turned at the mention of his brother's name, checking to see where his father was. Mr. Percheron had stopped and was staring at the tower in the morning sunlight as if to catch a last glimpse of George.

Mr. Braye stood by him. He touched his shoulder. 'The patrol will be on the lookout. And listen. This is important. Don't say a thing about this, not even to your closest friends.'

'Would I?' Mr. Percheron cleared his throat and walked on, his boots crunching on limpet shells. Clem and Ginger followed him in silence, keeping low.

A gigantic explosion ripped the air. Among the pine trees, Joe's shack was blown to bits and the roof flew into the sky.

The morning patrol appeared from nowhere and tore towards it, guns aimed.

As soon as the soldiers' backs were turned, the boys and men fled across the beach up the slipway and into the shelter of the pine trees. Peggy hurtled after them, seaweed trailing from her mouth.

9.30am

Spinner was woken late the next day by Lizzie's cat,

purring into her ear. She got out of bed to start a letter to her mother:

Dearest Mummy,
The concert was even more of a success than you can possibly imagine. We had such an interesting audience, because there was a visitor...

But there she put down her pencil because her father's favourite record was playing downstairs. 'Your Feet's too Big,' she joined in sleepily, pulling on clothes.

There were voices in the kitchen and one of them was German. Definitely. She could always tell. Her heart began to pound as it had so many times since the enemy had arrived. But as she crept to the landing, the music was turned down.

Mr. Braye said loudly, as though warning her, 'We saw the sergeant staggering towards the gullies and we all spent the night looking for him. It's dangerous among those rocks, Captain Von Pernet. The children came to help. It was brave of them to risk breaking curfew for one of your men.'

'I do not like to think of your children out in that storm. You should have told us, yes? We could have helped.'

'No time,' replied Mr. Braye. 'We had to beat the tide. Pardon me, but none of you understand how the sea works round this island.'

Spinner tiptoed downstairs, holding her breath.

'That is correct. We do not.' Von Pernet cleared his throat. 'So... You risked your lives for... well, a terrible man, if I may be so direct.' He lowered his voice, adding, 'I am aware that Sergeant Krause... Viktor... has a well-deserved bad reputation.' Then he raised his voice again 'If you find anything on the beach that indicates he is gone for good, I should be grateful… grateful for this knowledge.'

The kitchen door was closed, but Spinner kneeled on the hall carpet and watched through a crack in the wood.

Mr. Braye muttered something, his face very serious.

Then Spinner watched the German move towards the outside door.

However, as he turned the handle, he hesitated and cleared his throat again, taking a step back into the kitchen. He glanced out of the window at the lane and said, 'I feel that since we are being direct, it is my duty to speak. I, er, I trust we can keep this conversation to ourselves?'

Mr. Braye looked grave. 'I am trustworthy, Captain Von Pernet.'

There was a long pause. The captain patted his shirt pocket, above his heart. 'As you know, I have children too, Mr. Braye.'

Captain Von Pernet's voice was so quiet Spinner had to cup her ears. He pulled a couple of photographs from his pocket and showed them to her father.

'It must be very hard for you,' said Mr. Braye, politely studying the pictures. 'He indicated the chair beside him and Captain Von Pernet sat down, taking back the pictures and gazing at them.

'I love my children so much, like all of you in this island. I would die if they…' Here, his voice dropped to a whisper. 'If they were hurt… I could not…'

Spinner moved to the keyhole, putting her ear to it.

There was a sound of chairs being dragged as though the two men were moving a little closer, as though they didn't want anyone to hear.

Her father said, 'If your children were hurt, you could not live yourself. That's what you mean. You could not go on… and you are right, I would be the same. We fathers all think our children beautiful.'

'Indeed we do, Mr. Braye. Indeed we do. And we would do anything, anything, to keep them safe.'

Spinner bit her lip, then she looked through the crack in the door again.

The German was fanning his face with his hanky, looking very anxious. He said, 'I am afraid there are soon to be more men like Sergeant Krause arriving in the island. Terrible men.' His voice shook again. 'Please, Mr. Braye, I beg you. I *beg* you. I know about these men. Please, tell your children to be sensible when they see them. I know that they had an old pistol, a Luger. I was told in confidence and I worried…'

Mr. Braye pushed a cup of tea towards the German, his hand trembling enough to make the cup rattle. 'That old thing?' he said lightly. 'I thought that had vanished years ago. They played with it when they were small.'

Von Pernet looked serious. 'We threw it over the cliffs, Josef and I. So, please, tell them…' he paused, moving his chair roughly backwards. He spoke rapidly. 'Tell them that while we may not know about the sea around the island, we *certainly* know about seagulls and they must please, please put away their catapults. And they must take care of their lovely pigs.'

Spinner gulped, thinking of Peggy, safely in her sty after her triumphant night.

Captain Von Pernet's voice was very serious. 'These men that are coming… they will not take kindly to trouble, even from escaped animals who know no better. They will not hesitate to take *grave* action against anything or anyone that… well, that inconveniences them. I am sure you understand, Mr. Braye.'

Spinner saw that her father's knuckles were white as he gripped his cup, and she wanted to rush into the kitchen and show him she was all right and he mustn't worry.

But he nodded at the Captain calmly, saying, 'I am sorry that you have to say this. I am sorry that such people represent your great country.'

Captain Von Pernet acknowledged this with a small shrug. 'Mr. Braye, make all the children understand, even the cheeky little Joe and the big farm boy. Let them know that drawing the letter V in lipstick on walls doesn't make the Germans at all happy. They do not think it funny.' He picked up the cup and drained it, then nodded his thanks.

'I'd be delighted,' said Mr. Braye, his voice unsteady. The chairs scraped again on the floor. 'Goodbye, Captain Von Pernet, and thank you. This conversation has not taken place. Of course.'

Captain Von Pernet opened the door to go out. He patted the pocket above his heart again. '*Guten Morgen, Herr* Braye.'

When Spinner heard the captain's footsteps fading down the lane, she rushed into the kitchen.

'Dad,' she said, 'there's nothing to worry about… we…'

Mr. Braye looked at her, his face grave. He stroked her arm, and said, 'Spinner… we must talk about this.'

But just as she was dreading a one to one conversation and wondering how she could lie her way out of everything, Clem knocked at the door and walked straight in.

Plasters were stuck over the worst of the cuts, but he grinned at her, flinching at the pain as the smile pulled the plasters. 'Morning Mr. Braye. Thank you very much for your help last night.' Without waiting for an answer, he turned to Spinner. 'Want to fetch the animals with me? They spent the night away, remember?'

Mr. Braye frowned. 'What will you say about your cuts if you meet the patrol?'

'I'll say I went sleep walking.' He managed a tight grin. 'Walked into a rose bush or something.'

'Joe tells me his den was hit by lightning. How amazing. I would have thought the other houses nearby would have been hit as well. That shack was quite low.' Mr. Braye looked at them thoughtfully over his glasses.

Clem and Spinner glanced at each other.

Mr. Braye suddenly gripped them by the tops of their arms, so that Clem paled and Spinner's eyes widened.

'Never, ever take the law into your own hands again, *do you understand*? You have no idea how dangerous it is to do that on this island at this terrible time.' He dashed a tear from his face, repeating quietly, 'No idea, thank God, and I never want you to know.'

Spinner turned white. She'd never heard him sound so scared. She looked him in the eyes, saying, 'Sorry, Daddy.'

'I mean it. Please don't do anything like that again. Carting the enemy around in a sort of wheelbarrow? With a pig? *Ridiculous*. Thank God I'd given Viktor so much cider. We can't even begin to think of fighting men like him.'

As they left the kitchen, Clem murmured, 'Whatever he says, your father's fighting already, in his own way. He's been sending information to England with George for months, using the Le Carins.'

Spinner nodded as they walked into the sunshine. 'I thought something like that was going on.'

'Let's pretend last night never happened.' Clem stopped and put his hands on her shoulders. 'Look at me, Spinner. Father says we must use the situation to make us stronger. Perhaps it was weak of us to do what we did to Viktor.'

'Weak?' Spinner raised her eyebrows. 'How could we be stronger than that?'

'It was weak, I think, because we gave in to anger. You see, we've got to smile and sing like all that Girl Guide rot...'

'It's not rot...'

'I know. But we've got to show the soldiers we don't care. That we're above them. That we're real, strong Jersey people and they can't beat us.' Clem thought for a moment. 'And they can't crush us. That's what I mean. If we start killing them or hurting them, they'll have won.'

'I suppose so.' Spinner nodded slowly. 'Anyhow, I haven't any more time for guns or pistols for that matter. I'm going to start my soup kitchen. Joe's supplying conger and sand-eels.' She was about to mention Percy and how he'd help, when there was a loud tapping on the window of Ginger's flat above them.

Ginger peered out, his head swathed in bandages. 'I had fourteen stitches.'

'*Fourteen?*' Clem sounded envious, before asking, 'Come with us to fetch the animals?'

Ginger shook his head with care. 'Doctor's orders. No bumping about. Got to stay indoors and read. Suits me.' He winked painfully, then added, '*Per Ardua ad Astra*, and all that.' Then he closed the window.

Spinner looked puzzled.

'Through Adversity to the Stars,' explained Clem. 'Ruddy professor!'

As they set off towards The Trotter Club, Joe charged through the yard and up the hill. 'Oi, you two! Wait. I got something to tell you. Horrible stuff.'

'*Viktor?*' stammered Spinner. 'He isn't back, is he?'

Joe laughed. 'Course he isn't back. He'll be in prison already, in England. George will make sure of that.'

Clem whooped and punched the air, yelping at his smarting cuts. Suddenly, Peggy raced towards them out of the orchard. She made a strange noise, a bit like a cheer, then she looked at them, each in turn, a smile playing on her hairy lips.

'*She's smiling,*' gasped Spinner. '*I always said she would.*'

'Pigs don't smile, you twit. I told you that, ages ago,' said Clem. However, he looked closely at Peggy. 'Ruddy hell, Spinner. You're right. She is. She's blimming smiling. What a great pig.'

Peggy smiled once more, then dashed back to the orchard.

Clem roared with laughter, then turned to Joe. 'So, what's so really horrible? What's worrying you?'

'Auntie Vi. She's in a real bate, a temper. Blimey, you should see her, red as a beetroot.'

'Why?' Spinner frowned. 'Has a soldier hurt her?'

'Nah,' said Joe. He lowered his voice in case Auntie Vi was lurking in the hedge, 'She can't find her last Custard Cream, those biscuits we gave to Peggy. She thinks there's a thief about.'

Spinner's eyes were like saucers. 'I bet she's laid a trap.'

'Buckets of water on the door, coal in the biscuit tins,

you name it,' said Joe, leading the way to the top of the path. He pushed open The Trotter Club door and gazed at the rows of chairs. 'Blimey, it's going to take all day to put this lot back.'

'We won't take that red one that Viktor sat on,' said Clem. 'I reckon it's infected. Got a match, Joe?'

Joe pulled out a cigarette and lit up. 'I'm giving up fags. This is my last. Mum wanted me to stop. So I will. I reckon she helped us last night.' He chucked the matches at Clem, blowing a couple of smoke rings before they dragged the red chair into the sunshine. Then he crumpled a piece of paper and tucked it into the seat, ready to light. 'Carry on, Clem.'

Spinner stared at Clem. 'You can't set fire to a valuable chair like that. Whatever will your mother say? And Auntie Vi?

'Auntie Vi would say, *THERE'S A WAR ON*,' replied Joe.

Clem gave his big, lazy smile and struck a match on a stone. 'Fires are banned. So why not?'

As it flared, Joe shouted, 'Stop. I can hear the warning signal.' From the farmyard came three short blasts on a trumpet, the warning they'd planned before the concert. Spinner clung on to Clem, as Joe muttered, 'Jesus. Viktor must have escaped.'

'Don't say *Jesus*, like that,' said Clem.

Joe looked down the hill, his face puzzled. 'It isn't Ginger making the signal. It's my dad. What's the old blighter doing playing the trumpet? I thought he was helping George with Viktor then off to join the French Resistance and all that rot.' He peered down the hill again. 'But he's back. Just my luck.'

'He's waving,' said Spinner, 'and he's pulling something

on a rope.' Then she gave a sigh of joy and tugged Joe's filthy shirt. 'A puppy! He's got a beautiful puppy with him. It's barking and barking, as if it knows you.'

Joe didn't move. He stared down the hill as his father beckoned him, pointing at a bouncy black puppy which was pulling its rope, yapping and looking up at The Trotter Club. 'A puppy?' Joe whispered. 'I always wanted a puppy, but Dad said we couldn't feed one.'

'Give it limpets. That's what everyone else does,' said Spinner.

'Go on then,' said Clem, urging him forward. 'Say hello.'

Spinner squeezed his hand. Then Joe wiped his eyes with his filthy cuff, dropped the cigarette and flew down the hill. As he raced towards the puppy, he cried, 'Beaufort! Come here, boy.'

Afterword

Jersey is the largest of the Channel Islands, nine miles long and five miles wide. It's about eighty miles south of England, close enough to France to see houses and cars on its coast. The islands are British, but used to be part of Brittany.

The island is famous for its flowers, cows and potatoes and also was once known for its outdoor grown tomatoes. If you visit, you will see French signage and might even hear the old Jersey language, Jerriais, which Joe and Clem speak.

The Channel Islands were invaded by Germany on July 1st, 1940 under Adolf Hitler's orders.

For five years the islanders were cut off from the outside world. Their only communication with friends and families in Britain was by Red Cross letters, which took months to arrive and were only twenty five words long. It was as if the islanders had been put into a prison, with the surrounding sea for walls.

From 1942, radios were confiscated and listening to the BBC was banned.

In the last years of the occupation, some people died from malnutrition and others from lack of medicine. The bare necessities were in short supply: food, clothes, fuel. Power and gas was strictly rationed, there was little paraffin and few candles. It must have been hard for parents as they tried to comfort crying babies in the dark on freezing winter nights. Children wore home made clogs or went barefoot. Soup kitchens opened and bowls were made from dried milk tins.

Often, there was no toilet paper, shampoo, washing powder, toothpaste or soap. Imagine trying to keep clean!

As well as many other deprivations, there were thousands of rules.

By 1945, the German occupiers were as hungry as the islanders, fed up and homesick.

The occupation was meant to be a model one. On the whole the islanders were treated with respect, but anyone who broke the rules was punished, sometimes severely. I have given the hint of this with Percy. In occupied Holland, fourteen year old boys were deported to Germany to work in Hitler's factories – but many of them escaped home overland. In reality, this would have been impossible for Percy because of the sea.

There were Nazi men like Viktor in the islands, but most of the occupiers were from the regular German army and many officers secretly disapproved of Hitler. However, some islanders were sent to prisons in France or concentration camps in Germany and died in terrible conditions.

As their island was despoiled with concrete bunkers and gunsites, the residents witnessed in horror the harsh treatment of Russian and other prisoners, who they fed and rescued.

I think the islanders were so courageous and resilient, showing immense humour and patience in the face of adversity.

As a teacher, I've found that children on the mainland, that is England, where I've taught all my life, don't know this happened. I wanted them to hear about it so I ran occupation workshops in schools as part of WW2 History projects. The children were amazed and wondered how they would have reacted in the same situation.

So I began to write this book. You must understand that it was difficult. I didn't want to make light of that hard time.

For this reason, I only wrote about the first year, the easiest, and hinted at what was to come. I didn't use real Jersey names and I shrunk the island a little for the story, but there is still east and west, important if you are an islander. All the background facts are true and the children's actions are based on stories people told me over the years, including my relatives.

Many of these stories were funny, but there were silences too. I understood that things happened which people wanted to forget and still do.

So I wasn't sure if it would be possible to finish what I'd started, although I had so much material. However, Bernie Robert, who I quote at the beginning of the book, said, 'A little artistic licence doesn't matter. Please, just tell our story.'

My uncle said he 'would have been shot' for some of the things he and his friends did during those years, before he escaped in a small boat. I like to imagine that teenagers like him might have planned to kidnap a soldier and take him out to Icho Tower on a low tide.

Who knows if anyone tried that? No-one would have admitted such a thing. What do you think?

Acknowledgements

I would like to thank the people of Jersey, especially those I interviewed, including Bob Le Sueur, Pam Butler, Robin Stevens, Jo Le Marquand, Bernie Robert and others. I read every book I could on the occupation, including the farming diary written by my father's first cousin Nan Le Ruez.

As I wrote, I remembered our grandparents and parents, our Jersey heritage. I wanted this book to be in memory of them and our two uncles, Jack Crill and Arthur Candlin. They died as young men on active service during the war. Like so many, they never saw their beloved island again.

I am grateful to my friends and family for keeping faith over the book and for reading, checking and proof-reading, in particular John Cole, Alan Collins, Becky Sandover and many godchildren, young cousins and pupils. Thank you also to Gilly Carr, the Percy Street Writers and the Faber graduates and also to Liz Flanagan and Mel Darbon for their careful editing on the early drafts and their support.

None of this would have been possible if my lovely

agent Ben Illis hadn't found me Elaine Bousfield of ZunTold Publishing. She and her illustrator, Isla Donohoe, took huge care with their ideas for the jacket and illustrations and Elaine's publishing edits, enthusiasm, commitment and love for the book have been outstanding.

Thank you everyone!

For more insightful books you'll love,

head to

zuntold.com